CIRCLE OF DISHONOR

GWEN MAYO

MYSTERY AND HORROR, LLC
TARPON SPRINGS, FL

CIRCLE OF DISHONOR
Revised Edition

Gwen Mayo, Author

Sarah E. Glenn, Editor
Jessy Roberts, Pill Hill Press Editor
Copyright © 2015 by Mystery and Horror, LLC
Published by Mystery and Horror, LLC

ISBN-13: 978-0-9915825-2-5

(Mystery and Horror, LLC)

Library of Congress Control Number: 2014906696

Printed in USA by Mystery and Horror, LLC
(www.mysteryandhorrorllc.com)

DEDICATION

This book is dedicated to the memory of my dear friend Dr. Richard Haydon, III, who thoroughly enjoyed having Nessa's best friend, the medical examiner, named for and based on him. I hope in some small way the Nessa stories ensure a brilliant and talented physician is never forgotten. My friend, I will always miss you.

- Gwen Mayo

CHAPTER ONE

"NO!" my mind screamed, but the word could not get past the raw anger choking me.

Incessant pounding jarred me from another nightmare. I sat up and wiped my sweating face on the sleeve of my nightshirt. It took a moment to grasp that the racket emanated from the back door, rather than inside my skull. I groaned, sat up, and groped for my dressing gown.

"Why is it that nobody needs a detective during daylight?" I grumbled, pulling on my robe and grabbing my spectacles from my bedside table.

For a split-second I considered checking my appearance in the oval looking glass above the mantle, but decided that anyone coming to see me after midnight wasn't worth the effort. Besides, in the darkness my thick robe disguised any traces of womanly curves. In truth, a handkerchief could have disguised my womanly figure. The flat bosom bemoaned as a young woman had proven to be my greatest advantage in assuming a man's identity.

In my family, everyone tended to be wire thin, with mops of curly red hair and big ears. I didn't mind a build that resembled a scarecrow, but could have done without the big ears. With my hair cropped short, my ears stuck out at a most unattractive angle.

My visitor's impatience was becoming evident. I didn't bother turning on the gaslights as I rushed downstairs. The screen door wasn't going to survive much longer if the fool didn't stop banging on the frame. Besides, I really wanted whoever was creating the racket to stop before my head exploded.

"Hold your horses," I yelled. "I'm coming."

"Hurry," an agitated voice shouted through the closed door.

I recognized Belle Brezing's voice immediately. My pace quickened. Five months ago, Belle found me half frozen and nearly dead from a knife wound. I don't know how she got me to her rooms, but I awoke on lavender scented pillows with Belle's delicate hands pressing a cool compress to my fevered brow.

Life had been hard for Belle. She was a young mother, alone and desperate. Despite her impoverished circumstances, Belle had been reluctant to accept money for helping me. Only my argument that her daughter needed to eat impressed her enough to grudgingly accept the bank notes proffered.

On Christmas Eve, Belle reached the limit of her endurance. Leaving her daughter in the care of a neighbor, she gave up the tiny rooms she rented on Mill Street and went to work in Miss Jenny Hill's bawdyhouse.

We had met on the street once or twice since she moved to Miss Hill's. She hadn't spoken, but I always tipped my hat to remind her that she had at least one friend in town willing to acknowledge that friendship in the light of day.

With my head still pounding, I threw open the latch, and motioned Jenny Hill's most popular girl into the kitchen, curious to discover what brought her to my door at such an unpleasant hour.

"Miss Hill sent me to fetch you. Something awful happened at the house. We need your help." The urgency of Belle's voice wiped the traces of sleep from my eyes and forced me to focus on something other than the nightmare that haunted me.

Although speculation was pointless, endless possibilities of what 'something awful' could mean in a house of ill repute were irresistible. It was an act of willpower to focus my mind on my visitor.

Belle was tiny, maybe five feet tall, but unlike me, her lush curves drew all eyes in her direction. In the eerie half-light of the kitchen, the contradictions of her appearance were striking. Belle Brezing's large dark eyes and masses of black curls created a sharp contrast to her innocent face. Her facial features appeared almost ethereal, while her low-cut gown and expensive perfume bore witness to more earthy aspects of the eighteen-year-old prostitute's life.

"Would you like some tea?" I asked, noting her trembling hands and agitated state. "Or…perhaps something stronger?"

I knew I needed something stronger. The nightmare along with too much bourbon and not enough sleep had left me in a sorry state.

Belle's voice rose, jolting me from my misery.

"There's no time," she said. "You've got to come right away. There's been a shootin' and you know the law will be looking to blame one of us. Miss Hill's right beside herself. The old biddies here in Lexington would love to pin a murder on her. They're looking for an excuse to run all of us out of Fayette County, out'a Kentucky if they could."

I grimaced at the thought of a murder adding fuel to the battle being waged to clean up the city. Only last month, the crusading women of the Lexington Ladies' Club had joined forces with the Abstention Society. Together, the two clubs had launched a full-scale attack on saloonkeepers and brothels.

I didn't care much for the godly claims of teetotaling and anti-pleasure crowd. Theirs was a faith without compassion, concerned with finding fault in the lives of others. The clubs seemed full of angry people who like to blame women like Jenny Hill for the vices of their loved ones. I suspected that if they succeeded in ridding Lexington of all the other "sinners" they would attack each other. Their natures would not permit them to do otherwise.

"Whoever's dead won't be any more dead when we get there," I said as I helped myself to the bottle of bourbon sitting on top of my icebox, then held the bottle out to Belle in case she had changed her mind.

The trembling girl shook her head.

I shrugged, poured myself a generous shot, and placed the bottle back where I kept it.

"I know you want to get back," I said, as Belle paced the kitchen floor, "but I don't want to have to explain to the police what I'm doing at Miss Hill's establishment in my nightshirt. They're liable to think your boss has taken to providing for the more varied tastes of her gentlemen callers."

For a moment, the thought of me working at a brothel made Belle forget her troubles. "Those gents would likely want their money back," she replied, as she followed me to upstairs. "You do a right passable job of acting like a man, Miss Nessa, but you wouldn't be as convincing without your breeches."

"Only passable?" I asked, pretending to be offended. "I've gotten away with it for more than fourteen years."

I was relieved to see a trace of a smile at the corners of her mouth. People talked more freely when they were comfortable.

"Well," she said, "Miss Hill thinks you dress like a nancy-boy, but she doesn't seem to know that you're a woman, and she's a real good judge of menfolk."

She took a seat on the edge of my bed while I pulled on the padded tunic, which broadened my shoulders and thickened my midsection to more masculine proportions.

"I can tell, of course," she said after pondering the question a moment, "but that don't really count. I had to undress you to stitch you up last winter."

Her full lips pursed as she studied my tall thin frame. "I suppose anybody who knew your brother would know you weren't him. I was little when he was alive, but I remember his hands, and his smile. When he was in town, he played cards almost every night in Papa's saloon. Of course, he weren't really there to play cards. He would have been detecting like you, right?"

I nodded. Talking about my twin always brought a lump to my throat. It grated that fourteen years of searching had not brought me anywhere near identifying all his murderers.

"I remember the way he used to roll coins through his fingers," Belle said. "He caught me watching him from behind the pickle barrel once and threw me a nickel. I knew right off that you weren't who you said. Your hands are big for a woman, but your fingers ain't as long as Ness'. He had the longest, nimblest, fingers I ever saw."

Holding back my tears took tremendous effort.

Belle looked up at me and smiled. "I'm not sayin' anything you don't already know. I've noticed you keep your hands in your pockets most of the time."

"So you saw right through me, did you?"

"Well…I knew right off you wasn't Ness Donnelly when you told me that lie," she said confidently. "But I was a little taken aback when I unbuttoned your longjohns and found that padding you wear. Probably saved your life when you got stabbed, but don't it get awful hot in the summer?"

Her plain speaking made me blush, but what could I say? My whole life was built on a lie.

Belle noticed my embarrassment. Her tone softened.

"You look a lot like Ness. A little softer around the face. I figured you were kin of some kind, maybe a younger brother. I guess you did fool me. For a little while anyway."

"You'd make a good detective," I replied, a little surprised at the girl's memory and keen skill of observation. She couldn't have been more than five when Ness was murdered.

"Shucks, no!" Belle exclaimed, laughing. "I got all the wrong curves. You couldn't pad me enough to ever pass as a man."

I laughed. "You're right about that, but you don't need to be a man to detect. During the war, I worked as a nurse. Alan Pinkerton hired women operatives and sent them all kinds of places. I hear that his sons want to get rid of them. They probably will when they take over the agency. A pity. I learned a lot working for Mr. Pinkerton. He was very smart, for a Scotsman. Smart enough to know women are more observant than most men, and that we could go places men couldn't. It was Mr. Pinkerton who sent me to work as a nurse and collect information from the Confederate soldiers that came through the field hospital. He believed wounded men would confide easily in any woman who was willing to listen. You'd be surprised how much I learned, talking with them and writing letters to their families."

"I doubt it," she said. "If listening is all it took, I could out-detect you. I think you might be shocked by what men tell me in bed."

"Looking for a new occupation?" I asked, as I grabbed my hat.

Belle grinned and stood up.

"We should both stick to trades we're good at," Belle said, "at least as long as they let us. I don't know how town folks feel about women detecting, but those goody-two-shoes at First Baptist keep trying to reform us whores. Not that they want to succeed. The only thing they rank lower than a working whore is a reformed one."

Her bluntness surprised me, but she was right. If she gave up prostitution tomorrow the congregation might sing her praises during the service, but nobody would invite a former whore home for Sunday dinner or offer her respectable work the rest of the week.

"Why don't you tell me what happened while we walk?" I asked as we headed downstairs.

The fear was back in her face in an instant. Her lower lip trembled and traces of tears appeared in the corners of her dark eyes. Belle blinked them away quickly, then swallowed hard.

"I don't think it happened there," she said. "One of us would have heard."

I placed an arm around her.

"Leave the thinking for later," I said softly, as I opened the door. "Tell me what you know for a fact. Just what you personally saw and heard."

"Well, I didn't hear much, that's a fact. And I would have heard too, if there was a gunshot. There weren't. There was just the usual sounds 'til Rachel screamed."

I was grateful for the darkness. It hid the color flushing my cheeks. I wasn't entirely sure what the usual sounds in Miss Hill's house might be at this time of night, but my mind conjured up unseemly pictures of half-dressed men cavorting with Miss Hill and her girls.

"Is Rachel one of the other girls working at Miss Hill's?" I said, trying to regain my composure.

Belle nodded.

"She's the tall girl you saw me coming out of the dry goods store with last week. Came from over Danville way. Her pa kicked her out."

I remembered the tall blonde I had seen with Belle, her strong chin jutting slightly, her eyes proud and defiant. Part of me wondered if the fierce spirit so evident in her features was the reason her father had cast her into the street.

"You heard Rachel scream," I prompted, slowing my pace to match hers.

"A deaf man could've heard her scream three counties away!"

"What happened then?"

"Then everybody came runnin'. Rachel was standin' in the middle of the front hall. Starin' at…" There was a break in her voice as if she were looking for the right words. "…this dead man."

Her hesitation bothered me. It usually indicated uncertainty or secrets. Experience told me it was the latter. She was holding something back.

"Go on," I said.

"He was plumb naked. Just layin' there in the middle of the floor looking like he fell out of the sky or somethin' except for the bullet hole in his chest."

Belle paused mid-step and caught hold of my sleeve.

I turned to look at her.

"Someone plugged him, Miss Nessa. I swear it wasn't any of us. You gotta' help us. You know the law won't look elsewhere if they think they can hang a murder on one of us."

"Of course, I'll help," I promised without thinking. I owed Belle my life.

Later, when the cold pre-dawn air had lessened my headache, the reality of the promise I had made to Belle started to sink in. I had agreed to place myself between the law and a house full of whores. What was I thinking?

CHAPTER TWO

Conversation lapsed as we made our way through dimly lit streets. Preoccupied with my own thoughts, I plunged my hands deep in my pockets and hardly noticed my companion until her chattering teeth broke the silence. In the rush to fetch me, she must have forgotten to grab a wrap.

March in Kentucky was not as cold and damp as I remembered Chicago being this time of year, not even in the wee hours of the morning. Still, the night was cool enough to make me feel sorry for Belle. Her gown was sleeveless and cut low, revealing most of her bosom. I slipped my topcoat off and placed it around her bare shoulders before she had the opportunity to refuse.

As we walked, I turned over worries in my mind. Over the last fourteen years, I had built a reputation for being able to find the truth. My detective agency was born from the search for my brother's killers, but it had succeeded through my hard work.

Ness and I had been Pinkerton operatives during the war. Near the end of the hostilities, Ness was shot in the back several times. He had been investigating the army payroll robberies perpetrated by the notorious Copperhead Society known as the Knights of the Golden Circle.

After Ness was shot, I tried to pick up his investigation. It wasn't easy, but I was determined to find his killers. It didn't take long to realize that the wall between the worlds of men and women was a barrier Nessa Donnelly couldn't cross. So I buried my female identity with my brother's body, dressed in his clothes, and learned to pass as a man.

I had not intended to live the rest of my life pretending to be him. But the Circle proved more elusive than I anticipated. Necessity forced me to take on other clients to pay for the investigation that mattered. In the meantime, my manly charade became so convincing that sometimes I forgot the truth.

There were lean years, when only a handful of cases kept me going, but in time I grew more successful than Ness or I could have imagined while growing up in the Sisters of Mercy Orphan Asylum on the edge of Chicago's Irish slums.

This case frightened me. My business had grown and profited from having a good working relationship with the police. Now that relationship could be lost as I tried to prevent someone in a houseful of social outcasts from being charged with murder.

Was my friendship with Belle really worth the risk I was taking?

I glanced back at her, tromping along in my oversized topcoat. She looked small and frail. She was tougher than she appeared, but this was a murder. Maybe Belle was the only one I was really concerned about. She certainly had reason to be concerned.

Belle had already come under suspicion of murder in the death of one of her admirers. When the matter was ruled suicide, I deliberately resisted looking closely at what might have happened. Now I found myself wondering if there was any truth to the gossip about Belle shooting her lover. Not that the truth mattered; Belle's involvement meant there were enough similarities between Johnny Cook's shooting and this case to create plenty of fuel for a new police investigation.

It troubled me that I was still thinking about the Cook shooting when we reached the bawdyhouse. If I couldn't stop wondering about my friend's involvement, would anyone else give her the benefit of a doubt?

Jenny Hill's house looked respectable enough from the outside. It was a fashionable three-story brick home in the Federalist style, considerably larger than the new house I had built on the west end of Short Street. The bawdyhouse was rumored to have once belonged to the late President Lincoln's father-in-law. I didn't know if the rumor was true or not, but it struck me that it was just the sort of respectable front Miss Hill's late night visitors would like. She offered the local gentry all the comforts of their fine homes, and the added attraction of being able to indulge in prurient appetites their wives would have found unthinkable.

I paused on the doorstep and started to knock, but Belle pushed past me and opened the door. Three feet into the foyer, a rotund body-shaped lump was clearly outlined under a crisply starched white cotton sheet. I wondered which of the women had been thoughtful enough to drape a covering over the deceased.

The front hall was crowded. Around the corpse, half a dozen courtesans were standing like a circus imitation of pallbearers waiting to carry the murdered man to his final resting place. It was a ghoulish thought, but there it was. Everything about the scene was somehow grotesquely wrong.

Miss Hill was sitting at her writing desk, adjusting one of the pins in her auburn hair. Her silk brocade evening gown and full-length gloves made her appear more ready for an evening at the opera than a murder investigation.

"Thank you for coming, Mr. Donnelly," the madam said, standing to greet me. "I suppose you will want to talk to Rachel first." As she spoke, her hand waved toward a tall girl who visibly winced at having my attention drawn to her.

The unfortunate Rachel was clustered with two other girls. Her long blond hair fell loose around the shoulders of her uncorseted dress. At least she was wearing a dress. Her two companions wore only their silk undergarments. I tried not to stare, but seeing their painted faces and exposed limbs gave the murder scene the solemnity of a sideshow humbug.

"Later," I said. "I would like to look at the body first."

Seeing her confusion, I fumbled for a way to explain.

"I don't mean to be rude, Miss Hill. I will need to hear what all of you have to say, but the body is a silent witness to what transpired. The less information I have from the living, the more clearly I can grasp the testimony of the dead."

I wasn't sure she understood what I was trying to say, but she nodded and went back to her desk.

For a long moment, I just stood in the doorway taking in every detail of the scene. The brass gaslights lining the stairs cast a soft glow on the pale blue velvet flocked wallpaper and reflected off the sheet. My eyes kept coming back to the oddity of that clean white sheet. There was no blood; none pooling on the rug or seeping through the sheet. There was no trace of blood between the planks of white ash flooring, nor were there any droplets of blood trailing from the door to where the body rested.

I got down on my knees and looked closely at the floor to see if there was any evidence that someone had attempted to clean up the aftermath of a shooting. Here and there I found traces of shoeprints, both men and women's, though none clearly identifiable as being made by whoever left the body.

The variety of shoe prints scuffing the polished floor told me that nobody had tried to remove any evidence of a murder from the heavily travelled hallway. When I examined the boards more closely, I could see some faint traces of something being dragged into the house. I surmised it had been the body, since shiny streaks were visible from just inside the front door to where the sheet rested. When I had committed the details to memory, I lifted the lower end of the sheet.

The skin of the victim's toes had been scraped and small fragments of something clung to the flesh. Perhaps Doc Haydon, the county medical examiner, could tell me more when he had studied the injuries. In any case, it was an indication that Belle was right about him being killed somewhere else. I dropped the sheet back into place and stood up.

There were never any clear answers in the eyes of the dead, but the haunting emptiness always compelled me to meet their gaze. Perhaps I hoped for some hint of what they saw in that last instant of life. My hopes were never quite fulfilled.

When I lifted the sheet from the dead man's face, I saw only the wide-eyed expression of a man unexpectedly confronted with his imminent death. I wondered what horror caused the shocked expression fixed in his features. But there was no escaping those sightless brown eyes staring up at me as I examined the rest of the body. Shutting out thoughts of what they last saw was an impossible task. My mind grappled with images of what might have caused the shock detailed in his facial features. All I could surmise with any degree of certainty was that he knew his killer, and had clearly not expected violence from that quarter.

Belle had been accurate in her description of the body. The man was stark naked and had what appeared to be a bullet hole just above his heart. More testament to Belle's theory – that he was already dead when he was put into their hall – was the pattern of blood pooled in his extremities. Front and back, his ankles and feet were dark with blood. After spending four long years as an army nurse, I had seen more than my share of dead men. My nursing experience told me this man had been dead for several hours, and that someone or something had kept him upright after the shooting long enough for the blood to settle downward in his limbs.

With no sign of bleeding, I couldn't even be sure the wound had happened while he was still alive. It was remotely possible that he had died of natural causes and someone wanted to make it look like Miss Hill or one of her girls was responsible. The idea was farfetched, but not impossible.

I cleaned my spectacles with my handkerchief, bent close, and examined the bullet wound. There was a faint scent of lye soap clinging to his skin. Someone had scrubbed vigorously around the wound, hard enough to leave scratches in the flesh.

I wondered if the bullet were still lodged in the body. It might provide some clue to the shooting. Judging from the size of the injury, the fatal shot must have been fired at close range. I was itching to turn him over and see if the bullet had gone clean through his body. Only my knowledge of Doc Haydon's temper kept me from satisfying my curiosity. He would be extremely perturbed to discover I had disturbed evidence before he arrived.

"How much time passed between the time you found him and when you sent for me?" I asked, covering the body and directing my attention to Miss Hill.

The madam shifted slightly, rearranging her skirt so it showed her shapely ankles to their best advantage and gave me a clearer view of her black silk stockings. She was a comely woman, despite the rouged lips. I could see how effective her actions could be at distracting a man. I smiled at the effort she was wasting on me, as I waited for her to answer my question.

"Belle left right away, Mr. Donnelly," she said after a long pause. Then she returned my smile with such eagerness that mine instantly vanished from my face. Involuntarily, my gaze dropped. I could feel color creeping up the back of my neck.

"Do you remember the time?" I asked, trying to regain a professional demeanor.

"Oh – not more than an hour ago," she said, uncrossing her legs and leaning forward slightly in her chair.

"You're sure?" I asked, glancing around the room instead of at the bosom she was obviously displaying for my benefit.

I studied each girl's face. "None of you laid eyes on this man till an hour ago?"

Under my intense gaze, the women edged further away from the body, but nobody spoke.

"If anybody knows him or what happened to him, this is the time to speak up."

"It's plain enough he was shot to death," one of the girls beside Rachel said, bringing a weak laugh from her near-naked companion.

"Is it now?" I said, fixing my gaze on her. "And would you be knowing that for a fact, seeing as how there is no blood a' tall around the hole in his bosom?" My tone was becoming sharper, and I realized I had slipped back into the Irish pattern of speech I had fought so hard to break myself from using.

The natural sternness of my expression, coupled with the sharp words, made her gasp. She took an involuntary step backwards.

I willed myself to calm down before continuing.

"I'd say that either he was dead before he was shot, or somebody cleaned him up afterwards. Either way, it is plain that he was killed elsewhere and left in this hallway."

Nobody said anything.

I took a deep breath and let it out slowly.

"Has anybody sent for the police?" I asked. "They've got to be notified."

"We were hoping you would fetch them, Mr. Donnelly," Miss Hill said, "seeing as how my girls and I are regulars at the city jail. It just didn't seem right for one of us to walk into the police station. Not of our own free will."

The comment brought on nervous tittering from more than one of the girls.

I could see her point of view. The bribes paid by Miss Hill and fines levied against her girls supported the salaries of at least a third of the police force. Still, I couldn't help feeling that Belle had very cleverly maneuvered me into the position of shielding her and her friends from the law. I, on the other hand, was standing in the direct line of fire in the battle that was sure to erupt over this case. One glance at the overly innocent expression on Belle's face confirmed my suspicion.

"All right, I'll notify the police," I said, "but first, you ladies are going to have to tell me everything. You're hiding something from me. If you want my help, I have to know the whole truth."

I had addressed all of them, but my eyes never left Belle.

"His name is Nate Buckner," she said softly, moving her head ever so slightly toward the body. "He's some sort of big wheel down at the cigar company. I'm not sure what he does – did there, but afore James run off…my husband, James, worked for him."

"So you knew him."

Her chin tilted up with a proud defiance until our eyes met and locked.

"I knew him. And, afore you ask, there no love lost between me and Mr. Buckner."

"Bad blood?"

Belle sighed. "Do you remember when Johnny Cook died?" She didn't wait for an answer. "The feller that shot himself at my back gate?"

Belle's eyes never left my face, but I noticed her hands clenched into tight little fists as she spoke.

"Mr. Buckner was the ringleader of the bunch trying to get me hanged. He never believed that Johnny pulled the trigger. At the inquest he called me a murderer. Right out loud. In front of half the town," she added with indignation.

Her chin tilted higher in a gesture of defiance to anyone who dared believe she was guilty of the charge.

"I never seen him since then…not afore tonight. Never wanted to either."

This was even worse than I suspected. I knew Nathaniel Buckner by reputation. I had also clipped the newspaper accounts of the young man found dead at Belle's former home, filing it away as I did with all crime stories. It was a habit from my days with Pinkerton that had proved very useful when I went to work for myself.

The *Lexington Gazette* had speculated wildly about the Cook shooting. Belle was a favorite topic of the editor. The fact that the shooting had taken place just nine days after her wedding sold out several issues of his paper.

I suspected the newsmen were the main reason her new husband had hightailed it out of Fayette County two weeks after marrying her. It didn't help silence the gossips that a small photograph of Belle and love notes she had written to Mr. Cook were found in the dead man's vest pocket. It must have shamed her husband beyond his ability to endure to have his new bride's former suitor shot outside their home.

Local gossipmongers had thrived for months on Belle's troubles. Johnny Cook was even rumored to be the real father of Belle's daughter. Although the inquest ended in a ruling of suicide, the public was unsatisfied with that decision. Having the man most adamant in calling her a murderer shot and left in the hallway of her new residence was certain to make Belle the chief suspect in his death.

"Did anybody else know Mr. Buckner?" I asked. "Was he perhaps a regular visitor?"

Jenny Hill shook her head.

"He is not a customer here," she said, "and I don't think knowing him is the right way to put it. Not so as I would recognize him on the street. I knowed the name though--when Belle told me who he was. Mr. Buckner was president of the Abstention Society...you know, those prudes trying to close down all the saloons and bawdyhouses. Buckner told the newspapers that we were a threat to the morality of Lexington's youth. Shucks. Lexington's youth don't want their morals protected any more than their elders did when they were young. Maybe one of them younguns plugged him so as he would quit spoiling their fun."

This pronouncement brought a round of laughter.

My head throbbed with a vengeance. This case was going to be a public spectacle. Every saloonkeeper and whorehouse in town had reason to want Buckner silenced. Unconsciously, my fingers rubbed my aching temples. By this time tomorrow, the news would be all over the state that Nathaniel P. Buckner, vice president and part owner of the largest cigar manufacturing company west of the Alleghenies, crusader for temperance, and pillar of the community, was found dead in the front hall of Miss Jenny Hill's whorehouse.

Perhaps I would have been better off if I had died of that knife wound last year, instead of being stitched up and nursed through it by Belle Brezing. But Belle had saved my life, and kept my secret, something few people would have done. If I'd sought medical attention and survived, I could have faced prison for impersonating a man, maybe even a hanging. Unless it involved marriage, it was unusual for a woman to hang for impersonating a man, but every legal contract I had signed with my brother's name, each bank deposit, even the purchase of property and the house I had built, were illegal acts. In my own way, I was breaking the law almost as often as anyone else in the room.

Besides, I had promised Belle my help, and I never went back on my word.

CHAPTER THREE

I didn't think much of Commander James William Slayton's management of the Lexington Police force. When the city finally decided to create a full time police force, Slayton was appointed because of his ties to several prominent families. He was one of the local gentry, but his family's money had been tied up in the breeding and selling of slaves. His background left an unpleasant taste in my mouth that was not improved by getting to know him. Slayton was angry at the world for his own shortcomings.

Slayton had never been one of the city watchmen, which had recently been reorganized into a full-fledged police force. He had no experience in police work. For that matter, he didn't seem to have any experience in any sort of work. The end of slavery left him nearly penniless. His skills left him ill-prepared for making his way in a world that no longer allowed him to trade in human lives. The fields of his family farm grew wild with brambles while he spent his days attending social gatherings.

I, and many other business people, thought Lexington would have been better off with an experienced lawman at the head of our new police force. But some of the more aristocratic elements of Fayette County society had pressured the mayor to appoint a member of the Bluegrass nobility to lead the city's new department. Slayton was the mayor's choice. Perhaps because Slayton was willing to let city officials continue to take bribes from Miss Hill and her ilk.

He hadn't proven a bad choice in some respects. The man knew more about making social appearances than he did about keeping the peace, but also seemed to know his limitations. He left the day-to-day running of the stationhouse to his two sergeants while he attended the speechmaking and ribbon-cutting events in his brass-buttoned uniform.

Both of his sergeants and most of the officers in the twelve-man force were veterans of the late War Between the States, which gave the force discipline similar to a military unit. They took great pride in the new stationhouse and kept exacting order in most of the city. Irishtown and the Bottoms were within the city limits, but nobody expected a force of only twelve men to keep those wards orderly. City leaders were satisfied if the police could keep the property damage confined to Lexington's slums and the impoverished residents inside their wards after sunset.

I was hoping Sergeant Wilfred Hamm, the usual night sergeant, would be on duty when I reached the stationhouse. Single men of my age lacked the respectability to associate much with married friends outside of work, but Sergeant Hamm and I frequently consulted on cases. Over the years we had developed an odd friendship, which was only hampered because Mrs. Hamm had taken upon herself the impossible task of finding me an appropriate wife.

Mildred Hamm's efforts to marry me off to one of the local spinsters had redoubled since I became a homeowner. These days I tended to avoid the Hamms, but tonight I needed the sergeant's help enough to seek him out. I resigned myself to the awkward position of being hounded by his matchmaking wife. The Buckner case was going to be difficult, and I wanted him in charge.

Unfortunately, Sergeant Hamm was nowhere to be seen when I arrived at the station house. The officer manning the front desk was fair-haired with a pinched face and narrow eyes. As I waited for him to acknowledge my presence, I couldn't help wondering how he got the job. His thin, delicate hands and neat penmanship seemed more suited to a law clerk or bookkeeper than to an officer of the law.

After waiting for a moment for him to stop writing, I cleared my throat.

When he finally looked up from the report he was laboriously completing, I realized that one of his gray eyes wandered to the left, so that even when he was looking at me he appeared to also be studying the wall.

"Can I help you, sir?" he asked.

It took effort not to sigh. I knew the police force had been adding some part-time officers to the ranks in preparation for next week's centennial celebrations, but the young man in front of me did not seem to be the sort they were choosing. Sergeant Hamm had told me they were looking for men with sharp eyes and the ability to spot pickpockets and other unsavory sorts flocking to Lexington to prey on the thousands of visitors arriving to participate in the festivities. This officer looked as if he would be an easy mark for the shills. I glanced quickly around the room, desperate to catch a glimpse of some other member of the force that I could more readily trust with such an explosive case. Seeing nobody else, I resigned myself to the inevitable.

"I'm here to report a murder," I said.

Horror flooded his face.

"M-murder, sir?"

He sprang to his feet so abruptly that his wooden chair toppled backwards to the floor with a loud bang. A new round of pain shot through my head.

"Yes. Murder," I said firmly, clenching my fists inside my front pockets. "Is there perhaps someone you could send with me to investigate, while you go wake Doc Haydon?"

My suggestion was a thinly veiled attempt to find a more competent officer, though to be fair we would need the services of the medical examiner before the body could be moved. I was secretly enjoying the thought of waking the good doctor so he could suffer along with me. After all, his contribution of a keg of bourbon barrel ale to last night's poker game was partly responsible for my present condition.

"There's nobody here but me. Sergeant Hamm and Officer Watts went over to break up a fight 'tween a couple of drunks at the new marketplace. I doubt they'll be back for at least…"

He stopped abruptly, realizing that he should not have told me the activities of his sergeant. His pale face blushed a deep rose shade that glowed along the edges of his ears.

"Then you need to lock up and go wake Doc Haydon," I said. "Tell him that Ness Donnelly sent for him. Ask him to meet me at Jenny Hill's."

His eyes widened at the mention of the bawdyhouse, but to his credit he composed himself enough to follow my instructions. At least, I hoped the instructions I gave him were not too difficult for him to remember. I followed him out and waited for him to lock the door before I went in search of Sergeant Hamm.

"Mother of Christ, don't let that fool meet anybody he can blab to on his way to find the doctor," I muttered as I watched him walk off in the direction of Upper Street.

I didn't have to go very far to find Sergeant Hamm. Less than half a block from the stationhouse, I spotted him at the corner. His round nose and droopy mutton-chop mustache were unmistakable, as was the spit shine on his riding boots. Hamm had worked hard for his rank and hoped that, when the force grew, he might become the first man promoted to detective sergeant. In the meantime, he and Officer Watts worked to keep the peace and make such arrests as were necessary on the night shift. The two of them were returning with a pair of local drunks.

I signaled to the sergeant, and waited for him to arrive.

He gave a low whistle when I explained what had happened.

"You've got yourself in a bit of a pickle this time, Mr. Donnelly," he said. "I can't say I'm sorry to see it. Having you for the high-falutin' to vent their spleens about is going to take a lot of the heat off the Commander and make life less unpleasant for us poor policemen."

"I don't imagine you'll be too comfortable, Sergeant Hamm. We already have a lot of reporters in town to cover next week's Centennial Celebration. I'm sure they are going to have a grand time making your commander squirm when this story gets out, and it will get out, too. There is no way to keep it quiet, considering the circumstances."

Our voices had gotten louder in the exchange and Officer Watts was watching us closely. The sergeant noticed him staring and walked over to where he waited with the prisoners.

"You'd better take these two and find them a nice cell to sleep it off in," he said, "I'm headed over to Jenny Hill's. There's a situation there that needs police attention. I might be a while." He didn't elaborate, just turned on his heel and headed down the street. "You coming, Donnelly?" he yelled over his shoulder.

By the time we reached the bawdyhouse, Doc Haydon and, to my chagrin, the young officer from the stationhouse had arrived. The boy was leaning against the wall gawking at the room full of suggestively dressed women as though he were a hungry five-year-old on his first visit to a sweet shop. His good eye rested on Belle's ample bosom, not that I could blame the boy. If the neckline of her gown were a hair lower, Sergeant Hamm could have arrested her for indecent exposure. At least Rachel had put her hair up and her companions had gotten dressed while I was away. I could imagine the boy's reaction if they were still parading around in their unmentionables.

Meanwhile, Doc Haydon was kneeling over the body. He looked up when we entered. There was only about ten years' difference in our ages, but the stubble on his face held more gray than brown. The lines around his bloodshot eyes seemed to deepen each year.

"I guess you can call for the death wagon, Sergeant," he said gruffly. "Have them take him to my autopsy room where I can examine him more closely. There are some peculiarities about the cause of death that I need to reflect upon."

"What sort of peculiarities?" Sergeant Hamm asked, glancing from me to the doctor.

Doc Haydon frowned.

"I'll give you a full report when I have had time to examine him more thoroughly, Sergeant," he said coldly. "If you'll excuse me, I would rather get home before daylight." He walked out before Hamm had the opportunity to ask him another question.

When the red-faced sergeant looked my direction, I was deeply occupied studying the floral design of Miss Hill's velvet-flocked wallpaper, giving him no chance to direct his frustration toward me.

If I had been of a mind to, I could have told Hamm that the doctor wanted to get away under cover of darkness because he was seriously hung over, and did not want to be forced to walk home in the daylight.

He and I had spent yesterday afternoon at the Kentucky Association track and most of the evening playing poker at Michael Flannery's saloon. He'd picked up those dark circles under his eyes consuming half a dozen mint juleps at the track, followed by far too much bourbon barrel ale at the weekly poker game. Haydon was not any happier about having his sleep interrupted than I was when Belle had rousted me. Besides, the doctor was aware that it was unprofessional for a physician to be seen coming out of a bawdyhouse, no matter what his reasons for entering the establishment might have been. I didn't think he would appreciate my sharing this information with the sergeant, so I contented myself with studying the wall while Sergeant Hamm fumed.

"Officer Kent." Sergeant Hamm shouted.

"Yes, Sergeant?" the young man from the stationhouse replied.

"Go fetch the death wagon. And be quick about it."

"Yes, sir."

I stayed close to Sergeant Hamm while he questioned Miss Hill and the ladies. Once or twice, I had to bite my cheek to keep from laughing as they told Hamm where they were and what they were doing when the body was discovered. Not one account included the normal activity of a bordello, or the mention of anyone other than the ladies being on the premises.

Three of the girls claimed they had been sound asleep when the body was discovered, and hadn't left their rooms until Rachel's screams woke them. Emma swore that it was her turn at kitchen duty and she had been washing dishes at the time. Belle might have been telling the truth when she said she was in her room sewing. She was an excellent seamstress. In any case, she said that she had torn her gown earlier in the evening, and was busy mending it when Miss Rachel screamed. Miss Hill was in her office entering sums into her household account ledger. The unfortunate Rachel swore she had been writing her dear mother, and had just come downstairs to fetch a glass of water when she stumbled upon the deceased.

Rachel's account of her activities struck me as the most unlikely of the lot. I could not imagine that her father would allow any communication between his wife and the daughter he had cast out of his house.

Sergeant Hamm dutifully wrote the explanations of their whereabouts into his notebook, giving no indication of whether or not he believed their stories. He couldn't really expect them to admit they were engaged in an illegal activity or give him the names of their visitors. Still, it was frustrating that nobody admitted to hearing or seeing anything before Rachel screamed.

I hoped they would be more forthcoming with me. It was going to be next to impossible to clear the ladies if they refused to tell me who they had seen this evening or what they were really doing when Rachel discovered the body. I thought I might have better luck getting the truth if I spoke to each woman individually when the police were not present.

It was past dawn when Officer Kent returned with the death wagon. Undoubtedly, the presence of the black wagon was going to draw the attention of early morning dray drivers and workmen on their way to their jobs. Officer Kent and the driver made sure the sheet hid the body as they loaded Buckner onto the stretcher, but his bulky shape made it easy for onlookers to tell it was not one of the ladies being carried out of Miss Hill's establishment.

One glance at Sergeant Hamm told me he was thinking the same thing.

"I guess I had better go break the news to the widow," he said quietly. "She is bound to be wondering why her husband didn't make it home last night. From what I have heard of him, he was a man of regular habits."

CHAPTER FOUR

A gray mist shrouded downtown, muffling our footsteps. Sergeant Hamm and I walked along Main Street toward the city limits. Neither of us said anything. Sergeant Hamm hadn't expressly invited me to accompany him to the Buckner home, but when I followed him out of Jenny Hill's, he didn't refuse my company.

I suspected that he was somewhat reluctant to face the formidable Mrs. Buckner with the news of her husband's demise. I couldn't help wondering what he would tell Buckner's family about the circumstances under which the body had been discovered. Certainly telling his widow that he had been found naked in a brothel was going to require a great deal of tact. This was not a trait Sergeant Hamm was known to possess.

In any family, such news would be difficult, but for a family as socially prominent and morally crusading as the Buckners, the scandal would be ruinous. Folks of Mr. Buckner's social class were firmly convinced that their status set them above the human frailties of the less fortunate. The illusion didn't stop them from having the same failings as the rest of us, but it tended to make them unforgiving of their own when scandal drew attention to their vices. Once their veneer of respectability had been stripped away, the power and privilege of the Buckner family could never be fully restored.

By midday, Mrs. Buckner would discover that invitations were being discreetly withdrawn under the pretense of respect for her period of mourning. Later, when no legitimate excuse could be given for excluding her from social occasions, the snubs would be more direct. The whispers that had previously been hidden behind closed doors would pointedly take place in her presence. Should a member of the Buckner family call upon their neighbors, their call would be declined on the flimsiest of excuses. I couldn't help feeling a tinge of sympathy for the family as I watched the lines of pink and orange creep slowly over the horizon.

As we neared the east end of Main Street, I tried to sort through the tangle of questions. Why was Nathaniel Buckner shot? Why move the body? Was he dressed at the time of death? If so, why remove his clothing? Was placing Buckner's body in a brothel intended to bring ruin upon his family, or upon Jenny Hill and her girls, or was it more than that?

The sun was getting higher. Small tendrils of the morning mist drifted like fading ghosts over the grounds of Ashland, the late Henry Clay's magnificent estate which sat at the city limits. Beyond Ashland's carefully groomed lawns, the city's merchants had built fine houses among the oaks lining Richmond Road.

There on the outskirts of the city, the newly rich were building a stately neighborhood. At this hour, their live-in servants were just beginning to stir. Now and then Sergeant Hamm and I would catch the scent of salt pork frying or hear a snippet of some housekeeper's haggling with neighborhood pushcart vendors over the price of eggs or fresh milk. The iceman was driving his team of mules slowly down the street, delivering his frozen blocks to kitchens equipped with the newfangled iceboxes Mr. Thompson's freezing plant had recently made popular.

I couldn't help thinking of just how far the mile or two of cobblestones had taken us from the world Sergeant Hamm and I occupied on the west end of town. Neither of us had ever been impoverished enough to live in the Lexington slums of Irishtown or Davis Bottoms, where many of the servants who kept these great houses returned every evening, but we were interlopers on Richmond Road. Not quite the outcasts that Belle and her companions would be, but not respectable enough to be allowed into the parlors of the well-to-do merchants. It struck me that in their own way, the Buckners had just become as much social outcasts to this place as Jenny Hill and her girls. The Clay family was part of the old aristocracy, and could look the other way at the late Senator's well-known love of gambling and good bourbon, but the newly rich were not as comfortable with wealth and lacked any tolerance for public vices among their contemporaries.

When we reached the Buckner residence, Sergeant Hamm started to go around to the tradesmen's entrance. I knew this, but ignored his intentions and walked directly to the front door, pulling the bell before he had a chance to catch up to me.

A colored maid opened the door. Her eyes widened at the sight of Sergeant Hamm's uniform. I watched her mouth gape open next as I dropped my calling card into the small silver tray in her hand. I tried to overlook her shocked expression, bowed slightly, and met her eyes.

"Would you be kind enough to let your mistress know Ness Donnelly and Sergeant Wilfred Hamm are here on urgent business?"

She closed the door in my face and retreated with the card.

"What the devil are you thinking?" The sergeant hissed between clenched teeth. "Do you know what the Commander is going to say about us marching up to the front door like we were paying a respectable call on the family?"

"Were you planning to be disrespectful?" I asked, feigning ignorance of what he meant.

Before he had the chance to utter the obscenities that seemed to balance on the tip of his tongue, the door opened and a younger, thinner version of Nathaniel Buckner forced him to bite back his words.

"Mr. Donnelly?" the young man said, taking my card from the pocket of his dressing gown and reading my name from it as if he couldn't be bothered to remember who I was without prompting. The tone of voice and the way he tipped his head so he was looking down his long nose at me was intended to put me squarely in my place. "My mother is not receiving at this hour. If your business is indeed urgent, I will relay a message for you."

Nothing sets my teeth on edge quite so quickly as having a boy of twenty looking down his nose at the people who made his comfortable life possible. My fists clenched and plunged deeper inside my pockets as I struggled to keep my temper in check.

The sergeant and I had been up all night dealing with his father's death. We had just hiked two miles to talk to a family that was keeping us waiting on the doorstep, and treating us like insubordinates.

"I'm afraid that won't do, sir," I said icily. "Our business is not the sort that should be discussed on a doorstep. Of course, if you and your mother are not concerned about why your father didn't come home last night, I suppose the good sergeant and I could go home and wait until his absence is deemed important enough to his family to initiate a police inquiry. By then, I am sure the whole state will be aware of matters you might prefer to have known first."

Buckner's dark brown eyes betrayed the emotions his breeding refused to allow him to express aloud.

For a long moment he stood staring at us. "You have news of Father?" he said at last. His gaze dropped to his toes as he stepped back to permit us to come in.

Allowing us over the threshold of his home was Buckner's only concession. He led us to a small, unheated room and closed the door. Despite the hour and the long walk, he did not invite us to sit.

"Well? What is it, Officer?" he said, ignoring me and perhaps deliberately failing to acknowledge Sergeant Hamm's rank.

Sergeant Hamm took off his hat and held it awkwardly, clutching the brim with both hands. He cleared his throat. His gaze drifted toward me as he shifted uncomfortably from one foot to the other.

I understood his dilemma. It was difficult enough to tell a family a loved one had met with an accident, or been caught in some misdemeanor which landed them in jail. I could see his ears and the back of his neck turning red as he struggled to find a way to explain the circumstances of the late Mr. Buckner's demise to his son. He glanced at me again, and since I had already taken a strong dislike to the young man, I nodded my consent to being the one to tell him of his father's death.

My decision to break the news to the family was not entirely for Sergeant Hamm's benefit. Long years of experience had taught me that behind the carefully constructed mask respectable families wore in public there often lurked cold-blooded murderers. I wanted to be in a position to watch young Mr. Buckner's face carefully for signs of guilt.

"I regret being the bearer of bad news, sir, but sometime yesterday your father had the misfortune of being on the wrong end of a gun," I said, my studied gaze taking in every detail of his demeanor.

At the mention of the gun there was a nearly imperceptible flicker of fear that flashed through his features before disappearing, replaced instantly by an expression akin to the unreadable gaze of a riverboat gambler.

Buckner said nothing.

The men who sat across the card table from me at last night's game would have marveled at the speed with which Buckner could master his emotions. It made me wonder what reason a man of his age would find it necessary to develop such a skill. I was going to have to press him very hard indeed to break through that poker face.

"His body was discovered by Miss Rachel Elliott early this morning." I said. "He had been dead for several hours."

"Miss Elliott? I am not acquainted with a Miss Elliott," he said, in a tone that made me think that if he was not personally acquainted with her, he at least was familiar with her name and occupation.

Gentlemen frequently denied knowing any of the residents of Miss Hill's West Main Street establishment once they departed the company of the ladies residing there. What surprised me was that young Mr. Buckner's first response was to deny knowing Miss Elliott. Was he really more interested in protecting his own reputation than he was in the news of his father's death?

That callousness placed him at the top of my suspect list. He wouldn't be the first son to want to dispose of his father in order to gain an inheritance. Of course, his behavior didn't explain the location of the body. Creating that kind of scandal in his family would take hatred deep enough to be willing to see his own name dragged through the mud in order to exact revenge upon his father.

"Miss Elliott is a resident of a bawdyhouse that caters to men of social prominence, Mr. Buckner," I said, hoping to provoke a reaction. "Would you happen to know if your father frequented her employer's establishment?"

"My father was a man of the highest integrity, sir," he said with the same cold tone he used at the door.

The arrogant up-tilt of his nose and haughty voice would have been more effective if his hands had not been trembling. Buckner's carefully constructed mask had finally cracked. His muscles stiffened and shades of crimson crept along protruding veins of his neck.

I inched closer, crowding him as I spoke. "Never the less, Mr. Buckner, his body was carried out of a brothel at dawn this morning, wearing nothing but the sheet that one of the women had been kind enough to cover him with."

The words were hard, perhaps harder than necessary, but I

needed to find out if Buckner held any affection for his father. My own expression remained impassive as our eyes locked.

"There are questions that must be answered, sir. Since you have chosen to meet with us instead of allowing us to speak to your mother, we can be more direct. It is better that we ask you the difficult questions, rather than discussing the indelicate circumstances surrounding the discovery of your father's body with her. Don't you agree?"

The breath he had been holding escaped in a rush mingled with the scent of breakfast bacon and stale cigars. His face paled as is lungs deflated, but he didn't answer.

"I should think it would be difficult enough for your mother when news of this murder becomes public," I said, pressuring him further. "I ask you again sir, do you know if your father was a frequent visitor to Miss Hill's establishment?"

"No," he said, sinking down into one of the nearby armchairs.

"Did he have any vices that might explain the circumstances of his death?" I asked less harshly. I had won the battle of wills but took no pleasure in gaining more information.

"My father is--was usually home by half past seven unless called away on business or fulfilling a social obligation."

"Were there business difficulties, rivalries, that might have made him enemies?" Sergeant Hamm asked, his tone kinder than my own.

"I don't really know much about his business. I have an office at the cigar factory, but I've only joined the company this spring. Father wanted me to learn the business from the ground up. As a result, I spend most of my time with warehouse workmen or on the floor of the cigar factory overseeing the cutters."

"I see," the sergeant said. "What can you tell me about his associates outside the factory? Can you think of anyone at all who would wish him harm? Is there anyone who would want him dead, or gain from his demise?"

"I'm sorry," he said. His body slumped further in the chair, as if the news of his father's death was finally beginning to sink into his consciousness. "I should know him better, I suppose, but I don't know anyone who would do this. Father hardly does anything but work and attend church or meetings."

"Can you tell me when you last saw your father?" I asked.

"At noon yesterday. We had lunch together at the Phoenix

Hotel. Afterwards, he asked me to find my own way back to the office. He said he needed to send a wire to Frankfort and take care of some business at the bank."

"Did he seem worried or angry when you last saw him?" Sergeant Hamm asked.

A rueful smile played at the corners of the young man's mouth.

"I cannot say I have ever seen my father when he wasn't angry about something," he said. "His temper is well known. It takes very little provocation to rile Father."

It was reassuring to hear the young man still talking about his father in the present tense. Most men have a hard time thinking of loved ones in the past tense, but I have often noticed that men guilty of murder first commit it inside their own minds.

"I see," I said. "Was there anything in particular that provoked his temper yesterday?"

"If there was, he did not see fit to confide in me. We talked mostly about how things were going at the factory. We have lost a lot of the colored workers to the free land promises Kansas has been making. Father has been experimenting with hiring some of the girls from Irishtown to roll cigars, and wanted to know how they were working out. He listened to me for a couple of minutes, then his attention drifted. He seemed to have more interest in watching one of the other customers play with his eating utensils than he did in the new factory girls. We barely finished one course when he called for our check. He said he needed to send a telegram, and that I should tell Mother not to wait dinner for him – he had a board meeting at the bank with Mr. Peltmutter."

"Did you see who captured his attention?"

"Not well. He was sitting behind me," the young man said.

"Could you describe him at all?" Sergeant Hamm asked. "I would like to question him."

"He was built like a blacksmith, broad shoulders, barrel chest. His clothes were better though, not good, but not a workman's clothing."

"Did you see his face?" the sergeant asked. "His hair?"

"I don't recall anything distinctive in his features. His hair was thick, brown, touched with gray. He might have been Father's age."

"Thank you," Sergeant Hamm said.

"Where does he do his banking?" I asked.

"National Bank, of course. Father's on the board." There was a trace of pride in the way he spoke of his father's position.

Sergeant Hamm was closing his notebook when I glanced his direction.

"Did you have any other questions, Sergeant?"

"Not at the moment," he said. Thank you for your time, Mr. Buckner. We will need to call again later, after we've had a chance to speak to his business partner and his bank. We will wait until then to question your mother and the rest of the household. Unless you would prefer we break the news to her…"

"No!" he exclaimed.

I tried not to smile at the expression of horror on his face. He must have believed we would break the news to her as baldly as I had to him.

"There is no need to trouble her until we find out if he did indeed meet with anyone at the bank yesterday afternoon. We'll need to visit again, Mr. Buckner," Sergeant Hamm said, glancing at me.

I nodded, closed my notebook, and dropped it back in my vest pocket. I intended to visit the telegraph office, but there was no need to share that with him. If Buckner did send a message yesterday, I was hoping the operator would remember.

CHAPTER FIVE

The sun burned away the last traces of fog as we made our way back downtown. I could see the mule trams pulling out of Central Station and beginning their rounds of Main Street. Keen-eyed drivers perched ready to capture any likely fare. It didn't take long for one of them to spot us.

Sergeant Hamm and I climbed aboard, dropped nickels into the driver's box, and found a seat. Thankfully, my headache had retreated. I would have hated to face daylight in the condition I had been in when Belle rousted me from my bed. I plopped into one of the wooden benches just as Sergeant Hamm's stomach let out a growl that made me wonder how long it had been since his last meal.

The sergeant had been up all night, and I had barely slept three hours. We were hot and tired and no closer to figuring out the truth than when we left Miss Hill's.

Aside from taking an instant dislike to young Buckner, I hadn't any solid reason to think he was involved in his father's murder. In fact, my conversation with him led me to believe he was probably innocent. I couldn't blame him for wanting to shield his mother from police questioning. Later, it might prove necessary to question the household. For now, it seemed more prudent to leave them to their mourning.

Except for the rumbling of his stomach, Sergeant Hamm was quiet on the ride back to town. I was grateful for the silence. It gave me time to think about what happened between the time Buckner and his son met for lunch and the murder. Did he make it to Ambrose Peltmutter's office? Was he killed inside the bank? Why scrub the body so carefully that no trace of blood remained? Most curiously, why had the murderer dumped the body in Jenny Hill's front hall? If I didn't find answers quickly…

I retreated from the thought of Belle being hanged, and focused on what I needed to accomplish.

"Why don't we retrace Buckner's steps, starting with the Phoenix Hotel?" I suggested to Sergeant Hamm. "I would like to find out if anyone remembers the Buckners dining there yesterday. Besides, I could use a good meal. I'll treat you to breakfast while we poke around to see what we can turn up."

"Well, if you're buying," the sergeant said, smoothing his thick mustache, "I could use some hot coffee and a bite to eat."

"Good. We will start with the hotel, then the telegraph office. I am curious about that telegram."

"It's just around the corner," Sergeant Hamm said. "It shouldn't be difficult to investigate both."

"By the time you finish your report it will be way past your bedtime."

"Past that now," Sergeant Hamm grumbled. "The day sergeant's duty started afore we left Miss Jenny's. My missus will be thinkin' something dreadful's happened. You're a fortunate man to not have a wife thinking you're laying dead every time you don't get home on time."

"If that is your way of telling me your wife is getting ready to try finding me a good woman again, I'll consider myself warned."

Sergeant Hamm laughed.

"Millie says it ain't natural for a man your age to be single," he said, climbing down. "It's un-American, what with so many women left to spinsterhood by the late war."

I glared at him but he ignored me.

"Besides, you're a man of property," he added, "That new house of yours could do with a woman's touch."

"I am sure my housekeeper is perfectly capable of giving it as many womanly touches as it needs," I said crossly. "Besides, weren't you just pointing out how fortunate I was to not have a wife?"

"Bachelorhood ain't all that wonderful," he said. "Beulah can set a fine table but a man needs a family if he wants to be a respectable member of the community."

He stopped and looked me in the eye.

"Donnelly, you should give some serious thought to what you

are doing with your life. Your only friends are Doc Haydon and Belle Brezing. I will grant you that Miss Brezing has charms, but that's not the sort of woman who will improve your social standing."

"I wasn't aware my social standing needed improving," I snapped.

"Donnelly, think about it. You don't attend church regular. Being Catholic and all, you're not likely to be invited to join the Masons or any of the other clubs. Even the Oddfellows shy away from single men, except for the occasional priest. How does it look to potential clients to know the outrageous sums of money they pay you is spent at bawdyhouses and racetracks?"

My eyebrows shot up. Hamm thought I was a customer of Belle's.

"That really isn't any of their concern." I was peeved that Hamm wouldn't have believed me if I denied visiting Miss Hill's before the murder. A gentleman was expected to deny association with prostitutes.

"People talk, Donnelly," Sergeant Hamm said. "And don't think that I haven't noticed you got ambitions. With a good wife, your business would double inside of a year."

"I suppose you or your wife knows just the woman?" I asked sarcastically.

He frowned and said, "Millie thinks her cousin Kate should make your acquaintance. I do too. Mary Kate's pa is Irish."

My eyes narrowed.

He gave me a badly faked hurt expression. "I should think you'd be pleased to meet a nice Catholic girl."

"Why?" I asked.

He laughed.

"Kate's a strong steady girl, the sort that a man could be proud to have as a wife."

"Humm," I mumbled noncommittally. "I suppose that means she is pig headed and has the Irish temper?"

"She is a nice girl, Donnelly. You don't have to take my word for it," he said. Why don't you come to dinner next Sunday and meet her for yourself?"

"No offense, Sergeant," I said, "but I really don't have the kind of life that is suited to marriage."

"Look here, Donnelly, the war left big holes in men's lives. You think it was your fault that your sister went into nursing. She followed you into the war and all."

I started to protest, but Hamm cut me off.

"I didn't know her. I consider myself fortunate to have come through the unpleasantness without being wounded. I heard a lot, though, from men who remember the way she would go out on the battlefield under a truce flag helping carry the wounded to the hospital. My cousin Ezra is alive today because of her. She must have been a fine woman. Strong too, had to be to nurse the kind of wounds she saw. Ezra said that after working all day, she would sit up nights talking or reading to the men. She even wrote letters home when they couldn't write for themselves."

His hand rested on my shoulder in an almost brotherly fashion.

I opened my mouth to speak but he didn't let me.

"Being twins and all, I know you were close to your sister. But the war's been over nigh on fifteen years. Don't you think it's time to give up this fool notion of finding out what happened to her? Get on with your life."

I didn't know what to say to this. In a way, the men who killed Ness had ended my life too. Even if I succeeded at finding his killer, the old me was gone forever.

What had I become?

Not Ness; I shuddered at the thought of how appalled my brother would be at the coarseness of my behavior.

I was a mess, a circus freak, treading halfway between man and woman and not belonging to either world.

Sergeant Hamm's voice was kind.

"Come to dinner Sunday. If you don't find Kate to your liking, there's a passel of other women out there who would be happy to accept an offer of marriage."

I was relieved when we reached the hotel, until I realized that Sergeant Hamm had finally stopped his speech and was looking at me expectantly.

The lump in my throat made it impossible to speak. Besides, what was I to say to his glowing commentary on my wartime activities or about the impossibility of my ever getting married?

I couldn't very well tell him that the Pinkertons had carefully reviewed every letter I mailed, or that I wrote details of those intimate bedtime conversations into reports for the Union army. Nor could I tell him that it was Ness who had been murdered and that I would be committing a hanging offense if I found myself a "nice wife." I had chosen my road when I buried my dresses and put on my brother's clothes. There was no turning back after all these years.

The sergeant mistook my silence for consent.

"Good," he said, grinning at me. "Millie will be pleased to see you. She thinks you need fattening up. Five o'clock sharp. She don't like to keep dinner waiting. Besides, I have Sunday duty this week. I wouldn't want to have to leave before we've had a proper visit."

I paled a little at the thought of what he considered a proper visit, not that Hamm noticed. The aroma of fresh brewed coffee and sausages had his full attention. I had to hurry to keep up with him as we entered the hotel dining room.

Half a dozen colored waiters were scurrying around the room when we entered. Some carried four or five plates laden with hot buckwheat pancakes, sausages, steaming bowls of porridge or grits, and eggs cooked in a number of ways.

"Good morning, gentlemen," the headwaiter said. "Would you like a table, or have you come for beaten biscuits and country ham at the bar?"

My mouth watered at the sight of a tray of beaten biscuits and country ham passing a few feet away. I had never had beaten biscuits before coming to Kentucky. Now I considered them the only way to have country ham. I was sorely tempted to vote for dining at the bar, but my feet put up a strong, painful, argument for sitting at a table.

Sergeant Hamm spoke first.

"A table," he said, "but first I need to know if you worked lunch yesterday."

His broad smile vanished and his eyes grew large at Sergeant Hamm's question. In that instant the waiter's starched white collar became too small for his neck.

I was tempted to say something. Deep down, it bothered me that colored men in the city had reason for their inordinate fear of the law. The Klan was everywhere, including in the ranks of the police department. Hardly a week went by without a lynching somewhere in the Bluegrass.

I supposed the war hadn't changed much in their day-to-day interaction white men. Maybe it was because Negro and white units had fought for different reasons.

Chicago was full of immigrants who believed deeply in the need to preserve the Union. But many immigrants, particularly the

Irish, resisted conscription. Some even rioted rather than being forced into the Union army. Most Irish didn't care if the South left the Union. Freed men were just more competitors for the day labor jobs open to immigrants.

The war was different for the colored. They had fought first for the right to join the battle, then for a place in ranks that did not welcome their participation. They didn't really care about the Union or the rights of individual states. They fought and died for their freedom and that of their families. What they got was a mixed bag of good and evil. When the war ended, both sides knew trouble between the races was just beginning. It took all my willpower to stand back and wait for Sergeant Hamm to realize that the man was afraid to answer his questions.

"I was told that Nathaniel Buckner and his son had lunch here yesterday," Hamm finally said, in an effort to explain the purpose of his questions. "I am trying to find someone who might be able to verify that. I know Mr. Buckner is a regular customer, and a member of the Lexington Club. I'll try not to use what you say as evidence, but I was hoping you or one of the waiters might know him by sight and remember seeing him yesterday."

"Yes, sir," he said, noticeably relieved that we were not looking for him personally. "Mr. Buckner came in 'bout half past twelve. He was in a powerful hurry. Didn't even stay for coffee. Just paid his check and left the young man to eat alone at the table."

"Did he speak to anyone besides his son?" Sergeant Hamm asked.

"Not that I know of, sir."

The sergeant thanked him and glanced at me to see if I had any other questions.

"Where was Mr. Buckner sitting?" I asked.

"At that table," he said pointing to a table in the section reserved for members of the Lexington Club.

"Which way was he facing?"

Sergeant Hamm gave me a look that said I had lost my mind, but I ignored him.

"His back was to the window," the waiter said. "The young man was sitting there," he indicated the seat directly across the table from Buckner.

"Humm..." I murmured, "Do you know who was sitting there?" I asked, looking at the table directly behind the one occupied by the Buckners.

"No sir," he said, looking confused. "I never saw him afore."

"It was one man?"

"Yes, sir," he said.

"Can you describe him?" I asked.

"No sir," he said, shaking his head.

The fear in his face was palpable. Who could blame him? The laws which denied colored men from giving testimony against white men in court had been struck down, but the Klan considered such impertinence a lynching offense. There was nothing to be gained by pressing him for details.

"Did he speak to anyone?" I asked.

"No, sir," he said, "Commander Slayton said howdy on his way out. Couldn't say if he knowed the man. Commander's right sociable with everybody."

"Thanks," I said. "I think we are ready for that table now."

"Yes, sir," he said, picking up a couple of leather-bound menus. "This way, gentlemen. Jim here will take good care of you. Got some prime steaks in this mornin', if you're interested. They look mighty fine."

Sergeant Hamm laid his menu on the table.

"I won't be needing this," he said. "Those steaks sound just right. I'll take a side of potatoes and three eggs over easy. Coffee too, and some buttermilk biscuits with honey and loads of butter." When he had finished with his list he looked at me. "Do you know what you want, Donnelly?"

"I'll have the sausage links and a short stack of your buckwheat pancakes," I said. "If you have fresh milk, I would like a glass."

"What was that all about?" Sergeant Hamm said, as Jacob left to fetch our meal. "Why does it matter who sat behind Buckner at lunch yesterday?"

"Maybe it doesn't," I said, "but it bothers me that Buckner ran out of here in such a 'powerful hurry' yesterday. You told me he was known as a man of regular habits. Taking off in the middle of his meal doesn't fit. Any time the facts of an investigation don't fit they needle me."

"Grown men having milk instead of coffee for breakfast, don't fit either," he muttered as the waiter set a tall glass in front of me. "That stuff is for babies. A man needs something to put hair on his chest."

"I don't know about you, but I intend to sleep just like a baby later," I replied.

He laughed and said, "The difference between us is that you get up and sleep when you please, Donnelly. By the time I finish my report for the Commander, it'll be noon or later."

"It takes about as much time to write up a case as to do the investigating," I said.

"That's a fact," he said. "I'll be happy if the coffee keeps me awake long enough to do all the danged writin' the Commander wants. You mark my words, Donnelly, the day is comin' that it won't matter how good a man is at his job. All anybody will ask is how well he wrote his report."

"Umm," I mumbled noncommittally. Hamm wasn't often talkative, but on this subject he reminded me of a politician making a stump speech.

"I'm serious. Education is going to be the ruination of this country. The normal schools are turning half the girls out there into teachers. And what does that amount to? Just look at that new officer the Commander gave me. The boy can't even see straight. He got himself beat to a pulp the only time he ever tried to break up a fight. And God help us all if he has to use his gun. But, he writes real pretty."

His long face puckered into a disgusted expression.

"The Commander says he graduated high school and is thinking about saving up to get more schooling. If that don't beat all: grown men still going to school. And the Commander thinks that is something to be proud of, just cause the boy is a shirt-tail cousin of his."

I pretended to choke on my sausage to hide my laughter. I didn't share his views on education, but Sergeant Hamm's assessment of Officer Kent mirrored my own. My instincts told me it was one thing for the sergeant to insult one of his officers, and quite another for an outsider to do so. It was far more prudent to settle back in my chair and finish eating.

Getting to my feet after breakfast was a challenge. I had walked close to five miles since Belle rousted me from my bed. My lower limbs were starting to feel like dead weights. I told myself that just a little longer, and then I would go home and finish the sleep Belle had interrupted. Maybe this time my dreams would not take me back to the night my brother died.

The telegraph office was just around the corner on Main Street. We had to dodge workmen hanging flags from each lamppost and spreading red, white, and blue banners across the front of downtown buildings. The city council had voted to honor Daniel Boone during the festivities and every shop window and street corner seemed to sprout some vestige of him. Lexington was spending lavishly on the Centennial week celebration. I, along with every other businessman in town, had kicked in a handsome contribution to cover the expenses.

Sergeant Hamm frowned.

"I'll bet every pickpocket in the country is headed to Lexington for this fool party," he grumbled. "Did you notice the tents going up on the lawn of the fairgrounds? They are renting them out for seventy-five cents a night. All the hotels and boarding houses are out of rooms."

"Maybe I should rent out my spare bedrooms for the week," I joked. "If a tent is going for that price, imagine what I could make on a room with a real bed."

"Don't joke about it. Millie is fixing a pallet on the floor for the boys and renting their room to a couple from up Maysville way. They are paying her more for a week's room and board than I make in two months."

"I may have to speak to my housekeeper about it," I said, pushing open the door to the telegraph office. "Beulah could probably use a little extra money."

I had noticed that when it came to interviewing ordinary citizens, Sergeant Hamm was much more comfortable than he was in the presence of the local gentry. At the telegraph office, I stood back and let him ask the questions.

Tommy Ellis, the young operator, grinned when we entered.

"Morning, Sergeant," he said, "You're up late today. On a case?"

"Tommy, I need your help," Sergeant Hamm said, in his most confidential tone.

The boy's eyes danced with excitement. "My help?"

I watched as he leaned over the counter and lowered his voice to make the conversation appear more confidential. I tried to keep my expression serious, but lacked the advantage Sergeant Hamm's drooping mustache and long face gave him.

"I need to know about a telegram sent to Frankfort sometime between noon to one o'clock yesterday by Mr. Nathaniel P. Buckner."

"Yes sir,' he said, looking confused. "It was just his usual business kind of message."

"Do you still have a copy of his message?"

"Yes, sir, the company has me put the date and time on all messages and file them, but I'm not allowed to show them to anybody. They're private, like mail at the post office."

"The police are allowed to confiscate mail, Tommy. I could go get the judge to put that in writing if you want, but it would be a lot easier if you just let me look at the message and any reply he got."

Tommy looked uncertain, but he pulled out the small box of messages and took out one addressed to one Isaiah Malthus at the Republican Party Headquarters in Frankfort. He handed it to the sergeant.

I had to adjust my spectacles slightly in order to read over his shoulder.

"Stewardship issue of mutual concern has arisen STOP KL arrived this morning STOP Implement contingent plan immediately STOP Buckner."

On the surface, the message seemed harmless enough, but I had sent enough of these kind of cryptic messages to Allen Pinkerton's offices during the war to know that this one was probably a warning. The trouble was I didn't know of anyone with the initials "KL" and with all the new arrivals in town it would be impossible to find one new face among the thousands. I wrote the message into my notebook exactly as it appeared on the yellow telegraph form, and waited while Sergeant Hamm finished his own notes.

"Was there a reply?" the sergeant asked, as he handed the page back to Tommy.

"No, sir. See?" he said, pointing to a small stamp at the bottom of the page. "That means the message was undeliverable. If you want, I'll telegraph Frankfort and ask if Mr. Malthus was found."

"Do that," Sergeant Hamm said.

We waited while Tommy tapped in the series of dots and dashes that identified Frankfort as the station he wished to contact, then the long seconds of silence while we listened for the corresponding call signal for Lexington. Tommy's fingers tapped his question with a precision of a musician, then picked up his pencil and carefully copied down the response from Frankfort Station.

"Nobody has been able to find Mr. Malthus," he said. "It is causing a ruckus in Frankfort. Seems he missed a big meeting with the Republican legislators last night."

I couldn't remember exactly what position Isaiah Malthus held in the Republican Party, but his not showing up at a political meeting didn't sound good. Maybe it was nothing, or maybe that telegram was a warning to get out of town. I placed two bits on the counter on top of one of my calling cards.

"Tell the Frankfort operator to keep you posted if there is any news at all of Mr. Malthus's whereabouts. My address is on the card. There is a dollar in it for you when you bring me news."

Sergeant Hamm looked at me like I was the village idiot. The boy probably didn't make much more than a dollar a week. A Sergeant of Police barely made twenty-one dollars a month, but I had a bad feeling about Malthus being mixed up in what happened to Nathaniel Buckner.

As we left the telegraph office, I made up my mind to ask the Commander about the stranger Mr. Buckner was watching at the Phoenix Dining Room. He might remember some detail of the man's appearance. Maybe the man was of no importance, but Buckner's primary interest seemed to be in business. He had invited his son to lunch for the express purpose of discussing the new factory girls. Yet Buckner had been too distracted by another diner to listen to what his son had to say. It was out of character and that alone made it of interest to me.

Commander Slayton was in a foul mood when Sergeant Hamm and I arrived at the stationhouse. I couldn't blame him. The city was overrun with reporters covering the centennial festivities and the newsmen were finding Buckner's murder a much better way to sell papers. Normally the Commander would have insulated himself behind a couple of broad-shouldered officers, but in the hoopla of the centennial his officers were needed elsewhere. Only Officer Kent remained at the stationhouse, and the lad was of little use in keeping reporters away from his cousin's door. Two of the more enterprising reporters had the Commander of Police cornered in his office and were hammering him with questions, while Officer Kent issued ineffectual threats of what would happen if they didn't leave the premises immediately.

Sergeant Hamm grabbed the nearest interloper by his shirt collar and pulled him from the Commander's office.

"Kent, open the door," he ordered.

The young man obeyed.

Sergeant Hamm grabbed the crotch of the man's breeches with his free hand and flung him bodily into the street. A look of horror crossed his companion's face when the sergeant returned to Commander Slayton's office. He fled before Sergeant Hamm could throw him out.

"Thank you, Sergeant," Slayton said.

Hamm nodded, walked back to his desk, and sat down to fill out the report he detested writing.

Officer Kent closed the stationhouse door and stood facing the small window watching the newspaper men shake their fist at him. His shoulders drooped under the weight of his ineptitude.

This was not the best time to ask the commander questions, but I was unlikely to find a better opportunity without renting a horse and riding out to his home. I drew in my breath and plunged in before good sense stayed my tongue.

"Sergeant Hamm and I have just come from the Phoenix Dining Room," I said. "The waiter there tells us that you were there for what was probably Mr. Buckner's last meal."

"Was I?" he asked. "I don't recall."

"Lunch yesterday."

"I suppose I was," he said, "I don't see how it is of any concern to you."

"Miss Hill has hired me to look into Mr. Buckner's death."

Commander Slayton looked up from the report he was reading. His expression was grim as he met my gaze.

"I don't cotton to anyone meddling in police business," he said. "If you get in the way of my officers I'll have them throw you under the jail. Is that clear?"

"I just wanted to know if you had noticed the man sitting at the table next to Mr. Buckner," I said. "Buckner's son told us that his father seemed distracted by him, but neither he nor the waiter could give me a description of the stranger."

"What difference does it make?" he asked. "If you want to help Miss Hill, stop wasting my time with stupid questions and figure out which of her girls is guilty of murder. You might start with that Brezing woman. Men seem to have a way of getting shot when she's around."

Gaining control of my temper cost me valuable seconds. Slayton stood up and grabbed his hat.

"I'm going home," he said. "Send Officer Kent to fetch me if I'm needed."

"Yes sir," Sergeant Hamm replied.

My fists clenched inside my pockets as he walked away. It was obvious that Slayton had made up his mind that Belle or one of the other women had murdered Buckner. He had no interest in looking elsewhere.

I had hoped to see Mr. Peltmutter at National Bank on my way home. Unfortunately, the teller informed us that Mr. Peltmutter had been called away on some urgent business and was not expected to return today. There was a prickling at the back of my neck that made me wonder if the urgent business had anything to do with why Mr. Malthus couldn't be found.

Perhaps Belle was right. The police would, out of duty, follow Mr. Buckner's activities in the final hours of his life, but it would be with the expectation that Buckner's trail would lead them back to Jenny Hill or one of her girls.

I probably should have gone to sleep, but I wanted to organize my notes on this morning's activities while the investigation was still fresh in my mind. Although my skill with a charcoal pencil was never as good as my brother's, I had managed to teach myself to do a passable rendering of faces. Most of the day slipped by as I sketched the faces of each person who might have reason to kill Buckner. One by one, I added the details of my interviews to the reverse side of the card bearing their likeness.

There wasn't much to review. A prostitute, a whorehouse madam, an arrogant son, a banker and one large question mark graced the front of my cards. I had not ruled out Belle Brezing or Jenny Hill. Either, or both of them together, could have killed Buckner. Young Aaron Buckner was not overly fond of his father, and still ranked among the known suspects.

I had sketched Ambrose Peltmutter's likeness from the portrait of him hanging in the lobby of National Bank. As far as I could tell, he was the last person to see Buckner alive.

The question mark interested me more. Someone, or more than one person, was still in shadow. There should be a face behind Buckner's rushing out of the Phoenix Hotel Dining Room, a face behind his telegram, maybe another behind his meeting at the bank. The question mark would remain in my case file until all the people were filled in but for now the only details I could add to the card were the message in Mr. Buckner's telegram and the initials "KL." The rest remained a mystery.

CHAPTER SIX

I woke the next morning to the music of a hard spring rain drumming on the slate roof and the familiar sound of Beulah singing in the kitchen. She and her husband, Amos, had crept away from a Cynthiana businessman's home after learning that President Lincoln granted freedom to colored men and their families for joining the army.

Beulah had ostensibly worked as a cook for the field hospital, though she spent more time nursing the wounded than cooking. She discovered I was a spy early on and found it immensely satisfying to bring me tidbits of information overheard from men who didn't pay attention to the presence of a colored woman.

My reason for becoming a battlefield nurse was the first of many secrets Beulah kept for me. She had become so practiced at assisting in my deception, that most of the time she forgot I was not the man I pretended to be. I wished it were as easy for me.

For a long time, I lay there listening to the slow sorrowful words of a Negro spiritual floating upstairs on my housekeeper's rich soprano voice. Little by little the self-doubt drifted away, leaving only the familiar aching loneliness. It was an uncomfortable way of waking up after a long sleep. I turned my face away from the slate gray skies outside my window as I searched for less troublesome thoughts.

The rain made me wish I could spend the morning with a pot of hot tea and a good book. A brand new copy of Mr. Twain's latest work waited downstairs. The chocolate-brown cover and gold leaf lettering called to me from the shelf in my office. Cheered by the prospect of losing myself in a new novel, I pulled on my dressing gown and slippers and reached for my spectacles.

Beulah met me at the bottom of the stairs.

"There was a youngster here earlier with a telegram for you," she said, holding out the envelope. "I told him that you was sleepin' and I wasn't gonna wake you cause you don't get enough sleep to keep a body alive."

Her fist was resting on her ample hip and the look in her eyes dared me to argue with her.

I knew better. Good housekeepers were hard to come by and a good friend even harder. Beulah was the best of both. I was impatient to get my hands on the telegram, but not foolish enough to cross her.

Beulah flashed me a brilliant smile as she placed the envelope in my hands.

I ripped the telegram open and stared at the contents. Tommy had more than earned his dollar with the news he brought from Frankfort. Isaiah Malthus' body had been found shortly after dawn, whipped and bloody, hanging from the Republican Party headquarters sign. I read through it again, trying to think. The only connection I had to these two men was the telegram Buckner had sent; a telegram that had not been delivered.

"Beulah, I need to catch the Frankfort train," I said, "Please pack me some lunch for the trip while I change."

"Not before you have breakfast," she said indignantly, this time with both hands firmly planted on her hips. "I done baked biscuits and set out ham and some cherry preserves. There's tea warm on the back of the stove, too. You got time to sit down and eat first. The Frankfort train don't run for more than two hours."

Most colored folks wouldn't have dared talk to their employer that way. Beulah wasn't most. I could not spend my days working and still manage to keep the house in good order. Lexington had plenty of war widows in need of jobs, but all of them together weren't worth one of her.

She had pointed out more than once that no skinny Irish girl could work for a bachelor and still keep her reputation.

Beulah didn't need to remind me that none of them were likely to assist me the way she did. Without her help, I would never have been able to convincingly transform myself into Ness Donnelly. She gave me my first haircut, fashioned the padded tunics I wore, and made adjustments to my clothing that helped me with my disguise.

She was one of a kind.

I was lucky to have her in my employ, and we both knew it. Besides, her husband was giving serious consideration to moving to one of those new colored towns being formed in Kansas. I was not about to give her any cause to want to move away from Lexington. I shook my head, tucked the telegram into the pocket of my dressing gown, and took a seat at the kitchen table like a properly trained schoolboy.

I was just licking the last of the cherry preserves off my fingers when Beulah came back to the kitchen.

"This appears to be a morning for curious happenings, Mr. Donnelly," she said, rolling her eyes.

"Oh?"

"There's a skinny policeman out there who done brought you this letter. I showed him to your office. Do you want me to fetch him some tea while you get dressed?"

Her eyes traveled disapprovingly down my dressing gown, resting on my slippers.

"It ain't respectable to be seeing visitors in your night clothes, 'specially in the middle of the day."

I scowled at her. Perhaps she was deliberately trying to pick a fight. Nine o'clock in the morning was hardly the middle of the day by my reckoning, but I wasn't giving her the satisfaction of arguing.

"See if he wants tea," I said, taking the letter from her as I headed upstairs.

I knew I was letting her take liberties, but somewhere along the line I had given up control of the day-to-day running of my household. I wasn't sure I wanted to change the situation. It was rather comfortable to know that between six in the morning and six in the evening Beulah was in charge of everything and everyone who entered my home, including me. She was always respectful in front of visitors, but when we were alone, I was alternately mothered, scolded, bragged upon, and ordered about as affectionately as a child.

Her own children had been sold away from her during the years of slavery. I felt a familiar twinge of guilt that I had never tried to discover what became of them. If the children had been half as sassy as their mother… My mind pulled away from thoughts of what could have been done by an unscrupulous slave owner. I would find them somehow, or at least find what became of them. I owed her that.

I tossed the unopened letter on the bed and changed into a fresh suit, then packed a small traveling bag. I wasn't sure I would need to stay overnight in the capital, but decided to prepare for the possibility. When I was finished, I picked up the letter and read it:

Dear Mr. Donnelly,

I am writing on behalf of my cousin, Officer Thaddeus Kent, who has expressed a keen interest in learning to be an investigator. Since you are currently working on a case that is of mutual interest to yourself and the Lexington Police Force, I have assigned Officer Kent to assist you. I am sure that in the interest of cooperating with the ongoing police investigation you will show him every courtesy until the case has reached a satisfactory conclusion. In return for your mentoring my cousin in his efforts to become a better investigator, I have instructed my officers to share such information as they discover with you.
Sincerely,
James Slayton
Commander, Lexington Police

"Of all the…" I stopped abruptly. No word sprang to mind that suited the underhanded, despicable way Kent had been inserted into my investigation.

Commander Slayton hadn't expressly said he would stop the police from sharing information with me, but the threat was implied. How was I supposed to get anything done with young Kent dogging my heels? After a few minutes of throwing a private tantrum, I composed myself as best I could and went downstairs to speak to Officer Kent. I wasn't sure what I was going to say to the presumptuous little twit, but I could not afford to offend the Commander of Police. In my line of work, the police were an invaluable source of information.

"Officer Kent," I said, perhaps a little more forcefully than absolutely necessary.

Startled, the young man leapt to his feet.

"Yes sir!"

I looked him over carefully before saying anything. Kent was maybe twenty years old, probably closer to eighteen, with sandy brown hair and a pinched nose that was entirely too narrow to be attractive.

Thaddeus Kent had the kind of eager puppy dog expression that made it hard to believe he would ever intentionally complicate the case. Instead, he seemed likely to inadvertently blunder into trouble. He was the sort who would be looking for an adventure. Still, the boy had been bright enough to use his cousin to advance his prospects. If I could get past the distraction of having his small gray eyes look in two directions at once, he could be of some usefulness.

"Do you own a suit?" I asked.

"Yes, sir," he said, looking slightly confused.

I didn't bother to explain. If he was going to be working with me, he had to learn to follow my orders.

"Good. Go home and change. Pack a grip in case we have to stay overnight. Meet me at the Main Street Depot in half an hour."

"The Depot, sir?"

"Yes, the Depot, and don't be late. The Frankfort train isn't likely to wait for you and neither am I."

"That ain't enough time to go home, sir," he said. "I got some regular clothes at the station house, will that do?"

"It will have to," I said. "We don't want to raise questions about what a Lexington policeman is doing in Frankfort."

When he was gone, Beulah came in with a bundle wrapped in brown paper.

"I put a few extra victuals in so you be sure to share with the boy. He is near as skinny as you. Honest, Mr. Donnelly, I don't know what I'm going to do if you don't put some meat on your bones. You're giving my cookin' a bad reputation."

"Yes, I suppose I am," I said. "After tromping around in the rain all day I am also going to be giving your ironing a bad name. Face it, Beulah, working for me going to be the ruination of your reputation."

"Now you had best watch out, Mr. Donnelly. Yer collars was clean and starched when you left this house, and they better not come back all sodden. If folks start saying I don't do right by you, I just might as well join that new group going to the Nicodemus Colony. I won't be staying in a town where I ain't able to hold my head up in church no more."

The thought of Beulah heading off to Kansas with the settlers hit me hard. My stomach knotted.

"Now, why would you want to go running off to be a sod

buster? Forty acres and a mule might be fine for farmers, but you and Amos know less than I do about farming."

She glared at me.

I doubted that she could think of a retort. She'd grown up in a large house on the outskirts of Cynthiana. Beulah had spent most of her life working inside the houses of her owner's various family members. Amos, her husband, had been hired out to a cabinetmaker. Neither of them had ever tended so much as a kitchen garden. I cringed at the thought of offending her, but could not stand silently aside and let her leave for a life she was ill-prepared to lead.

"I was only five when we left Ireland. About all I can remember of farming is gnawing hunger, the smell of rotting potatoes, and the sight of whole families eating grass while wagonloads of grain rolled by us to feed the British army. That's no life for you and Amos." I said solemnly.

She turned away, but I put a hand on her shoulder.

"I don't lie to you, Beulah. "You know I'm not telling you this just because I want you to stay. I do want you to stay. Farm life is harder than anything I'll ever ask you to do. Please don't do this."

"I ain't afraid of hard work."

"No. You are the hardest worker I have ever seen. But what would you do when you found snakes in your hen house or garden? You hate snakes worse than anybody I know. Then there's the grasshoppers that can wipe out a whole year's work in a day. I don't believe the men planning this venture thought it through very well. I haven't seen any evidence they have planned for reseeding or a crop loss."

"I suppose you could plan better?"

"Beulah, it's nearly April. By the time you get settled in Kansas, it will be awfully late in the season to try to clear fields and plant any kind of crop. If you and Amos are dead set on going, I won't stop you, but please find out how folks plan to eat this winter. You need to know if those already settled there will help newcomers through the winter. I don't want to think of you feeling the kind of hunger that drove my family from Ireland."

"Humph!" she said, and marched back to the kitchen.

Part of me wanted to follow, try again to persuade her to stay, but I had a train to catch. Besides, she and Amos had to decide for themselves. I could only hope that she had listened to my warnings about this colony. Something about the plans for this settlement set off alarm bells in the back of my mind, but I could not come up with any solid reason why it rankled.

It was past time for me to leave for the station. I took one last longing look at my unopened book and the fire before heading out into a cold spring rain.

On my way to the station, I stopped by the telegraph office to pay Tommy and find out if there was any further news from Frankfort. There were a couple of other boys in the office when I arrived, and I realized that overnight the young telegraph operator had risen in stature among the clerks and errand boys.

I hid a smile. No doubt the news of Buckner's murder had circulated around town since yesterday and Tommy was making the most of his being questioned by the police. I laid a silver dollar on the counter.

"Thanks for your assistance," I said with as much sincerity as I could muster. "Has there been any other news since this morning?"

"No sir, Mr. Donnelly," he said. "Should I bring it round to your house again if anything else comes over the wires?"

"You'd best take it to Sergeant Hamm at the station house. Officer Kent and I are taking the twelve o'clock train to Frankfort."

As I left the office I couldn't resist glancing back to watch his admirers gather closer to get a look at the shiny silver dollar in his hand. For a while at least, the task of being a telegraph operator would hold some glamour to boys with otherwise dreary lives.

CHAPTER SEVEN

Cold spring rain had turned the skies slate gray and blackened the bark of nearly leafless oaks. Here and there I could see splashes of spring color on dogwood or redbud blossoming at the corner of a house, but mostly the road was dark and gloomy.

My traveling companion occupied himself with a dime novel, its yellow cover emblazoned with the image of a dashing young officer riding into the roaring cannons of war, pistols drawn. Officer Kent was too young to know how unlike real battle such scenes were, but those cheap action-packed novels were amazingly popular with young men. He held the book up close to his nose and focused his one good eye on the page, moving only now and then to turn to the next page of his book.

Just outside Midway, I untied the bundle Beulah had packed and examined the contents: a smaller bundle of beaten biscuits, one of dried apple slices, another contained thick slices of country ham, the sweet scent of maple permeated the last and traces of butterfat soaked through the brown paper. I resisted the urge to open the maple one first.

True to my promise to Beulah, I invited Officer Kent to join me. Over slices of country ham and beaten biscuits, I tried to get to know him.

"What made you decide you wanted to learn to be an investigator?" I asked

He got a strange expression on his face. For a moment, I thought the question might have offended him.

"I need a skill I can make money with," he said quietly.

"There are lots of ways to earn a living," I said. "Why detective work?"

"I'm from up near Pikeville. Except for farming and the coalmines, there's not much work."

"So you decided to try your luck in the city?"

He nodded.

"My Ma said I wasn't cut out for the mines or for farming. Since there isn't much else to do in the mountains, she sent me to Cousin James, hoping I could learn a trade."

"Then Commander Slayton suggested that you become a detective?"

"It wasn't like that," he said.

Officer Kent licked his lips and swallowed hard, his hands resting in his lap as he looked at the floor.

"I am not a very good police officer, Mr. Donnelly. I can't see well enough to shoot straight, and I am not much of a fighter. The men don't say anything, with the Commander being my cousin and all, but I can see that they don't really want me around. If it weren't for family obligations, I doubt that Cousin James would keep me on the force, either. He sometimes talks with me about the things that go on at the stationhouse and gives me advice about what to put in my reports. I think he is just being kind because he knows I send most of my pay home to help Ma."

I realized I had underestimated his intelligence. He was young, and understandably, a little too eager to please, but painfully aware of his shortcomings.

"But why detective work?" I asked again, as I undid the wrappings on the maple-scented package.

Inside the bundle, thick chunks of Beulah's maple fudge greeted me. The delicacy was a specialty of my housekeeper and a weakness of mine; so much so that she kept it hidden in the kitchen and only doled it out in small amounts. I had been known to search out her stash from time to time, but not often enough to have her stop making it.

There were only two pieces in the package. Reluctantly, I offered one to Officer Kent.

The look on his face when he tasted the creamy maple fudge

loaded with tiny pieces of hickory nuts almost made it worthwhile to part with some of my treasure.

"This is really good," he said, still not answering my question.

I nodded my mouth too full to speak.

The engineer blew the station signal before I could ask him again.

I realized we were approaching Frankfort, gathered up the wrappings from our lunch and began getting my things together.

Officer Kent blanched slightly when I took a derringer out of my bag and dropped it into my coat pocket. I didn't like guns any more than he did. Unlike my companion, though, I was a fairly good shot. I was also determined to stay alive. Two violent deaths in two days were enough to make me aware of the danger. If it was the same killer, he was unlikely to hesitate about leaving another body or two behind him. The derringer wasn't much of a weapon in a gunfight, but at close range it could make the difference between living and dying.

Frankfort Station was a small brick and limestone depot about two blocks from the public square. Normally a town the size of Frankfort would rate little more than a wooden railroad platform and a whistle stop, but when the legislature was in session the town doubled in size. The prominence of those who attended the session gave the town a prestige that went beyond the status its size merited. For three months, the depot and the livery stable across the street were overwhelmed with visitors.

I had learned from past experience to find a room for the night first thing, and then attend to whatever business brought me to town. It was better to pay the price of a room I didn't use than to wait until I needed one to start looking. Waiting usually meant sleeping in someone's hayloft, if you were lucky enough to find anyone willing to rent out that space. Freshmen legislators frequently ended up sleeping on the floor of their offices.

"At least it isn't raining here," I said.

Thaddeus Kent nodded.

"I guess that's good. If you don't mind my asking, Mr. Donnelly, why are we here?"

"Looking for the truth, Officer Kent," I said.

The puzzled expression on his face made me smile.

"Would you mind if I call you Thaddeus? Back in Lexington

you are a police officer, but here, you are just another young man visiting the center of state government. It won't do to keep referring to you as Officer Kent, and you are a bit young for me to address as Mister."

His ears turned a little pink.

"Nobody ever calls me Thaddeus," he said, "except my ma. When she is really mad my name is Thaddeus Andrew Kent, the rest of the time I'm just Tad."

"I will keep that in mind, Tad," I said. "Now, we are going to go find rooms for the night and then see what we can find out about the last person we know Buckner tried to contact. He sent a telegram to a man by the name of Isaiah Malthus. Mr. Malthus was found hanged this morning."

"Murdered?"

"It seems so," I said.

I purchased copies of the Louisville, Frankfort, and Bowling Green papers from the newsboys working on the station platform, and tucked them under my arm to read later. I doubted if any of them had reports on Mr. Malthus' demise but I wanted to see what was being written about Buckner's murder.

We walked along the edge of the road leading into the hills overlooking town. The trees had not yet developed spring foliage and I could see all the way to the muddy green waters of the Kentucky River.

From previous visits to Frankfort, I remembered Thompson's Boarding House. It was a rambling, slightly run down, farmhouse that sat on the outskirts of town. The long, uphill climb to reach the boarding house made Thompson's the lodging place least favored by those with business at the State House, which made it the one most likely to still have rooms to rent at mid-legislative season.

It was a wise move. Mrs. Thompson was down to her last two empty rooms. She was reluctant to let me have both, but I paid twice the season rate for room and board, in advance to secure her promise that we would not be asked to share. The extravagance shocked Tad, but I had no intention of sharing a bed with him or anyone else.

As Tad and I walked to the telegraph office, I mulled over the latest murder. I was uncertain Isaiah Malthus had any connection to the murder of Nathaniel Buckner or that I would be able to find out anything about him. The only thing I could say with any certainty was that an unsolved murder was not common in Kentucky.

Kentucky had a national reputation for violence that was not entirely unearned. But when a man was shot, it was usually common knowledge who shot him and why. Between the Regulators and the Klan, lynching parties were a regular occurrence. Duels still caused a few deaths, though thankfully those were becoming rare. There were always feuds brewing in the mountains. Lately, we had been having more than our share of political assassinations. Still, the murder of ordinary citizens for unknown reasons was an altogether different kind of violence.

Buckner's telegram to the murdered man was too much of a coincidence. Within a day of each other, both the sender and the intended recipient had met violent death. My gut told me there was only one motive behind two prominent men in two different cities being murdered and left in very public places. When I understood that motive, a web of secrets would unravel.

Abner Littleton, the telegraph operator, was older and less talkative than the Lexington operator. I suppose that with the legislature in session he had very little time to talk. It took more than half an hour of waiting for him to be finished with his customers long enough to talk to me at all. I introduced Tad and myself and explained the reason for my visit. Mr. Littleton didn't seem at all surprised that Buckner was murdered shortly after sending Malthus a telegram.

"Don't that beat all," he said.

I wasn't sure what he meant by the remark, but Littleton didn't bother to elaborate.

"What time did you deliver the telegram?" I asked.

"I didn't," he said.

Another message came in for Frankfort and he held his hand up for me to wait. Three messages later he looked up to see us still standing there.

"Yes, I know, you were unable to find Mr. Malthus," I said. "But what time did you first try to deliver the message?"

"I didn't. When the legislature is in session I've got no time to be gallivantin' around town looking for folks. A runner comes by for messages every hour. I gave it to him about eleven o'clock. He tried all day, but no luck. The sheriff took it this morning."

Another message was coming in, and I decided that any further questions were not worth the effort and set off to locate the local sheriff's office. Later, I might see if I could find the runner for Mr. Littleton and ask him about the telegram.

Sheriff Messer wasn't pleased when Tad and I walked into his office. He had just taken over the office of sheriff in a special election, winning the race largely because his predecessor was forced to resign after the murder of Judge Elliott. The judge had been shot to death on the steps of the State House during the last legislative session in front of more than eight hundred people.

Judge Elliott's murder had been a sensational case. It was easy to see why Sheriff Messer didn't want to draw the attention of newspapermen to this latest murder. Although the shooter who killed Judge Elliott had confessed to the crime almost immediately, much public sympathy was on the killer's side. His lawyer was claiming temporary insanity and there was a great deal of doubt that he would be hanged for the crime. The former sheriff had been forced out of office in disgrace. Now, Sheriff Messer was caught up in a case that was taking bizarre turns.

Messer had been the one of the previous sheriff's strongest critics, frequently pointing out that out of a crowd of people his predecessor had been unable to find a single witness who would admit seeing the fatal shots fired. Now, like it or not, this sensational murder case was his to deal with. Tad and I were only the first of many who would come asking him unpleasant questions about the new murder.

"I am sorry to bother you, Sheriff," I said. "I am Ness Donnelly, a private investigator from Lexington looking into the Nathaniel Buckner murder."

"What can I do for you?"

"Abner Littleton at the telegraph office said you had taken the message our victim sent to your victim shortly before he died. I was wondering if you would be willing to share information about the cases."

"Can't see as how it matters," he said. "Frankfort is a long way from Lexington."

"I am not certain it does, but there is a chance the two cases are related."

"Telegram isn't much of a link."

"No, not much at all," I said. "I hope the telegram can be

explained by some piece of ordinary business they were involved in, but so far we haven't found any explanation at all. A pity. The last thing the Lexington Police and I want is to have these two cases tangled together."

I hoped I sounded sufficiently doubtful about any link to make him think we could be persuaded to leave town quickly.

Sheriff Messer leaned back in his chair and fingered his whiskered chin thoughtfully.

"Well now," he said stretching in a way that made the buttons of his uniform pull tight across his potbelly, "I can't really see why you would come all this way over this." He laid the telegram out on the desk. "I've read it through. There is nothing even remotely suspicious about it."

"I'm sure you're right," I said, "but I have been hired to look into the case, and Police Commander Slayton thought it important enough to send his own cousin to assist me. Under the circumstances, we would consider it a great favor if you would share whatever you know about this murder with us, and perhaps let us have a look at the body."

Messer plainly liked the idea of having the commander of Lexington's police force indebted to him. I could tell he was weighing the potential embarrassment of having outside assistance in "his" murder case against the possibility of gaining a favor from Lexington's police department at some future date.

"I can't say we have any real evidence, Mr. Donnelly, just a few personal effects and the chain they hung him up with."

"Chain?"

"I thought it was a bit odd too," the sheriff said. "Rope is a lot easier to come by. Cheaper too. But that's how we found him, trussed up in slave shackles and hanging from the Republican Headquarters sign."

"Strange choice for lynching a man," I said.

"Not a regular lynchin' job. Poor devil, someone had stripped off his jacket and shirt and whipped him within an inch of his life before they hung him. We found his jacket and vest on the ground under his feet. His shirt was just hanging down from the waist of his breeches."

He paused and met my eyes.

"Are you sure you want to look at him? The undertaker has cleaned him up some, but it was a nasty killing."

"I'm sure," I said, "but could we see his personal effects first?"

He nodded, then opened the drawer and brought out a bundled handkerchief and untied it to reveal the small collection of items found on the body. As the sheriff had said, there wasn't much: a few coins, a money clip with several bank notes, a silver snuffbox, and a gold watch that looked as though it had been handed down in his family for many years. I picked up the watch and chain to examine it more closely.

The watch fob, which had been face down, turned over when I picked it up. My breath caught in my throat. I had not seen the markings for many years, but the image was indelible in my mind: a gold circle with a shield inside bearing the triangle and trowel crossed by a sword.

"What the…" I muttered under my breath.

"Curious, isn't it?" the sheriff said. "I wouldn't have taken Malthus for a Mason."

This was no Masonic symbol. I probably should have told the sheriff what I knew, but it didn't make sense. Malthus was a prominent member of the Republican Party Central Committee! A staunch Republican carrying a symbol of the Knights of the Golden Circle was as incredulous as seeing a Baptist preacher wearing a crucifix.

The gold fob Malthus carried was not cast with the crown and cross, worn by the general membership of the Knights of the Golden Circle. A far more sinister symbol lay in the palm of my hand. The sword was indicative of membership in the one of the elite militia "Castles," as the Knights called their lodges. These Castles were so secret and entrenched that no Pinkerton operative had ever been able to infiltrate one of their circles.

"I'm not sure he was a Mason," I said, after a moment. "The gold fob could be a war souvenir. It was amazing what men collected."

The sheriff grinned.

"That's a fact," he said. "I suppose it could be a lucky piece he picked up during the war."

I didn't think it was very lucky for Isaiah Malthus to be wearing one of the symbols of the Knights of the Golden Circle. The party of Lincoln was reviled by the KGC. But there it was, dangling from the gold chain on his watch. Either Malthus didn't know what the symbol meant, or he was a spy, a traitor, and a member of the

—

64

most notorious society in the entire Confederacy. Perhaps he was even a member of the KGC circle responsible for my brother's death. This was the symbol those men used. That thought sent a cold chill running the length of my spine.

The Knights of the Golden Circle were one of the largest societies working to form the Confederacy. Back in '61, the Knights had claimed to have over 400,000 members in Kentucky. Most of those had been duped into believing the Knights were simply ordinary Copperheads, peaceful Southern sympathizers trapped in a state forcefully held by the Union Army. Membership in the Knights wouldn't have seemed very different than joining any of a dozen other secret societies forming the peace movement across the country. Even as pockets of violence broke out, many still believed that the Union could be peacefully dissolved and a new confederation of southern states formed.

By the summer of '64, Pinkerton operatives were able to infiltrate a few lower ranking circles of the Knights and learn some of their secrets. The Knights lost much of their following when the evidence revealed circles within circles and splinter groups of powerful men who formed secret Castles intent upon taking over world government. As the truth was revealed, the Golden Circle was no longer a badge of honor for any man who deemed himself a son of the South. Many never learned, or never believed the evidence the Pinkerton's reported. It was believed that the master plan was so secret that it was only revealed to an inner circle of high-ranking Knights and the plans were never written down. Ness and many others that tried to infiltrate the ranks were killed before ever getting close to the core of the network. There were rumors, of course, but hard facts were hard to come by.

"It sure is a nice watch," the sheriff commented. "I wish I had one like that to pass on to my boy. Do you have a son, Mr. Donnelly?"

Jolted from my thoughts, I swallowed hard and tried to pull myself together.

"No, sir, I'm not married," I managed at last. "You're right though. That is one of the nicest timepieces I've ever seen." I handed it back to him. "From the looks of his possessions, I guess we can rule out robbery."

The sheriff laughed.

"If you ask me this one is a case of pure orneriness. Somebody just wanted to beat a man to death and Malthus was in the wrong place at the wrong time. Was it like that with your victim, Mr. Donnelly?"

I shook my head.

"No Sheriff, ours was shot to death and the killer didn't leave anything behind, not even his drawers."

"Well, if that don't beat all. You mean to say he wasn't wearing anything at all?"

"Not a stitch," I said gravely, as we stood to leave.

"Lordy, it takes thieving to a new low when they steal the drawers off a dead man."

I hadn't really considered what it meant to have no clothing or personal effects for Nathaniel Buckner until now. My attention had been focused on the telegram, but if Buckner and Malthus were connected through membership in the Knights of the Golden Circle, their deaths took on far more sinister implications. The thought was so intensely frightening that I hardly noticed where we were going until Tad caught my shoulder.

"We're here, Mr. Donnelly," he said, pointing to the undertaker's sign.

"Oh," I said, coloring slightly. "I'm sorry. My mind was elsewhere."

The sheriff chuckled.

"You'd better watch about getting distracted like that, Mr. Donnelly. In these parts that could get a man run over in the street. None of these legislators can drive a sulky any better than my missus, and she cleans out half the ditches in town regularly. "

My ears turned a shade pinker, but there was nothing I could say. No words could explain the cold fear I carried or the memory of arriving at our usual meeting place to find my brother's killers in full assault. I tried again to banish the image from my mind as I followed the sheriff inside.

As I looked down at the body of Isaiah Malthus, I wondered if his aristocratic features had masked his true nature. He was not a large man, probably no taller than me. Age had robbed his body of the muscles he must have had in his younger days. I could see the markings of the shackles around his wrist, and deep cuts where the whip had wrapped around his body, slicing into the ribs.

"Has the doctor given you his report yet?" I asked

"Doc Jenkins will present his findings at the inquest

tomorrow," he replied. "I don't think there is much to be said, considering how we found him. Like I told you Mr. Donnelly, it takes an ornery cuss to do this to a man. He better hope I get him before the Regulators do. Those boys don't take kindly to one of their own getting messed up like this."

The suggestion that Mr. Malthus was one of the Regulators got my attention. In my opinion, the Regulators were as bad as the Klan. One of the reasons Lexington had formed an organized police department was to prevent one of the vigilante organizations from taking over the city. We still had flare ups of Klan activity, but mostly the KKK worked quietly behind respectable masks. Thankfully the Regulators had never gotten a toehold in Central Kentucky. In some counties the Regulators had replaced all government officials in everything but name. Elections, county officers, even judgeships were under the complete control of the vigilantes.

"You think Malthus was involved with the Regulators?"

"I don't know that he was," the sheriff said, "I don't have no truck with vigilantes, even if they are doing the state a favor by keeping order in the mountains. I'm just sayin' that a lot of them boys that belong to the Regulators are Republicans. I can't really see how someone powerful as Mr. Malthus could avoid knowin' a few Regulators by their proper names. Some of them boys' help would have been needed to get his position in the state party. If this thing don't get solved fast, there's going to be a heap of trouble."

"Do you think Regulators would have the nerve to come into the state capital?"

"As near as I can tell, they was involved in shooting the judge here last month."

"Why do you think it was the Regulators behind shooting Judge Elliott?"

The expression on his face told me he thought I was a fool.

"Well sir," he said, "there was nigh on eight hundred people in the square when Judge Elliott was shot. Not a single witness has been willing to come forward. Folks are just plain scared. His killer was one of the Regulators sure as I'm standin' here. Otherwise, I'd have more witnesses than I could shake a stick at."

"I can see your point," I said.

He pushed a stray strand of hair back from his face.

"Nobody in this neck of the woods wants to cross them. The

governor has put up a new state militia post just outside of town. I expect he will go after the Regulators soon, if they don't come for him first. We have more mountain than city in this state and those boys keeping order in the coalfields are getting' more powerful every day. Governor can't afford to let that kind of power go unchallenged if he wants to keep runnin' things his self."

Regulators added a new dimension to the investigation. I had heard a little about the uprisings in the mountains. I could see the vigilante militia swooping down from Elliott or Pike County into Frankfort to lynch a man, maybe even deliver the beating Malthus had suffered, but it didn't make sense for them to leave Buckner in a bordello in the middle of Lexington.

I mentally added the Regulators to the growing list of inquiries. Between links to the KGC and the Regulators this was turning into more than the local sheriff or I were equipped to handle. The state militia were an unknown element. They were believed to be loyal to the governor, but they were small in number and widely scattered. How much control did the governor have when it came to calling them out to defend against their neighbors? For that matter, was it their neighbors or did the secret societies hold the militia?

I found myself wishing that Buckner's death turned out to be something ordinary. It would be easier if it were a disgruntled saloonkeeper or sporting house madam who shot him for meddling in their trades. There was nothing I could do but focus on the information available and hope something started to move the investigation in a different direction.

The years I had spent working as a nurse while collecting information for the Pinkerton Agency made me very familiar with the condition of bodies and the nature of injuries. I bent down to examine this one.

"He must have already been dead when they hanged him," I said. "There are markings on his neck where the chain cut into his flesh, but no sign of the bruising he has around his other injuries. I would say your hanging was done for effect, Sheriff. Did you notice the salt crystals clinging to the flesh around the whip marks? This wasn't just a beating. Your killer wanted Malthus to suffer a lot before he died. There's a large discoloration here behind his left ear. Someone gave him quite a blow to the back of the head. He may have been rendered unconscious before being shackled. The salt makes me think that his killers would have waited until he came to before they brought out the whip."

I looked up and noticed both the sheriff and Tad were turning a little green.

"I guess that is about all I need to see," I said, dropping the sheet back in place. "Thank you for your assistance, Sheriff. If you don't mind, I would like to attend the inquest tomorrow."

"It is open to the public. Scheduled for eight in the morning," he said. "It's my job to run the inquest. I'll get started quick as the Doc gets there."

"We'll be there early," I told him, as Tad and I turned to go.

I had seen enough of small town inquests to know that if we didn't get there early, we wouldn't get into the room. Court days drew large crowds into a county seat, but a murder added real excitement to otherwise ordinary lives in rural communities.

"What now, Mr. Donnelly?" Tad asked as we headed back down the street toward the telegraph office.

"I want to talk to the runner who tried delivering that telegram," I said. "I am curious about where he looked for Mr. Malthus yesterday."

CHAPTER EIGHT

I spotted the runner coming out of the telegraph office with a fist full of messages. While he wasn't actually running, I was some distance away. Tad and I had to sprint to catch up with him before he disappeared into the Capitol Building.

"Wait," I shouted, as he was about to cross the street.

"Can I help you mister?" he asked.

I took a moment to catch my breath.

Red-brown freckles, nearly the same shade as his thick curls, splattered like paint droplets over every exposed inch of the telegraph runner's skin. The lad was at that awkward age between boy and man, tall and lean with a crooked smile and eyes the color of cornflowers.

"I'm Ness Donnelly, a private investigator from Lexington," I said, when I was able to speak again. "I wanted to ask you a few questions about the telegram you tried to deliver to Mr. Malthus yesterday."

His eyes widened at the mention of the murdered man.

"I don't know nothin' about that," he said. "Honest."

"You didn't know Mr. Malthus? How did you go about finding him?"

"Oh, I knew who he was. An important man like Mr. Malthus gets lots of messages," he said. "But the sheriff had done cut him down by the time I tried lookin' for him at the headquarters buildin' yesterday."

"That wasn't the first place you looked?" I asked, in surprise.

His face reddened, turning his freckles nearly purple against his pink skin.

"No, sir," he said. "I checked the balcony first to see if he was watchin' the legislators."

I didn't say anything. Looking for Malthus at a state legislative session was unlikely to be causing him to turn such a rosy shade. But I didn't want to press him too hard.

He fidgeted with the telegrams in his hand for a moment before speaking.

"After that I went to Miss Ruth's place."

"Miss Ruth?"

"Yes, sir. She lives about two blocks down, toward the river," he said, not looking at me. "Mr. Malthus sort of lives there, when he's in town."

Tad's cheeks flushed when the implications of what the runner said sank in. I wondered if I was becoming jaded. Perhaps it was just that in my line of work expecting the unexpected becomes a habit, but I was not at all surprised that Malthus was keeping company with another woman when he was away from his family for several weeks at a time. There were probably a good number of other political figures that did the same every legislative session.

"Did you make any other stops?"

"Just the headquarters. But like I said, there weren't nobody there except the deputy."

"Thank you," I said. "I won't keep you any longer."

Whatever expectations I had when I knocked on Miss Ruth's door vanished from my mind along with any sense I possessed when the door opened. I stood dumbfounded before the most beautiful Negress I had ever met.

Hands the color of creamy coffee clutched tightly to a small black handkerchief. Though her door was not adorned with crepe, she was obviously mourning. Her gown was made of unrelieved black silk, ornamented with a tiny row of jet beads along the yoke. I could also see signs of hastily dried tears in the corners of her soft brown eyes.

"May I help you, sir?" she said, breaking through the fog surrounding my brain.

I was taken aback by the lilting tone of her voice and perfect diction. There were a few well-educated women in Kentucky, but educated colored women were a rarity.

"Is this the home of Mr. Isaiah Malthus?" I asked.

Suspicion instantly filled her eyes. Her back stiffened.

"If you have questions about Mr. Malthus, take them to the sheriff. I have nothing to say," she said frostily.

"Wait. Please," I pleaded, as the door started to close.

The plea persuaded her to slow her action.

"I am investigating the murder of a friend of his, Mr. Nathaniel Buckner," I added hastily.

She must have recognized the name. The door remained open just a crack and I could almost feel her mind weighing the truth of what I said.

I didn't know if she could read or not, but I took one of the calling cards from my vest pocket and extended it through the partly open door.

"My name is Ness Donnelly. I am a private investigator from Lexington. Officer Kent here is a Lexington Police Officer. Since they have no authority outside the city, his commander has asked that I allow him to accompany me."

She glanced at the card then opened the door a little wider. The warmth had vanished from her eyes when she looked at me.

"The last thing we know Mr. Buckner did before he died was to send a telegram to Mr. Malthus. If you don't believe me, you can ask the sheriff or the telegraph operator."

"I don't need to ask anyone, Mr. Donnelly," she said, moving aside so we could enter. "I was here when the telegram arrived. May I ask why you believe it is important?"

"I am not certain it has any connection to his death," I replied. "But the wording of the message and the proximity of their murders made the possibility worth investigating."

"You have seen the message?"

"The Lexington Police have a copy."

We were still standing just inside the front door. I didn't know if Mr. Malthus paid for the house, but it was clearly her home, not his. A portrait of her posed in a splendid gown, one arm resting gracefully atop a grand piano, hung above the mantle. Hothouse roses blossomed from a silver vase near the painting. I wondered if Mr. Malthus brought them to his mistress.

My eyes fell on a small pewter framed photograph that was almost hidden behind the roses. A boy, probably not much younger than Tad, stared solemnly out at me from the oval frame. He looked uncomfortable in the stiff collared uniform of a military cadet. Miss

Ruth was unlikely to tell me anything, but the picture spoke volumes. Certainly the fact that Malthus had a colored mistress was sufficient to explain the slave shackles he was hanged with, but to have a colored son passing for white was an offense he would not be forgiven for committing. It was no wonder that his killers had tortured him to death.

"You were telling me about the telegram," Miss Ruth said, moving to block my view.

We were descending into verbal fencing, testing out each other, and looking for weakness. This was not what I wanted.

"I'm not here to bring more grief," I said quietly. "I just need any information that might help me solve Nathaniel Buckner's murder."

She studied me for a long moment before speaking.

"I know the name, but not what sort of acquaintance Mr. Buckner was," she said. "They always met elsewhere."

"But he mentioned Mr. Buckner?"

"No," she replied. "He never talks business at home. But I have seen the name on papers from time to time."

"You can read?" Tad blurted.

I glared at him.

Color crept up his scrawny neck and his head dropped.

"I'm sorry ma'm," he said, looking at his toes.

Tears dampened her long lashes and crept slowly down her face, but there was a trace of a smile playing at the corners of her mouth.

"It's all right, Mr. Donnelly," she said. "There aren't many colored women of my generation who had the opportunity to learn to read. You shouldn't blame Officer Kent for being surprised."

"You're very kind."

"Not at all," she replied, dabbing her eyes.

"Do you have any of Mr. Malthus' papers?"

"No, I'm sorry," she said. "He kept his business and private life as far removed from each other as possible."

I nodded.

"Thank you for your time," I said.

She placed a hand on my arm as I turned to go.

"Would you do me the kindness of letting me know what you find out?" she asked.

"When the investigation is over," I said. "I can't share the details of an investigation with anyone until it is finished."

Tad and I arrived for the inquest before seven. He started to take a seat near the front but I pointed him toward a pair of wooden chairs near the west wall of the room. They were certainly not the best seats for watching the proceedings, but were angled in such a way as to give me an excellent view of the visitor's section.

"We can't see the witnesses from here," Tad grumbled as we took our seats.

I put my head in my hand and closed my eyes until I had carefully ordered my words.

"Tad, think this through," I said, rubbing my temples. "If you are going to be a detective, you have to learn to place yourself outside the crowd and focus on the important details of what you see. Do you know what is important here today?"

"The inquest?"

"No, the inquest is just a formality," I said.

The reason Commander Slayton wanted his cousin to accompany me was to learn detective work. I wasn't sure that I could teach the young man to think as an investigator, but I should at least try to keep him focused on the process.

"We already know the decision of the inquest will be murder by person or persons unknown. For us, the important part of what happens here today is discovering who else thinks the inquest is worth attending. We want to get a good look at the crowd. From our vantage point, we will be able to see most of the faces. Pay close attention to anything that strikes you as odd in expressions or behaviors. There is a very good chance the killer or someone close to him will be in this room listening to hear what the witnesses might have seen. We are looking for the killer and this is the first place we have been where we might actually see him."

"You think so, Mr. Donnelly?" he said. Suddenly he was very interested in who walked into the room.

"Tad, try to be more discreet about watching people," I cautioned quietly. "We want to catch the killer, not draw his attention to us."

The inanity of my words hit me even as they left my lips. The way his eyes wandered, no one could be sure what the young officer was really looking at.

By a quarter of eight, the room was crowded. Sheriff Messer

began promptly at the hour and kept the proceedings short and to the point. Testimony was sparse and offered no new details about the murder. Both the doctor's report and those of the men who discovered the body rehashed information I had already gleaned from other sources. I wrote down the names of the witnesses, but spent most of my time drawing crude sketches of people in the room. They were not great likenesses, but when added to the descriptions I carefully made of each person, they would help me recognize anyone I saw again.

It fascinated Tad to watch me sketch, and once or twice he suggested additions to the notes I made. Many of the sketches would never have a name to go with the faces, but it was possible that the killer had already made an appearance in my notes.

"What now, Mr. Donnelly?" Tad asked when the room was nearly empty.

"Now we pick up our things and catch the train back to Lexington. Later we may find something that confirms our murder is connected to this one, but we need to get back to Nathaniel Buckner's murder."

"Cousin James said this wasn't much of an investigation," Tad said.

"Did he, now?"

"No offense, Mr. Donnelly," he said, turning red.

"None taken," I said. "Your cousin has his opinion about Miss Belle, and I have mine. What you need to keep in mind is that he sent you to me to learn because I have a little more experience at investigating murder than he does. I can assure you that we are just getting started."

"What next?" he asked eagerly.

"By the time we get back, Doc Haydon should have finished his report. Then there are a few questions to ask Miss Hill and her girls. We still need to interview Mr. Peltmutter at National Bank. I want to look around Mr. Buckner's office, maybe ask a few questions of his partner. Then, my boy, we have to take on the most difficult problem of all."

"What problem is that, sir?"

"We have to come up with a way of getting the Buckners to let us search through any place Mr. Buckner kept private papers, without telling them what we are looking for."

"What are we looking for?" Tad asked, looking thoroughly

confused.

"The secret," I said. "Somewhere, in every case, is a secret someone thought worth killing to protect. When we know that, we will know our murderer."

"That's all, just find out who is keeping a secret?"

"Unfortunately, it won't be that easy," I said. "Looking for the one important secret leads to discovering a lot of other secrets that people are lying to you about. We have to dig through all those secrets to determine the truth."

"I don't understand," he said.

"I don't either Tad, but I will." I studied his face for a moment trying to decide how best to explain how I investigated a case to him. "When you are asking questions, you have to remember that everybody is going to lie to us about something. It may not be something important to us, but it makes our job harder. Sometimes people don't even realize they are lying. They may think they were ten or twenty minutes earlier or later than they really were, or leave out some detail that seems unimportant or unflattering. When we ask the right question to the right person or see a detail in a different light, then we will know our killer."

CHAPTER NINE

I telegraphed ahead, and let Sergeant Hamm know we were on our way back. He was waiting on the platform when we stepped off the train. His long face was showing signs of fatigue, making his expression even more solemn than usual.

"Discover anything interesting in Frankfort?" he asked.

"Nothing that tied our case to theirs," I said.

I considered telling him about the key fob, and Miss Ruth, but decided to keep it to myself. Like I said, everybody lies, including me. My reasoning was that I had no proof that the fob was anything more than a trinket. As for Miss Ruth, she intrigued me. I had not yet decided what to make of her.

Deep down, I harbored a fear that if a Castle of the Knights of the Golden Circle was still at work in the Bluegrass, anyone could belong to the KGC. Alan Pinkerton's admonishment to "trust no one" echoed through my mind every time I thought about the Knights of the Golden Circle. I remembered Ness lying face down in a pool of his own blood, plunged my hands deeper into my pockets, and changed the subject.

"Did you get Doc Haydon's report yet?" I asked.

"Yes. The Doc says that Mr. Buckner was shot once in the chest at close range. The bullet went clean through. He don't know what caliber. Most likely a large pistol. You were right about him being killed somewhere else. The doctor thinks that the body was kept upright for several hours, then moved to Miss Hill's."

Sergeant Hamm must have noticed my smug expression because he gave me a withering look.

"Of course, that don't mean it wasn't somebody at Miss Hill's place that did the shooting," he added defensively.

There was no point to arguing with Sergeant Hamm over the improbability that the ladies had killed Buckner and put the body in their own front hall.

"Did Doc Haydon find anything else?" I asked.

"He says Buckner was cleaned up after death. Whoever scrubbed the body left soap in the wound."

I nodded. "I would like to get a look at his report."

"The only other things the doc found were those scrapes you noticed on Buckner's feet. He says that happened sometime after death too. I don't know how he can tell."

"Lots of ways," I said.

Hamm held up both hands. "Don't say it. I don't want to know."

I shook my head.

"You're about as bad as the Doc," he said. "What is it that makes you want to go poking and prodding a body the way you do? It gives me the willies just thinking about the stuff you two tell me about dead folk."

"It is just basic medical science," I said.

"I don't care what it is, it ain't natural to go digging around in a man's innerds without feeling sick about it."

"Somebody needs to," I said. "Otherwise a lot of murders would go unsolved."

"Maybe," he said, "but I couldn't do it. I reckon I'll just take Doc Haydon's word on what he finds."

"What was his word on the scrapes, anyway?" I asked.

"The doc said there were bits of cobblestone in them. He believes Buckner's feet were dragged along a street or walkway here in town. That doesn't give us much to go on. The city buys all cobblestones from the same brickyard. Every street is paved with the same stones, except the streets around the new market house. They brought in those big slabs of limestone to pave the road there."

"It tells us that we are looking for a place on one of the paved streets or walkways. The sidewalks in front of Miss Hill's are wooden planks and Main Street isn't paved that far down. The cobblestones stop just one block past Broadway. From there on to Frankfort, the road is crushed limestone and oil."

"I'll grant you that," Sergeant Hamm said as he twisted the tips of his mustache thoughtfully, "but that still leaves us a good sized portion of town that could have been the murder scene. Any insight into how we go about narrowing down our search?"

"I would start with the bank."

"The bank!" he said, incredulously. "You think he was killed at the bank?"

"Have you spoken to Mr. Peltmutter? Did he arrive for their meeting? Has he given you some indication that Mr. Buckner was alive that afternoon?"

"No," Sergeant Hamm said glumly. "I tried twice yesterday but he was away."

I picked up my grip and headed toward Main Street with Sergeant Hamm and Tad following close behind me.

"As far as we know the last time he was seen alive, he was leaving the telegraph office and headed toward the bank. We have not been able to determine if he ever arrived at National Bank, but doesn't it strike you as odd that Mr. Peltmutter is always unavailable when we call?"

"Mr. Peltmutter is a busy man," Hamm said. "You can't just expect the president of a bank to be waiting around for us to drop by."

"Still, nobody I have spoken with saw Nathaniel Buckner after the telegraph office. The best lead we have at this point is Peltmutter."

I should have stopped there, but sometimes common sense doesn't catch up with my mouth in time to prevent me from planting both feet firmly in inside.

"Maybe you don't think the president of a bank would murder someone on the board of directors, but having his portrait hanging in the bank lobby doesn't exempt him from being a suspect. I think we have to keep at him until we know whether Buckner reached his meeting or not."

"Look here, Donnelly," Sergeant Hamm said, taking me by the shoulder and spinning me around to face him, "don't tell me how to do my job. I may not have been trained by the great Alan Pinkerton, but I know how to investigate a murder."

His anger made me realize I had gone too far. Still, it wasn't like Hamm to lose his temper.

"I apologize," I said, meeting his gaze. "I was out of line, Wilfred."

I hoped that the apology would defuse his anger and lead to

him telling me what was bothering him.

"Ness, I know you don't think Jenny Hill or her girls were involved," he said, "but you've got a blind spot when it comes to Miss Brezing. I reckon you should know that the Commander wants me to arrest her for the Buckner murder."

"Belle didn't kill him," I said firmly.

"That's what I mean about you having a blind spot. Everyone in town knows there was bad blood between her and the deceased," he said. "Mr. Buckner made a lot of people think Miss Brezing murdered Johnny Cook, and I, for one, am not sure she didn't shoot the boy."

He stopped talking and just looked at me for a moment.

"What I'm trying to get at is this: what was there to stop her from shooting Buckner, too?"

I frowned.

"What would she gain by it?" I asked. "Johnny may or may not have shot himself, but the court said he did. That decision isn't likely to be overturned. Granted, Buckner made a lot of accusations, but Belle is a prostitute. Nothing Buckner could say about her would tarnish her reputation any more than her occupation has."

The sergeant glanced across the street to where some two-dozen stone-faced matrons were passing out leaflets on the evils of drink.

I waited, knowing what he was about to say.

"You know Buckner was trying to get all the whorehouses closed down," Hamm argued. "Those ladies are with the Abstention Society. Buckner's death has given them new resolve. They have sworn not to stop until they run every prostitute and saloonkeeper out of Lexington."

"I know," I said.

"Buckner's campaign is reason enough to want him out of the way, wouldn't you say? He was attempting to put Belle out of business."

"Maybe it is reason enough for Miss Hill," I said. "It is her business Buckner was trying to close, not Belle's. Even if he was to succeed at his goal, that isn't a good reason for Belle to kill him. Why is the commander so determined to prove it was her?"

"Simple! Buckner was causing a lot of trouble for the ladies. If Miss Hill closes her doors, Belle is out of business and a home."

"Causing all of them trouble is not a very personal reason for her killing him."

"Men have been shot for less."

"Even so, just how successful do you think he would be at ridding the city of bawdy houses?" I asked. "If he closed down Miss Hill today, she would be open again before the weekend. If not, a dozen others would take her place. As long as men have desires, and they are willing to pay a woman to satisfy them, all the Buckners in the world won't stop prostitution."

"You're probably right," he said, embarrassed by the bluntness of my statement. "Still, Mr. Buckner was an important man around here. If we don't find a better suspect soon, I am going to have to arrest Miss Brezing."

"Let me talk to her again. Maybe my questions will help her remember something she hasn't told us yet. The only thing Belle is guilty of is being a whore," I said. "I am certain of that."

"She had better find herself a good lawyer," Sergeant Hamm said, as we neared the stationhouse. "When you talk to Miss Brezing, tell her that. I can hold off a day or two, but if something doesn't turn up soon I am going to have to bring her in. I can't stall the commander for any longer than that."

I nodded, but said nothing. Belle was going to need more than a lawyer. She needed me to find out who really killed Buckner, and I was no closer to that than I was when she woke me Tuesday night. I needed to find out more about Buckner and Malthus before I spoke to Belle. I strode off toward North Upper Street, trying to think of what I might have missed.

"Are we going to see Miss Brezing now?" Tad asked, his voice betraying an eagerness that made me smile. I couldn't blame him for finding Belle attractive; most men did.

"Later," I said, "Miss Brezing is probably sleeping. Besides, before I see her I need to pay a visit to Doc Haydon. I want to find out anything I can about our victims."

"Victims, sir?" Tad asked. "I thought you told the sheriff that you didn't see any connection between the two cases."

"I didn't," I said, "but not seeing a connection doesn't mean it isn't there. Until we know that they are definitely not connected, we must consider the possibility that they are."

"Do you think that Doc Haydon can tell you anything that he didn't tell Sergeant Hamm?"

"Maybe not, but I think I may ask him different questions.

Besides, I don't really know what he said to Sergeant Hamm. I only know what Sergeant Hamm understood him to say."

"Mr. Donnelly," Tad said thoughtfully, as we walked toward Doc Haydon's office, "Is this part of what you were saying about how everybody lies?"

I smiled. "We might just make a detective out of you yet."

Doc Haydon grinned when I entered his office.

"I was just getting ready to go to the track," he said. "Wissahickon is running in the third. I've got an eagle on her to win."

"That sounds like a safe bet," I said. "But I wanted to talk to you about Buckner."

"We can talk just fine at the track, Donnelly, not that there is a whole lot more I can say about him. The man died of a single gunshot wound to the chest. Most likely from a large caliber revolver fired at close range."

He opened the door. "The fillies are waiting, and I'm sure the bar has a julep with my name on it. Oh yes, bring the boy. He might learn something."

"Mr. Donnelly, I'm a Baptist," Tad whispered as we walked toward Race Street. "We don't hold with gambling or imbibing strong drink."

"Don't worry, Tad," I whispered back, trying to sound serious. "The Doc and I are Irish. We won't mind if you leave the whiskey and the horses to us. Besides, I never really gamble when I go to the track with the Doc. He's on downright friendly terms with all the horses, and they tell him whose turn it is to win."

I left Tad to ponder what I said and caught up with Doc Haydon. "Do you know what time Buckner died?"

"Only a rough guess," he replied. "I would estimate about twelve to fourteen hours before you sent for me. Rigor mortis had set in and the hypostasis indicates he was standing for some time after death, or leaning to be more precise. There are white spots among the bruising, places where the flesh was resting against something. If you want me to make an educated guess, I would say somebody shot him, then propped him in a corner until they had time to clean him up. I can't say that I have any ideas about why they decided to dump him at the whorehouse. That's about as peculiar as taking his clothes. I found fragments of cloth under the soap. He must have been dressed when the bullet struck."

"Doc, you've lived here a lot longer than I have," I said hesitantly. "Did you ever know of Mr. Buckner being associated with the Knights of the Golden Circle?"

Doc Haydon stopped abruptly.

"Where the devil did that notion come from?"

I reached into my pocket and pulled out the sketch I had made of the KGC symbol.

"Mr. Malthus, the man murdered in Frankfort, was carrying a gold watch fob with this emblem. I recognized it as one of the ones used by a particularly violent group of KGC operatives during the war."

The doctor let out a long low whistle.

"I thought you Pinkertons arrested all the Knights during the war. Can't say as I heard anything about them since they tried to burn New York City to the ground."

"Mr. Pinkerton arrested some of the ring leaders, after the fire in New York. The army caught a bunch more when they took over that train in Kansas, but we were a long way from arresting all the members of the fifth column."

"You think they are plotting something now?" he asked. "The war was a long time ago."

"I know," I said, "but they stole a lot of money from the Army of the Republic to finance a new Confederacy. Kentucky was a hotbed of activity for the KGC. I don't need to tell you that. The papers were full of stories about them and the 'shadow legislature' the Rebs organized down in Bowling Green."

He handed the drawing back to me.

"All I can tell you, Ness, is that Buckner is the right background and age to have belonged to the Knights. But the same could be said of every white man over forty born in the Bluegrass Region, including me. Almost everybody in Lexington supported the South. A lot of men were involved in the Knights back then. It doesn't mean much. Most of them would deny it now, but at the time," he shrugged, "belonging to the KGC was a method of trying to preserve our way of life."

Doc Haydon started to say something else, then stopped to listen.

"Shoot fire! That was the gate! Donnelly, you made me miss the start of the first race."

Without waiting for an answer, he took off toward the track at a pace I had to trot to keep up with.

"I didn't hear nothin'," Tad said, racing to keep up with us.

"I didn't either, Tad," I said as we hurried to catch up with the medical examiner, "but I would bet my life that he did."

Sure enough, the horses were coming around the final turn when we arrived. I left the Doc to watch the finish and I bought the first round.

The second race was about to begin by the time I carried the chilled glasses to Doc Haydon's box.

He didn't even glance my way as I handed him his julep.

I pulled up one of the wooden chairs and sat down beside him, watching the horses being lead to the gate.

Haydon was perched on the edge of his chair. One hand clung to the wooden frame around his box, the other clutched his drink. I didn't know if he had a bet on this race, but knowing his sporting proclivities I suspected that he had. The doctor preferred to place his bets before race day. That way, there was nothing to distract him from his two remaining passions; whiskey and horses.

The starting pistol fired, but my mind was not on the race. I was troubled by his reference to "our way of life."

Doc Haydon and I had been friends for a lot of years. Afternoons spent with him, watching the races and discussing the finer points of the sport, were a welcome diversion from the ugly side of human nature our work forced both of us to examine.

The Knights were part of that ugliness. I wanted to be certain that he was never associated with them, but didn't dare say anything until the race ended.

The horses were nearing the finish. Doc Haydon's clear blue eyes were fixed on the chestnut moving up on the inside. The veins on the side of his neck glowed purple against the red flesh. He didn't breathe or even move until the colt nosed out in front. "Come on, Harold!" he shouted, instantly on his feet. As they crossed the finish line, the chestnut was pulling away, winning the second race by a head.

I held my glass up for our usual toast. The glasses clanked together.

"It does the heart good to see a fine horse running on a beautiful spring day," Haydon said, downing his julep in a single gulp. He was grinning. "I guess the next round is on Harry. What do you say lad?" he said, looking at Tad. "Will you have a drink with us? Isaiah mixes the finest julep that can be found in this part of the state."

"No thank you, sir, but I would like a glass of water," Tad replied, his one good eye looking at the doctor. "I mean no offense, sir," Tad added quickly.

Doc Haydon frowned.

"Have you injured that eye or has it always been that way?"

"What?" Tad said.

"Your eye, lad. Have you always had difficulty moving it in the direction you're looking?"

Tad blushed. "I-I suppose it has always been like that, sir."

The doctor's frown deepened.

"Donnelly, could I trouble you to fetch those drinks? I want to get a better look at the boy's eye."

"You think it's curable?" I asked.

"I think I would like to have a closer look," Haydon replied, "From this distance, I can't tell if there is any scar tissue."

When I returned with the julep cups, Doc Haydon was slowly tracing a line through the air with his finger while intently watching Tad. The boy had one hand over his good eye and was trying to follow Doc Haydon's finger with the other.

Race fans from the surrounding boxes were so intent upon watching the two of them that they were paying little attention to the horses being led out for the third race.

After a moment, Doc Haydon noticed me standing there and took one of the drinks from my hand.

"I hope you don't mind that I finished your last one," he said. "The ice was starting to melt and I was obliged to drink it before you let one of Isaiah's juleps get watered down."

"I see," I said, handing him the fresh drink. "And what did you decide about Tad's eye?"

"Oh, the lad has amblyopia," he replied.

"Would you care to put that in English for him?" I asked.

"He has a lazy eye," Doc Haydon replied between sips. "There was an interesting article about it in the most recent journal the Royal Academy sent. I can't say that I have ever seen a case as bad as this before. His is so striking I had to get a better look."

I grinned. Doc Haydon was as curious as I was, and almost as persistent.

"So, is there something you can do besides look?"

"If he were still three or four," he said, frowning, "it might have been correctable. But there's no point in speculating. Medicine is a developing science. When he was a young tyke, we wouldn't have known how to treat amblyopia. Now that we know how to approach the condition, the lad is nearly eighteen and the muscle controlling his eye movements has atrophied too much to fully recover."

He didn't even look at Tad as he spoke.

"If he religiously does the exercise I was just showing him, and wears an eye patch over the good eye for the next couple of months, he should be able to regain most of the function."

"That's good," I said.

"You could take him to see the doctors at one of the big eastern medical schools, after he builds up the muscle some. See if they can grind him some lenses to correct the vision; that first problem is at the root of his condition. Harvard's medical school has a Department of Otology and Ophthalmology. They might be able to correct the vision distortion so his eyes work together better."

"Why should I take him?"

Doc Haydon leaned back in his chair and took another sip of his drink.

"No reason. I didn't think he would go East alone. Assumed you were interested. I thought you liked the boy."

The third race was starting, but I was too perturbed to pay attention. My drink sat untouched on the floor beside my chair. My hands clenched inside my pockets. For all intents and purposes, Thaddeus Andrew Kent was a teenaged foundling. Two days ago Commander Slayton had dumped his cousin on my doorstep with a note asking – no, telling – me to look after him. Two days, and Doc Haydon was assuming I had taken the boy to raise.

Worst of all, even as I fumed over the outrage of his presumption, I was growing attached to the lad. Out of the corner of my vision, I could see Tad dutifully practicing his eye exercise. He was trying to improve his lot in life. It reminded me of the way Ness and I had worked to erase our Irish brogues and rise above the poverty of our childhood. If Tad conducted himself well on this case, I would at least ask Doctor Haydon to write to the doctors at Harvard on his behalf.

Thinking of the case reminded me of the question I had

intended to ask Doc Haydon.

"Doc, what did you mean earlier?" I asked after the large bay I didn't recognize crossed the finish line three lengths ahead of the favorite.

"About what?"

"About the Knights, when you said our way of life?"

"I can't explain it," he said, a little wistfully.

His eyes gazed out over the infield but I could tell he was focusing on something deep inside. I leaned back in my chair and waited for him to order his thoughts.

"The war killed what was left of innocence," he said, after a long pause.

"Were you part of a Circle?"

"No," Haydon replied. "I didn't want any part of the insanity that tore this country asunder. Not that anyone could entirely avoid the unpleasantness. But I am a surgeon. I cannot look at a bleeding man and see an enemy, no matter what color his uniform. I just fixed up my patients as best I could and tried to get through the insanity without losing my own mind. I was doing pretty well until typhoid swept through the hospital. Maybe that's the difference between us, Ness. Truthfully, I don't know which side brought fever. So I blame both sides for the war and death while you just blame the Knights for killing your twin."

There was a thoughtful expression on his face as he turned to face me.

"I lost my sister, my daughter, and my wife to typhoid. The war created the conditions, but it was disease that killed them. I was never a Knight. I never wanted anything to do with the killing or the reasons people found to hate each other. I just wanted the dying to stop."

He held his cup up.

"A toast, my friend," he said softly, "to the walking wounded and those ghost ladies that haunt us. You will always see the ghost of Nessa in your mirror, and I will always mourn my dear Caroline. To the casualties of war, my friend, and to those ladies who made us who we are."

"Just who is that?" I asked, gazing into my Julep cup.

"You and I, Ness, we are the real crusaders. You want to vanquish crime, and I, disease. It has nothing to do with God or country. We want to obliterate them because they hurt us. We are both doomed to failure. Know it too. But we have to keep trying. It isn't in either of us to quit. Sometimes, we are even lucky enough to make a small difference."

CHAPTER TEN

Tad showed up at my office the next morning in his police uniform and sporting his new eye patch. The black padded cloth was about the size of a twenty dollar gold piece, flattened at the top where the tie attached. It looked slightly comical with his brass buttoned black uniform and tall rounded police hat.

Beulah showed great restraint in not grinning until after she had turned in a direction where Tad couldn't see her face.

I tried to look stern, but her smile was infectious. It took all the effort I could manage just to keep from chuckling

"Have you been on duty all night?" I asked.

"No, sir," he said, "I just had to help Sergeant Hamm rope off some walkways this morning. There have been a lot of complaints about visitors trampling flowerbeds and trespassing on private property."

"I noticed there was a circus setting up near the tents at the Fairgrounds. How is the sergeant holding up to having an extra city to patrol?"

"Two," he said, "there's another circus setting up at the black fairgrounds. They got their own tent town too. Cousin James has everybody working sixteen-hour days and we had to set up cots at the old munitions warehouse to handle all the overflow from the city jail. The sergeant doesn't complain about the work, but his temper is a mite short. He thinks Cousin James should ask for help from the guard, but the city don't want to pay for the extra men."

Knowing Sergeant Hamm's opinion of circus people, I suspected Tad was understating his mood.

"If you are needed elsewhere…"

"No, sir," Tad said, before I could finish the thought. "Begging your pardon for interrupting, Mr. Donnelly, but Cousin James wants me to stick with you. He said to concentrate on the murder."

"In that case, I hope you're hungry. Beulah is going to be disappointed if you don't have a generous portion of her biscuits and sausage gravy. She doesn't approve of skinny people."

His face had an odd expression as he looked at my slight build. Even with the padding I added to my upper body, the youngster was at least twenty pounds heavier than me.

"Are we working here this morning, sir?" he finally asked.

"No," I said, getting to my feet and leading the way to the dining room. "We are going to be going through the newspaper archives at the public library later. I want to look at anything about either Mr. Buckner or Mr. Malthus. I was thinking of starting with yesterday and working our way backwards."

"How far back, Sir?"

"I wish we could go back through everything, but we haven't the time. We will look over this year first. After that, why don't you start with December and work back through all of 1878? I'll look over '77. I don't think we can do more than that today."

"You want me to read a whole year of newspapers in one day!"

I laughed.

"You don't have to read the whole paper. Skip the short stories, poetry, advertising, births, and marriage announcements. Pay close attention to the business section and the political news, look over all the letters to the editor, and pay particular attention to those concerning those things we know are an interest of one man or the other. Any time you find either man mentioned, write down the date of the paper, the page number and the key facts of the story so I can find it again if I need to."

"That seems like a lot of work to find mostly useless information," Tad said.

"Tad, today you are going to discover that detective work is very much like prospecting for gold. Ninety-nine percent of what an investigation turns up is useless," I said. "The remaining one percent is the nugget that solves the case. Once you accept that sorry fact, the hours spent mining useless information to find the one useful bit become less difficult to face."

After spending half a day turning my fingers black on old newspapers, I was ready to concede that one percent was a grossly generous estimate of how much information I had mined from the newspaper archives. I had learned a great deal about tobacco prices and Republican politics, but discovered no connection between Buckner and Malthus. Not one article listed both men together or separately.

"Let's give it one more hour," I said. "If we don't find anything, we can give up the search for a while."

Tad had removed his eye patch after the first hour. Since then he had rubbed his tired eyes, spreading enough printers' ink around them to make his face resemble a raccoon's mask. When I looked up, I couldn't help laughing. I handed him my handkerchief.

"You might want to find the water closet and wipe the ink off your face." I said. "I'll look over this stack, then I think we had better go pay Miss Brezing that visit."

His expression brightened at the mention of Belle.

I sighed as Tad hurried off to clean up. Reluctantly, I picked up the next paper and started thumbing through the pages. Three papers later, I ran across an editorial letter urging the state legislature to enact laws prohibiting the sale of alcoholic beverages by the glass in grocery stores. Several notable citizens including the mayor and the commander of police had signed, but also both Malthus and Buckner. The letter was another tenuous link between the two victims. I made a note of the date it was printed, and decided that I would inquire of the other signers how well Buckner and Malthus were acquainted.

Tad returned, looking considerably more presentable than he had earlier. I noticed that while he was removing the printers' ink he had taken the liberty of combing his hair before visiting Jenny Hill's establishment.

Jenny Hill and her ladies were just finishing an early supper when we arrived. Belle took us into the large double parlor and closed the door.

"Have you found out anything Ness – Mr. Donnelly?" Belle asked.

"Nothing useful," I said, trying not to look directly into her dark eyes.

Instead of the sassy woman I was accustomed to seeing, today she seemed very young and frightened.

"Belle, we are running out of time. Sergeant Hamm asked me to convey a suggestion to you. He thinks you should find yourself a good lawyer because you may be arrested in a day or two."

"But I didn't kill Buckner," she said.

"I believe you," I replied. "You know I will do everything in my power to prove your innocence. Is there any reason you can think of that the real killer would leave the body here?"

She shook her head.

"Would anyone wish you harm, Miss Belle?" Tad asked, his voice quivering slightly.

Belle smiled at him demurely. "Maybe a few of the married women in town," she said. "I can't quite picture any of them carrying Mr. Buckner into the hall though. Can you, Officer…"

"Kent, Miss Belle, Officer Thaddeus Kent," he said straightening up and blushing.

In other circumstances, it would have been more amusing to see how smitten young Tad was with Belle, but right now I needed their attention on the murder. I cleared my throat loudly.

"Do you know a man by the name of Isaiah Malthus, Belle?"

"Our visitors don't always use their real names," Belle said. "I might know his face."

I showed her my crude drawing.

"I'm not sure. He might'a been here. What does this have to do with Mr. Buckner?" she asked.

"Maybe nothing." I said, "but Mr. Buckner was trying to contact him shortly before he died. Mr. Malthus was killed in Frankfort within a day of when Buckner was killed here. I am trying to find out if there are any connections between the two deaths."

She sat down near the lamp and examined the drawing again.

"No," she said, "I don't recall anybody who looks like your picture."

Her face looked so frightened that I knelt down and placed an arm around her shoulders.

"It will be all right," I said. "I promise."

"Rachel better not see you with your arm around me," she said, forcing a smile that didn't reach her eyes. "She thinks you're handsome."

I laughed at the silliness of the statement.

"Rachel needs an eye exam," I said, standing to go. "If you

think of anything that might help, let me know. Otherwise, I'll drop by tomorrow and let you know what I discover."

"Please do," Belle said. "Come anyway, even if you don't find anything. I conjure up all sorts of worries when I'm alone."

"I wish I could tell you not to worry, but this is serious, Belle. The Commander of Police is under a lot of pressure to find Buckner's murderer. With all the parties, balls, and other events going on this week, he hasn't enough men to do a proper investigation. Arresting you would save him the trouble of continuing the search. Besides, blaming you is a lot easier than finding the truth. You should take Sergeant Hamm's advice and find a good lawyer."

"I said I didn't kill Buckner," she protested.

"I know you didn't kill him, Belle. But being innocent and being charged with a crime are two different things. The Commander of police wants a fast arrest, your arrest. You need a lawyer," I said firmly. "And I need your help."

"My help?"

"Belle, the statements you ladies gave the police were amusing, but not exactly true."

She blushed.

"I need to know who was in this house when the body was discovered, and what all of you were really doing," I said.

Our eyes met.

"I need you to talk to the ladies and make a list of who was here and where they were. Particularly, what Miss Hill was doing."

"What difference does that make?"

"Think about it Belle. Her business is to know who is in the house so none of the girls can cheat her. She wouldn't leave that front hall unattended. How did someone get in here and out without being seen?"

"Oh!" Belle said, her eyes widening at the thought. "You think someone distracted her?"

"I think she has sharp eyes," I said softly. "Miss Hill collects a percentage of every girl's business. I noticed that she has mirrors positioned around the parlor she uses as her office. They reflect each of the downstairs rooms and the front hall. I think she keeps a close eye on who comes through that front door and which girl they go upstairs with, don't you?"

We left Belle to think about the answers to my questions. I

wasn't sure she would tell me who was there the night Buckner died, but she would at least have to consider what Jenny Hill knew about the killing.

CHAPTER ELEVEN

Ambrose Peltmutter was proving to be remarkably difficult to interview. My efforts to meet with him at the bank had become so frequent that the clerks hung their heads in shame each time they spotted me waiting in their lines. This morning, Tad and I arrived at the National Bank at nine o'clock sharp, determined to remain in the lobby until the elusive Mr. Peltmutter put in an appearance. Ezra Martin, the chief clerk couldn't meet my eyes when he gave yet another apology, explaining that Mr. Peltmutter had taken the day off in order to pay his final respects to Nathaniel P. Buckner and his family.

I had my doubts about Peltmutter having any desire to pay his respects to the Buckner family. The banking business was highly conservative and, even though Nathaniel Buckner had been on the board of National Bank for more than eighteen years, it was unlikely to reflect well on the bank for its president to be too closely associated with Buckner's family. He would probably, out of duty, put in an appearance at the funeral. I seriously doubted that appearance would include his family or that he would attend the cold supper at Buckner's residence. Beyond an appearance at the funeral, Ambrose Peltmutter would put as much distance as he could between himself and the scandal brewing around the Buckner murder.

I thought about Buckner and Peltmutter as Tad and I made our way over to Milward's Funeral Parlor. Leaving Buckner's body at Miss Jenny's had tarnished his memory. I had found lurid accounts of the murder featured in every newspaper I read. Over the last four days, the *Lexington Gazette* published such harsh accountings of the incident that I sometimes blushed reading them. Mr. Buckner's character had been so thoroughly destroyed by the press that there was little chance any of the ladies in town would risk having their own reputations tainted by associating with the Buckner family. I believed that was the motive behind leaving him at the bawdyhouse. I just couldn't understand why destroying his reputation was important to the killer.

At Milward's, I checked the guest book in the viewing room. It confirmed my opinion of Peltmutter. There was no indication on the page that he or any of his family had visited the mortuary. The near-empty guest book gave a sad accounting of Mr. Buckner's true friends. All the money and status he possessed in life had not provided Nathaniel Buckner with friends steadfast enough to risk damage to their own reputations in order to pay a final call on him.

I copied the handful of names listed on the page into my notes, and then with a brazen stroke I added my own name to the list of his visitors. I had no real acquaintance with Mr. Buckner, having never met him in life, but it galled me to know that the man was not yet in the ground and had already been judged so harshly by the community. The things I had learned about him while investigating his murder led me to believe that he would never willingly pass through Miss Hill's door. I suspected that his murder was somehow connected to the KGC. If he was one of them he probably deserved an inglorious death. However, I hated hypocrisy. Many of the men who were turning their backs on his widow had certainly belonged to the KGC and more than a few were regular visitors to Miss Hill's establishment. They pretended to be made of better stuff than the deceased, yet their absence at their friend's viewing belied the effort.

Tad and I removed our hats, and stepped into the viewing room.

Only Mrs. Buckner and her son were in attendance at this hour. Buckner looked very different laid out in his business suit. Mr. Milward had managed to ease the look of surprise from his face. I wondered if the small copy of the Bible had been placed in his folded hands as a statement from the family about the unseemly way he was discovered.

"I am sorry for your loss, Mrs. Buckner," I said, when I turned away from the coffin.

Her eyebrows arched slightly as she looked up at me.

She was a small woman, thinner than usual for a woman of her social position, and appeared deceptively frail unless one looked into her dark eyes. There was a fire in her, banked down, slow burning embers behind coal black eyes. I could see why she was reputed to be the force behind her husband's success.

"If you are truly sorry, Mr. Donnelly, why are you helping those women?" she asked.

"I assure you Mrs. Buckner, I am doing everything in my power to discover the truth. If it is any comfort to you and your family, I do not believe your husband entered Miss Hill's house of his own free will. The evidence so far indicates his body was brought there after death, perhaps to damage his reputation."

A spark of hope passed through her eyes. "Why would anyone commit such an atrocious act?"

"I don't know," I said honestly. "The answer might lie in his private papers. May I have your permission to call, after the funeral of course, and examine his office and personal effects?"

"Is this necessary, Mr. Donnelly?"

"Somewhere among his possessions could be the reason he was murdered and left in a place that would publicly humiliate him. Everyone I have spoken with tells me it was not in his character to associate with Miss Hill or the women in her employ. Yet the circumstances have been arranged to belie the truth. Someone went to a great deal of trouble to besmirch his reputation. I need to look over everything if I am to find the truth."

"To find the truth or to clear those women?" she asked coldly.

"Mrs. Buckner, you have my word, if I discover one of the women in Miss Hill's establishment is connected to this crime, she will not find my testimony of any help."

Her gaze burned my skin from under her black veils. She stood there studying me for what seemed an eternity.

"Very well, Mr. Donnelly, you may look through my husband's possessions," she said at last.

"Thank you," I said, and then turned to leave.

"Mr. Donnelly," she called after me.

I turned and met her gaze.

"Yes?"

"Find who has done this…unspeakable atrocity," she said. Her whole body trembled with barely controlled rage. "I will make it worth your while."

"I have a client, Mrs. Buckner," I replied.

"Those women? Why should they care?"

"I don't discuss my clients," I replied in a tone that I hoped would brook no further discussion, then turned again to leave.

We didn't bother waiting for the tram. The Peltmutter house was among the long established homes that lined the east end of Main Street, a short ten-minute walk from the mortuary. I needed that much time to order my thoughts.

Fortunately, Tad seemed to be growing accustomed to my need for silence. He walked along beside me with his hands in his pockets and his hat pulled low over the eye patch, not speaking until we were at the banker's front door.

"Where'd you get those?" he asked, when the maid who had taken my card retreated.

"What?"

"Those little cards like you gave her?"

"They are just calling cards. You can buy them at any print shop."

"Could I?" he asked, looking astonished at the possibility.

"Of course."

"Gee. Could I have one of yours to show 'em?"

I took one of the small white cards embossed with black letters out of my pocket and handed it to him just as the maid returned.

"Mr. Peltmutter has been called away on a family emergency," the girl said coldly.

I didn't believe it. If Mr. Peltmutter were truly gone, she would have told us immediately instead of leaving us standing on the doorstep for several minutes. There was nothing to be done, though.

"I see," I said. "When is he expected to return?"

"Ah-" the girl stammered, obviously not expecting to be questioned. "We don't expect him home afore next week."

She seemed satisfied that that was a sufficient answer, and closed the door before we could press her for more information.

The nature of the Peltmutter family's emergency struck me as being highly questionable. I considered investigating the excuse, and decided against it. There were better uses of my time than continuing to chase Ambrose Peltmutter when he so clearly did not want to talk to me.

Tad dutifully followed me down the walk.

"Are you just giving up on Mr. Peltmutter?" he asked.

"No, I'm not," I said, "but he is avoiding me. Continuing to hunt for him is a waste of my time."

"Don't seem right, him leaving town without telling the folks at the bank," he muttered.

"Maybe he drummed up some excuse to leave town so he could avoid attending Mr. Buckner's funeral," I said.

I turned up Mulberry Street toward Vine Street and the warehouse district. If I couldn't get an interview with Mr. Peltmutter, perhaps I could have a look around Buckner's office.

"He could be involved," Tad said. "I heard you and Sergeant Hamm say that Mr. Peltmutter was supposed to be meeting with Mr. Buckner the day he was killed."

"Indeed," I agreed, "I have every reason to believe that Mr. Peltmutter did see Mr. Buckner shortly before he died. The telegraph operator told us that Mr. Buckner left his office and headed down the street toward the bank. I also think he has some reason to want to avoid talking to me."

"I think that girl lied to us," he said.

"Good," I said. "I think so too."

"You do?"

"Yes. Mr. Peltmutter may, very well, be at home in his own parlor right now congratulating himself on getting rid of us," I said. "Unfortunately, there is nothing I can do to make him invite me into his home except keep digging for the truth until I find something compelling enough to change his mind."

I frowned at that unlikely event. Peltmutter was actively avoiding me. I doubted that anything short of divine intervention would get me an interview with him. Somehow I couldn't picture any heavenly host feeling obliged to intervene on behalf of confirmed sinners like Belle and me.

"What if we don't find anything to make him talk?" Tad asked.

"Our other option is to find him somewhere public, like the funeral."

Tad looked aghast.

"You'd corner him in church!"

"No," I said. "But I am willing to attempt cornering him at the cemetery."

We had walked only a few blocks from the center of town, but the streets were already becoming narrow and slightly seedy. Mingled scents of tobacco, hemp, coal, and leather lingered in the air and left a choking taste in the back of my throat. I wondered what it must be like for the warehouse workers who walked from the slums of Irishtown to work here every day. They left the stench of open sewers and swine running loose in the streets to work in this, and then returned to the slums each night. Tad coughed as the pungent odor of fresh tar added a new assault to our senses.

I glanced back to see how Tad was doing and noticed he had taken to regularly walking with his hands in his pockets and wearing his bowler at the exact same angle I wore my own. Had it not been for the hands pushed down into the pockets of his breeches I would have thought the angle of his hat was just an attempt to conceal the eye patch Doc Haydon had prescribed, but his whole posture was clearly an attempt to imitate me.

"New hat, Tad?"

"Yes, Sir," he said, adjusting it slightly, and smiling at me. "Sergeant Hamm helped me pick it out. What do you think?"

I thought I was going to have to have a word with Sergeant Wilfred Hamm before Tad's admiration became a source of jokes around the stationhouse, but it wasn't prudent to say so aloud.

"Nice looking hat," I said.

What else could I say? His new derby was practically identical to my own.

This had to stop. Getting the sergeant to quit encouraging Tad's imitation of me would probably require my agreeing to more dinners with his wife's many cousins, but I had to do something. I felt foolish and a little embarrassed at the prospect of posing as a suitor to end Sergeant Hamm's little joke, but not so embarrassed that I would refuse to cooperate if that was the price of ending this game.

The Lexington Cigar Company was a two-story red brick building half a block past the woolen mill. Horace Newman, the senior partner in the firm, was nearly seventy. I supposed that at some point we would have to question him, even though his involvement was improbable. Mr. Newman was far too feeble to help carry a man of Buckner's size. Besides, he was unlikely to have reason to want to be rid of his business partner. From all accounts, Buckner was running the business alone. Newman still kept an office at the factory, but rarely used it. If local gossip was to be believed, the only time Mr. Newman ever came to his office was when his wife's sisters visited Lexington. Business during those visits became so urgent that he was forced to put in long hours at the office. Buckner was the active member of the partnership.

Today black crepe draped the doors of the factory and a wreath of black posies hung from each window of business offices. Despite the absence of company managers, work still progressed on the factory floor. The mood of the office was subdued and the warehouse foremen all wore black armbands to show respect for Mr. Buckner. Two young clerks were the only office employees working. They sat side by side at small wooden desks working diligently on the account books.

"Good morning," I said, when one of them looked up. "My name is Ness Donnelly, and this is Officer Thaddeus Kent of the Lexington Police. We are investigating Mr. Buckner's murder and need to see his office."

"There's nobody here but us," one of the young men said nervously. "The office is closing soon, so employees can attend the funeral."

"We won't take long," I replied.

The clerk paled.

"I haven't the authority to let anyone into Mr. Buckner's office."

"I have Mrs. Buckner's permission to look over her husband's personal effects," I said. "If that isn't sufficient, I could send Officer Kent for a warrant." I pointed at Tad. "Commander Slayton has assigned Office Kent to assist me, which is why he is not in uniform, but he does have the authority to make arrests if necessary."

"A-arrests, sir?"

"Obstruction of justice is a crime," I said. "But I thought Mr. Buckner's employees would want to cooperate in resolving the questions about his murder."

The young man hesitated, looking at his friend.

"Since the two of you seem to have something to hide, I can wait here until Officer Kent returns with the authority to enter Mr. Buckner's office. I have to be sure nothing is removed before he returns."

My words were pure bravado. I was not sure the court would issue a warrant to search Buckner's office, and even if they did, I had no authority to guard the office in Tad's absence. Luckily, the clerks were flustered enough at the thought of being suspects in Buckner's death that they offered no further arguments.

"That isn't necessary, Mr. Donnelly," the clerk said, fumbling in his desk for the keys. "Mr. Buckner's office is just over here."

He stood up and we followed him to the office door.

"What are we looking for?" Tad asked, as soon as the clerk had left the room.

I took out my notebook and turned to the sketch I had made of Mr. Malthus' watch fob.

"This, among other things," I said. "If you find this symbol or any other enclosed in a circle, I want to see it. Look for correspondence between Mr. Buckner and Mr. Malthus, or any letters concerning Mr. Malthus. See if any of his letters appear threatening, angry, or otherwise out of place in a business office. For that matter, look for anything out of place. If you run across something that is not related to his work I want to see it."

We searched in silence for several minutes before Tad spoke.

"There is a folder here on the Nicodemus Colony. One of the letters is from Mr. Malthus."

My heart stopped, then started again. "Let me look at that."

Inside the folder were nine letters, some of them several years old, between various men concerning donations toward the founding and continued support of the Nicodemus Colony. Only one was from Malthus, dated November last. Another bore Mr. Ambrose Peltmutter's sprawling signature. One or two of the others were familiar, including one by James Slayton, and another by the mayor, but several were by men I didn't know. I read through them quickly, seeing nothing that drew my immediate attention. Since I had no authority to take the letters, I set Tad to the task of copying each into my notebook while I continued to search the rest of the office.

I sat down at Buckner's desk and started rummaging through the desk drawers as I considered the letters. There were a lot of prominent citizens that had contributed to the funds for the Nicodemus Colony. Some thought it would improve relations with the colored communities. Others hoped to put an end to the lynchings that were all too common in our city. I was not at all sure there was any benefit in helping the colored families settle in Kansas, but my views of farming were jaded by my own childhood memories.

What I did know was that two of the men helping this flow of settlers to the West were now dead. I was not sure what, if any, connections there were between the Nicodemus Colony, the Golden Circle, and the murders. Perhaps it was all just coincidence. Malthus could have kept the watch fob as a war souvenir. For that matter, the murders could be completely unrelated.

If my fingers had not happened upon a small amber colored bottle in the bottom desk drawer, I might have convinced myself that I was on the wrong track. I was going on instinct and experience. Instinct told me the murders were related. Experience told me that the highest ranks of the Golden Circle still believed they were entitled to rule the world. The moment I touched the cold glass, I realized that I was not mistaken.

The Golden Circle named itself for the imaginary circle that extended from the cotton and tobacco fields of the Southern States through the Caribbean and Mexico, all the way to the coffee plantations of Central and South America. Their dream of controlling the cotton, sugar, tobacco, chocolate, coffee, and hemp trade had not died. These men really believed that if they could gain control of the major New World crops, all the nations of the world would bend to their will. It was an insane plan, but the dream of controlling the world had not dimmed even when their plans had been foiled and the South defeated. These were ambitious men of the highest social rank, a moneyed aristocracy steeped in the values of the Old South, held together by dark secret rituals and an unflinching belief that they were the architects of a new world empire.

A tiny bottle, no bigger than a spice jar, rested in my hand. Inside, I could see a scroll, carefully bound with a golden string. It took all my willpower to fight back the temptation to open the bottle. Only the knowledge that the secrets of the Golden Circle were not that easy to capture stayed my hand. More than one of these bottles had fallen into the hands of Pinkerton men who discovered, much to their chagrin, that the scrolls inside burst into flames once the bottle opened. There had to be a way to remove the scroll, but nobody I knew had ever successfully retrieved one from its bottle.

There had been some successes at discovering secrets, but none that involved this sort of package. Once, the Pinkertons had been able to stop them from burning New York City, when a member of the Circle balked at murdering children. The plot was already being acted out and several buildings had been lost to the fires before the man came forward. On another occasion, the army discovered plans to invade Mexico and halted the train carrying the so-called Fifth Order, preventing them from reaching Texas. The men had disgraced themselves by becoming so frightened by the arrival of armed troops that they threw their weapons into the Missouri River without ever firing a shot. At the time, we thought that was the end of the Golden Circle. I now had the creeping feeling that we were wrong. I had to figure out a way to unlock the bottle's secret without having it evaporate before my eyes.

"I'm finished, Mr. Donnelly," Tad said, looking up from the letters. "What do you want me to do now?"

My hand closed around the little bottle. For a split second, a nagging touch of conscience told me I should put the bottle back in the desk drawer. I had no more authority to take it than I did to remove the letters. I didn't listen.

"Just put the file back where you found it," I said, slipping the bottle into my pocket while his back was turned. "Then see if there is anything else in the files. I am going to take a look at the bookcase, then I guess we can leave."

Ten minutes later, Tad and I were finished searching the office and on our way out. The bottle created only the slightest bulge in my coat pocket, though I had to struggle to keep from putting my hands on it while we were leaving. I knew we had to attend Buckner's funeral. Tad was eager to continue the investigation, but after the funeral I intended to go home and dig through old files. Somewhere in Ness's notes there might be an indication of what he had learned about the Golden Circle, or perhaps a key to opening the secret in my pocket.

CHAPTER TWELVE

Time had slipped away from me while we were searching Buckner's office. His funeral was at two o'clock. It was past noon when the clerk relocked the door. Tad and I had to hurry through streets clogged with booths selling coonskin caps and wooden long rifles to the throngs of festival goers. We were supposed to meet Sergeant Hamm at his office a quarter of an hour ago. There was an advantage in being late: I would not have to tell him what we had found.

The sergeant's military training had hammered punctuality into his mindset. He detested being late and considered perpetual tardiness a character flaw on par with drunkenness on duty. Today our tardiness would be particularly vexing, since Commander Slayton was acting as a pallbearer and would notice any disruption made by our late arrival to the service.

"I'm sorry," I said when we arrived at the station to find him pacing in front of the desk he shared with the other shift sergeant. "There were some letters of interest in Mr. Buckner's files. Tad was copying them while I searched the desk. Would you mind if we filled you in on the contents later?"

"Those letters had better be worth the wait," Sergeant Hamm growled, picking up his hat and heading toward the door. "The Commander is going to be mighty peeved if we show up late. It ain't respectful."

Wilfred Hamm was a good five inches taller than me. I was having trouble keeping up with him as we walked toward Buckner's church. As usual, Sergeant Hamm's uniform was spotless and his boots shined with the fine gleam that my most diligent efforts always failed to bring to my own boots. I was hot, dusty, and no doubt a disgrace to Beulah's efforts to make me appear to be a gentleman. It pained me to think that the sergeant had worked all night, walked at least as far as I had today, and still managed to remain as well turned out as he had been when he left home the previous evening. Meanwhile, word of my unkempt appearance would probably reach Beulah's ears before I got home, leaving me to deal with her displeasure as well as the sergeant's irritation.

At the thought of home, my fingers plunged deeper into my jacket pocket wrapped around the cold glass bottle I had removed from Buckner's office. Another twinge of guilt crept into my awareness. I had stolen it, and was now deliberately keeping it from the sergeant. This small bottle was evidence of the Golden Circle's continued activity in the state. It worried me more than I cared to admit aloud that Buckner and Malthus were involved with the KGC. They may have been involved in my brother's death. Their murders had closed yet another possibility for finding his killers.

I told myself that the two of them probably knew no more than I did about who shot Ness. Membership in the Knights had once included more than half the men in Fayette County. There was no way of determining how many men still had loyalties to the secret society. The tiny bottle in my pocket indicated that some of the Knights were still at work. I wanted to take the bottle home and try to figure out how to open it without losing the slip of parchment inside.

The scroll was probably coated in some compound that would burst into flame when exposed to air. I had seen something of that sort in a traveling medicine show. But my knowledge of chemicals was sparse. I needed help – but from whom?

My inability to trust anyone was forcing me to keep more and more discoveries to myself, intentionally shutting Sergeant Hamm out of the case. I wanted to trust him, but could not bring myself to do it. Not when the case so clearly involved the Golden Circle. Any of the men attending this funeral could belong to the Circle, including the sergeant. I could think of a number of reasons the KGC might have interest in a police officer of some rank. The thought made me shudder, but try as I might, I could not force it from my mind.

Hamm probably didn't know any more than I did about how to

open the bottle without damaging its contents. Conversely, if he did know the secret, the knowledge would make it even more likely he was now or had once been a member of the KGC. I decided that Doc Haydon was the only person I knew that might be able to assist. I would take the bottle to him at the first opportunity I found.

The Buckners attended one of the oldest and largest Baptist congregations in the state. Nearly a thousand people could be seated in the sanctuary, though I suspected today's crowd would be considerably smaller.

Lexington First Baptist was built atop First Hill, over the site of the fort where the original settlers erected their log cabins. It was constructed in the gothic style and, in my opinion, was the ugliest building in the entire city. I was reminded of this each day, since it sat less than two blocks from my home and I had to pass it each time I ventured into town. The stonewalls were mud brown, streaked with lines of black smoke from nearby chimneys. At night, bats flew through the arched windows of the bell tower. It was easy to believe reports that those first settlers, buried under the structure, rose up to haunt the surrounding community.

Even in daylight, I paused at the foot of the stairs leading to the sanctuary. The double doors of the huge gothic building were still open and I reluctantly followed Sergeant Hamm as he hurried toward the gaping mouth of the monstrosity. One of the ushers noticed us hurrying up the steps, and waited until we entered to close the heavy doors of the church.

It took a moment for my eyes to adjust to the dim light filtering through narrow windows into the vestibule. We slipped into one of the back pews as quietly as we could and glanced around the room. The crowd was noticeably void of female faces, but a combination of curiosity and duty made Nathaniel P. Buckner's funeral better attended than the number of mourners at Milward Funeral Parlor would have indicated.

Buckner's business associates attended without their wives and daughters, of course, but it pleased me to see that a respectable number of them had felt obliged to attend. Even the elusive Mr. Peltmutter had returned from his 'family emergency' to attend the funeral of a fellow board member of National Bank. I recognized him from his portrait, and pointed out the rotund banker to Tad.

Although the room was quite cool, the banker was continually dabbing droplets of sweat away from his beady little eyes. He was clearly perturbed by something and kept shifting nervously in his seat. Once or twice I caught him glancing my direction, but he quickly averted his eyes whenever his eyes met my own.

I secretly hoped it was our presence that made Peltmutter so uncomfortable. I was still annoyed about being turned away from his front door and denied a meeting in his office. Several times, as he glanced furtively around the room, I tried to see what he was looking at but was never able to determine the source of his fear.

"I intend to corner Peltmutter before he has a chance to escape and ask the questions he so blatantly avoided this morning," I said, quietly to Tad. "Stick close at the graveside service."

Tad nodded and fixed his good eye on Peltmutter.

I had always thought that Catholic services were long, but not even Christmas Eve Mass compared to the length of the sermon delivered over Buckner's corpse. Perhaps it was the circumstances of the case that drove Reverend Fletcher's need to extol the virtues of sobriety and stress mankind's need to avoid the appearance of evil. He talked for a good hour, ending with warnings of the fire and brimstone awaiting the wicked and an altar call that I would have thought out of place in a funeral service. Thankfully, nobody was sufficiently moved by the sermon to feel obliged to answer the call to repentance.

Sergeant Hamm shifted uncomfortably in the pew.

"Long-winded preacher," he whispered.

I nodded in sympathy.

My decision to pose as a man complicated the practice of my own faith; maybe it just gave me an excuse not to attend confession. There was no point to confessing sins I felt no contrition in committing. The church had long ago lost meaning for me. I could vaguely remember belief in God, but what nebulous faith I possessed as a child was lost somewhere between the coffin ships that brought my family to America and the war that filled my adopted country with as much death as the one we left behind. Only hollow rituals remained. This service didn't even offer the comfort of familiar rituals.

The way I figured it, two hours of suffering through Reverend Fletcher's sermon sufficiently served as penance for my sins of gambling and drinking committed earlier in the week. He had gone from making an altar call to giving a personal testimony that seemed as much bragging on his ill-spent youth as it was revealing of God's mercy. If he didn't stop soon, I was sure it would drive me to visit the track again just to commit enough sin to justify the amount of penance his sermon forced upon me.

At some signal unrecognized by me, the choir rose and began a sorrowful song. We stood and waited as the pews emptied. One by one, the mourners filed past the open casket for a last look at the late Nathaniel P. Buckner before exiting the church. From the back row, Sergeant Hamm and I watched them leave. Mrs. Buckner leaned heavily on her son's arm. With her face hidden behind the thick black veils, she seemed small and frail, a shadow of the woman I had met earlier. Behind the two of them, an elderly couple trailed quietly by.

"That's Newman, his partner," Sergeant Hamm whispered.

Tad started to say something as one of the men from the inquest in Frankfort drew near. I kicked his ankle before he got the chance to let the man know we recognized him. He was a tall man, muscular and broad shouldered. I estimated he was somewhere in his late forties, old enough to have belonged to the KGC, but he lacked the moneyed appearance of men in Buckner's social circle.

Except for the pallbearers, Sergeant Hamm, Tad, and I were the last to leave the church. We stood near the curb as Commander Slayton and the other pallbearers carried the casket out and placed it in the waiting hearse. Once the casket was loaded, and the carpet of hothouse roses was arranged over the coffin to afford the best viewing through the glass windows of the hearse, Mr. Milward assisted the Buckners into his waiting carriage. He then signaled the hearse driver to take the body to Lexington Cemetery for burial. The three of us stood silently watching as Buckner's elderly partner assisted his wife into their carriage. She and Mrs. Buckner were the only two women I saw in the funeral procession.

In single file, carriages, sulkies, and the occasional farm wagon joined the slow moving procession. No one spoke. The creak of wagon wheels mingled with the song of a distant mocking bird. Horses hooves, wrapped in crepe and burlap, landed with a muted thud on the straw strewn cobbles of Main Street.

As we passed under the huge Centennial banner emblazoned with the life-size vestige of Daniel Boone, I couldn't help thinking how strange it was to be walking in a funeral procession along a street gaily decorated for the city's Centennial parade. All along the route, festivalgoers dressed in pioneer garb stopped what they were doing, removed their coon-skin hats, and bowed their heads in silent prayer below the bright red, white, and blue flags that waved in the spring breeze. At the edge of my vision, I could see small children tug impatiently at their parent's hands, unable to understand the sudden pause in their adventures. I didn't blame them.

The sun was bright and warm and the sky such a clear blue that it seemed the heavens themselves rejected the solemnity of Buckner's passing. I wondered how much real sorrow there was among the mourners. The only genuine grief I had seen was in his widow's face. How many, like me, were drawn here in an attempt to glean a bit of knowledge into what really happened to Nathaniel Buckner on the last day of his life?

When the line of carriages had passed, the three of us fell into a companionable silence in the line of mourners following Buckner on his last ride. As a sergeant of police, Wilfred Hamm was issued a horse, but in deference to us had chosen to walk the short distance from the church to the cemetery. I held my hat in gloved hands, resisting the urge to glance at Jenny Hill's house to see if Belle was watching us pass below her window. I had maybe another day to find Buckner's murderer. It wouldn't be more than that before Sergeant Hamm would have to give into the pressure to arrest her.

Perhaps it was sheer stubbornness that made me believe Belle was innocent. I didn't think so. Belle was many things, but dishonest wasn't one of them.

Unlike the other prostitutes, Belle was even honest about her occupation when arrested. I had bitten my tongue to keep from laughing at the last court appearance I had witnessed from her. I had just finished presenting evidence in a theft case when Belle had entered with several other known prostitutes. Her case followed half a dozen other women who all claimed to be seamstresses. When her turn came, she proudly stated her occupation as prostitute. When the judge asked her how business was, she told him it was "plumb awful" because she had to compete with all the seamstresses in town. The judge had been so amused by her remark, he dismissed the charges.

If Belle Brezing had shot Nathaniel P. Buckner, she would have told me and would probably have had a reason compelling enough to argue justifiable homicide. I realized that was why I took the case, and why I never believed that she shot Johnny Cook.

Whatever it took, I was determined that one of the few honest people I knew would not hang for a crime she didn't commit.

CHAPTER THIRTEEN

Peltmutter was my best hope of finding the killer. I thought about this as we neared the heavy stone pillars supporting the gates to Lexington Cemetery. If he was not the killer, he was at least one of the last people to see Buckner alive. No matter how hard he tried to avoid me, I was going to corner Ambrose Peltmutter at the cemetery and find out what happened when he met with Nathaniel Buckner in his offices that final day. As I glanced up at the words "City of the Dead," which were carved into the stone above the gates, it occurred to me that this would be an ideal spot to press the banker for information. Foliage was heavy around the oppressive iron gates. Even in the afternoon sun, the shadows would make it hard for anyone to see more than a few feet. My mind set to work on how I could get Peltmutter there. By the time we reached the graveside the plan had taken shape.

The design of the gates and dense landscaping made it impossible to see oncoming traffic until the horses had moved though the heavy limestone gateposts. Each of the carriages had to stop at the gates while the driver looked for other carriages before entering Leestown Road. This left the carriage hanging back among the rhododendron bushes, budding dogwoods, and golden-flowered forsythias. It would be easy for Tad and Sergeant Hamm to secret themselves there and wait for me to deliver Peltmutter.

I quietly explained what I had in mind to Sergeant Hamm and Tad. The sergeant argued that we should take a more direct approach. I understood his reasons. As a police officer, he had the authority to question whomever he pleased, but Peltmutter had managed to avoid us for days. Once I pointed out how good the banker was at absenting himself when we wanted to ask questions, Sergeant Hamm reluctantly agreed to allow me to try my way of questioning the banker.

Near the end of the service, our plan was undone. Commander Slayton sent word to his two officers that he needed their assistance lowering the coffin. The sergeant didn't need to explain, but he showed me the note before putting it in his pocket.

"Duty calls," he said. "Questioning Mr. Peltmutter will have to wait another day."

He didn't wait for me to reply.

"Commander needs us," he said to Tad.

I frowned as the two of them slipped quietly away from the graveside and circled to where the Commander of Police stood. Sergeant Hamm was probably right about waiting. I, however, wasn't ready to give up on speaking to Peltmutter. I didn't like having to deal with Peltmutter alone, but didn't believe he would give me a second opportunity. The banker had proven to be very good at denying me chances to question him. He was likely to absent himself from the city if we allowed him to get away from us now. I had no intention of letting that happen.

Near the end of the service, I fell back toward the edge of the crowd, then circled around to the blind side of Peltmutter's carriage. While the coachman was talking to one of the fellow drivers, I climbed inside the carriage to wait for Mr. Peltmutter to return.

Peltmutter froze when he returned, opened the carriage door, and found me waiting.

"Get in," I said quietly, lifting my hand so he could see the derringer leveled at his heavy-lidded eyes.

His drooping jowls quivered as Ambrose Peltmutter stared openmouthed down the short barrel of my gun.

The fear was palpable, making me certain that I was right about Peltmutter's involvement. I might have felt sorry for him had it not been for his willingness to let Belle hang for a crime she didn't commit.

"Get in," I repeated firmly.

He still hesitated.

"The former members of Mr. Buckner's infantry unit are going to start firing a salute to him once the pallbearers finish lowering his coffin into the grave. One extra gunshot won't be noticed," I said in an icy tone. "You have until the first gun fires to make up your mind."

Peltmutter whimpered as he climbed inside.

The springs of the carriage groaned under his weight as he sat down on the blood-colored velvet seat across from me.

"Good choice," I said, running my free hand over the seat cover. "If you force me to shoot you, your widow won't need to get the carriage redone."

The last traces of color drained from his face.

"What do you want?" he asked.

"Just a little of your time," I said. "I have a few questions about your friend Buckner. Thought I would take you someplace quiet where we could discuss his death."

Outside, I could hear the driver calming the horses as the guns fired, then he climbed into the box, and waited until the procession started moving. When we stopped for the gate, I ordered Peltmutter to get out.

"Tell your driver to go on. Say anything else, and the next funeral you attend will be your own."

The driver looked puzzled when we disembarked and waved him on. Fortunately, the line of carriages behind him was sufficient incentive to keep him from questioning his boss. As the driver continued on, I pulled Peltmutter back into the shrubbery where the other departing mourners were unlikely to notice us.

My derringer was nearly invisible in my gloved hand, but Peltmutter was unlikely to forget it was there. He stepped away from the procession without making any attempt to escape. Together, we waited in the shadow of the stone front gate to the City of the Dead, until the sound of passing footsteps quieted. I stood close beside him, the barrel of my gun pressed into the soft flesh at the small of his back, not moving until the last straggler disappeared from view.

I still held out some hope that Sergeant Hamm would finish with the task his commander had assigned him and join me. If not, I was just going to have to persuade the banker to talk by myself. Peltmutter seemed to have a talent for avoiding questioning. Now that I had him cornered, I was not going to be thwarted again.

I moved carefully from behind him and chanced stepping out of the shadows. If someone lingered behind at the cemetery, the black barrel was small, and might easily be mistaken for one of my fingers by anyone but Peltmutter. The banker seemed to have little more than a nodding acquaintance with the truth. I wanted to look at his face while he talked.

Experience had taught me that most lies were written in the speaker's face. A tilt of his head, the hint of a smile, a slight shift of his eyes, or even the tightening of facial muscles could reveal that he and the truth had parted ways.

"Now, Mr. Peltmutter," I said, when I could see him clearly, "it is time for you to explain what happened when Mr. Buckner came to your office."

I saw his mouth gape open and watched it snap shut. He was trembling with fear, but seemed to be as afraid of talking as he was of the gun in my hand.

"I am asking one more time, Mr. Peltmutter," I said quietly. "What happened in your office?"

"Oh God," he croaked, beads of sweat running down his piggish face. "Nothing. Nothing happened. I swear it."

His whole body quivered as his small eyes darted wildly, looking for help. Seeing nobody to rescue him, Peltmutter whimpered.

"Please. I swear, Donnelly, he was alive when I left."

"You left?" My eyes narrowed. "It was your office, Peltmutter. Why would you leave?"

"I--" He dabbed at his brow with a moist handkerchief. "I misspoke."

He was plainly grasping for a convincing lie to tell me.

"I meant Buckner left. Please, please leave me alone. I don't know anything."

Two men were dead. One had obviously been tortured before being murdered. I was not at all moved by the pleas of the sniveling coward in front of me.

"Was someone else with him when you left the office?" I asked.

Peltmutter never got the chance to answer. A blanket, heavy with the stale scent of horses, dropped from the top of the limestone gate and landed on the two of us. I swore as I reached up to throw the blanket off. I didn't think anyone had seen us slip out of Peltmutter's carriage. I must have been wrong.

Before I could clear the blanket from my face, someone leapt on us from above. My attacker threw me off balance.

The derringer discharged as I fell backwards.

There was a groan. The bullet must have hit someone. I didn't think it was Peltmutter. The voice wasn't high and squeaky enough for the fat banker.

I doubted that the gun had inflicted any serious damage, firing through the blanket as I had; bullets fired from my little pistol lacked much velocity. I could only hope it had inflicted enough damage to slow my attacker down. I needed any advantage I could get.

The struggle was awkward, pinned under the blanket as I was. All I could do was punch blindly, with as much force as I could muster. I hated not knowing who my attacker was, or what was happening to the banker. The man I struggled with seemed too large and solid for Peltmutter. If this man was wounded, he showed no indication of injury. I struggled furiously, kicking and punching. One or two punches landed solid. Finally my right arm worked free of the heavy blanket.

I grabbed my attacker's tie and pulled until I could hear him choking. For a moment the fight turned to my advantage. He was still swinging, but the punches lacked any force. Just as it seemed the brute was going to pass out, someone stomped down hard on the arm still entangled in the blanket. There was a sickening crack of breaking bone in my forearm. I lost my grip on his tie.

My attacker pounded his forehead into mine. I swore, brought my knees up hard, and shoved with all the strength I still possessed.

The big man rolled off of me.

No longer pinned by the weight of his body, I struggled to get to my knees as I swiped at the heavy wool blanket hanging loose around my head. I caught a glimpse of the gathering gloom before something solid slammed into the side of my face. In an instant, the world faded from red to black.

"Miss Ness – Miss Nessa, you've got to help." I heard Belle whisper hoarsely. "There's not much time."

I groaned.

Why didn't people ever let me sleep it off when I had a hangover? It wasn't right, I thought as I tugged at my blanket. Somewhere in the back of my mind the stench of horse sweat, grass, and damp earth registered in my awareness.

"Miss Nessa, please," Belle's voice urged softly. "Try to get up. I heard them say they'd be back for you soon as they catch that other man. I can't carry you. You gotta try to move."

I moaned and swiped at something wet on my face.

"What the..."

"Shush!" Belle ordered in a hoarse whisper. "They might hear you!"

My head throbbed. I tried to open my eyes, but realized only one of them could open. My hand went to the other. I instantly regretted the move. Touching it hurt like the devil.

Disoriented and confused, I explored the side of my face with my fingertips. My right eye was swollen shut and caked with partially dried blood. Assessing the damage did not bring back any recollection of what had caused my injuries. The movements only made me want to retch.

"You have to get up!" Belle said. "You don't want to be here when they come back."

"Who?"

Belle didn't answer. She stood up, braced her back against the stone gatepost, and pulled my arms as hard as she could, half-lifting me from the ground.

I gasped with pain as she jerked my arm. It took all my willpower not to swear aloud. My whole body shook, but she got me to my feet before I succumbed to the wave of nausea that accompanied moving.

Belle propped me against the gate, quickly gathered up my gun and broken spectacles, and dropped them into my coat pocket. The fog was clearing a little from my brain as she wrapped my right arm around her shoulders and propelled me toward the gate.

Despite her admonishment to keep quiet, I didn't see another soul anywhere near the entrance. I vaguely wondered where all the carriages had gone and how long I had been unconscious as the two of us staggered from the Lexington Cemetery to Jenny Hill's house. There, with the help of the other girls, Belle took me to her room and deposited me on her big feather bed.

The effort of getting to Belle's room left me exhausted. I was out almost before my head hit the pillow.

I awoke with Doc Haydon bending over me. He extracted a plump black leech from the side of my face.

"Well, Donnelly," he said, lifting the half-curled leech up high enough to examine it, "about time you rejoined the living."

"Living?"

He laughed and said, "I think you'll live."

"The jury is still out," I replied.

He held the squirming leech high over my face.

"Nonsense. You'll be fine in a few days if you can manage to quit getting your head pounded in. My fat friend here has saved you from having a nasty bruise on the side of your face. Thanks to him, that cut on your head should heal a little faster too. Of course, this little fellow won't be of much use to me for a while. And you, my friend, will still have a big bump on your head for a few days."

"What happened?"

"I was going to ask you that. It isn't every day that Miss Belle comes to drag me away from my surgery. It is going to cause talk among my patients. You probably have me in trouble with half the ladies in town. The other half will come down with mysterious ailments this week requiring the immediate services of a surgeon just so they can pump me for information about you and Miss Belle."

"Belle," I said, attempting to sit up.

The room started to swim, and I fell back on her lavender-scented pillows.

"I wouldn't try that again for a day or so," Doc Haydon said, pressing a cool cloth to my face. "I stitched up your head, where the wire frame of your spectacles cut into the flesh, but you have a nasty break in the eye orbit. It is a good thing that your skull is so thick, Donnelly. This bump on the side of your head is almost the exact spot you hit last winter. As near as I can tell nothing is broken there, but it isn't good to get hit in the same place over and over again. The next one could kill you. I also set the ulna. It was a simple break so if you keep it taped, up look after it, and stay out of fights, you'll heal good as new."

"I'll keep that in mind," I said. "As for the head, what would you suggest I do, Doc? I really don't think telling the people trying to kill me that they shouldn't hit that side of my head is going to be of much use."

Doc Haydon shook his head, but I could see he was trying not to chuckle.

"I can see your point," he said. "You might try taking some less dangerous cases. Like I said, you were lucky. I have patched you up as best I can. Take care of that arm, or I'll tape it to your rib cage. That is, if I can find your ribs. You must be the most cold-natured man in town to still be wearing all those undergarments this time of year."

I turned deep red, thinking of how close I had come to being undone.

Doc seemed not to notice.

"I don't intend to let your shenanigans give my work a bad name" he said. 'I mean it Ness. Don't use your left hand any more than absolutely necessary. Is that plain enough? Get used to being one-armed for a while. It takes a few weeks to heal. I know it is inconvenient, but if you don't take care of your arm, it will punish you the rest of your life."

"Gee, thanks," I said sarcastically. "I always wanted to know what it was like to have only one arm."

"Look, Donnelly," Doc Haydon said, sitting down and pressing another cold compress to my brow, "This is none of my business, but I do care what happens to you. If you are dealing with some splinter of the Knights of the Golden Circle, you are in over your head. Give it up. Finding you in Miss Belle's bed is good sport, but I don't want to see you land on my autopsy table."

"I can't give it up, Doc."

"Yes, you can." His voice was hard. "Be reasonable. You were lucky that Miss Belle had the good sense to go looking for you when you didn't return from the graveyard. If she hadn't been hoping to talk to you, who knows what might have happened. Luck doesn't last forever. Next time there might not be someone there to pull your fat from the fire."

I reached into the pocket of my coat and pulled out the little amber bottle I had taken from Buckner's office.

"You see this?" I said, holding the bottle up. "Do you know what it is?"

"A note in a bottle?" he said dryly.

"I saw one of these during the war," I said, "the parchment burst into flames, and the bottle shattered in the man's hand when he opened it. The doctor had to take off three fingers because the flesh burned right through to the bone."

"Humm…spontaneous combustion."

Haydon took the bottle from me and held it up to the light.

"It looks like ordinary parchment. Probably treated with some sort of phosphorus compound."

"Phosphorus?"

"Most likely," Haydon said. "Maybe mixed with something to

make it cling to the skin if it is opened. That would explain the burns."

"So, how do I open it without losing my hand?" I asked.

"Beats me," he said, "if the compound is phosphorus based, you would have to either reduce the temperature below the flashpoint, or eliminate the combustible gasses. Of course, I am just guessing about it being phosphorus. A chemist might be able to tell you more. I could ask."

"No!"

I rose without thinking and immediately regretted moving.

When the room stopped spinning, I saw Doc Haydon standing over me, one eyebrow arched, waiting for an explanation.

"You said it yourself, Doc, members of the Knights were all over the Bluegrass during the war. Anyone you ask, anyone with enough knowledge to tell me how to open this, probably was a member, and could be part of the group that murdered Buckner," I explained. "I don't have so many friends that I can afford to lose one."

He smiled.

"So you have decided that I am not affiliated with the Knights?"

"Yes."

What made you decide to trust me?" Haydon asked.

"You did."

He grinned, and ran his fingers through his thinning hair.

"I'd love to hear how you came to that conclusion."

Sergeant Hamm burst in before I had time to answer.

The door slammed behind him, sending waves of pain vibrating along the side of my head. Bile rose in my throat.

In an instant, Doc Haydon's hand was placing a cold towel on the back of my neck.

"Easy," he said gently. "Breathe slow."

His hand lifted my head slightly and held me so I wouldn't choke until the wave of nausea passed.

The sergeant waited silently. His jaw was clenched so tight that his mouth vanished under his thick mustache.

"Whatever bee you have in your bonnet can wait until my patient is in better shape, Sergeant."

"No it can't," Hamm said. "The Commander sent me to arrest Miss Belle. We have to search every room."

"She isn't here," Haydon said. "I could have told you that just fine without your busting in here and making all that racket."

"Have you seen Miss Brezing?"

"Not lately," the doctor replied.

"How lately?" Hamm asked.

Haydon eased my head back down on the pillow and turned to face Sergeant Hamm. I could tell from the tone of his voice that he was close losing his temper.

"She came to my office to fetch me about two hours ago. I haven't seen her since," he said. "Come to think of it, I haven't heard or seen anyone but Ness in some time. Kind of odd, don't you think? I would expect the party to be in full swing at Miss Hill's this time of day. Wouldn't you?"

Hamm ignored the questions. The Sergeant looked from Doc Haydon to me.

"Did Peltmutter do that?" he asked. "I didn't think he had a good fight in him."

"Peltmutter had help," I said .

He stroked his mustache thoughtfully.

"What sort of help?"

"A couple of his pals threw a little party for me. At least I think it was only a couple…hard to tell from under the horse blanket they cast over my head."

"I don't think I would celebrate with his friends again, if I were you," Hamm said. "You aren't going to look very handsome for your date Sunday."

I groaned. Leave it to Sergeant Hamm to find a way to make me feel worse.

At the mention of a date Doc started to say something, but one look at my face froze the words on his tongue.

Hamm's expression didn't change.

"If you see Miss Belle, tell her it would go easier for her if she turned herself in."

"An easy murder charge?"

The sergeant's long face was grim. He reached up and stroked his mustache again.

"I guess 'easy' is the wrong word, under the circumstances. I just –I wouldn't want to have to shoot her," he said solemnly. "If she tries to run…"

He didn't have to finish the thought. I knew he was beginning to have his own doubts about Belle's guilt. But to Sergeant Hamm, orders were to be followed. He would do his duty no matter how much it personally pained him.

CHAPTER FOURTEEN

Storm clouds rolled through Beulah's dark eyes. She glanced around the ornate room Miss Belle usually occupied, then gave me a look that clearly said it would be a long time before I was forgiven for spending the night in a bawdyhouse.

Under her steady gaze, I felt obliged to pull the covers up under my chin and try to look as weak as possible.

My attempt to win sympathy was an utter failure. She planted both hands on her hips and shook her head.

"Mr. Donnelly, what am I going to do with you?"

"Take me home," I suggested, meekly.

"Humph!" she said. "If ya wanted to go home, ya might a sent word yesterday, instead of settling in ta this din of iniquity for the night. Course I don't reckon you thought much about that. What with your being all cozy in that Brezin' woman's bed."

"I wasn't really able to do much yesterday," I said.

"And just why was that?"

The expression on her face told me it was best to stay silent.

"Huh!" She snorted, "Gettin' yourself all beat up at a funeral, that's why. Your tomfoolery is goin' ta be the death of me."

She pulled back the quilt and scowled at my rumpled shirt and crushed tie.

"You been actin' like one of those no-accounts down in the Bottoms. I ain't gonna put up with it. No sir! Just how am I supposed to face the preacher after havin' to come fetch you out of a house full of fancy women?"

I didn't realize this one was a rhetorical question until I opened my mouth to answer.

Beulah glared at me.

My mouth snapped shut. I tried to look repentant as I waited for her to continue.

She shook her head and let out a long sigh.

"I jus' don't know what the world is comin' to," she said. "Thought I was workin' a respectable job. Then you go actin' like a hooligan. Fightin,' spendin' the whole night in a whorehouse, I jus' plumb give up. I ain't even gonna pray for you no more. You is beyond redemption."

Tad came in just as she was finishing her lecture.

"The wagon is downstairs," he said, then stopped abruptly in the doorway.

His face colored, as his uncovered eye caught sight of the silk petticoats hanging across the top of the black lacquer screen in one corner of Belle's room.

"Stop gawking at them unmentionables and give me a hand," Beulah ordered.

Even the roots of Tad's sandy hair turned blood red at the rebuke.

"I-I'm sorry," he stammered, suddenly finding every item in the bedroom a new source of embarrassment.

I couldn't help laughing.

Beulah gave me a look that would have withered cabbage.

"Humph! A lotta right you got to laugh. At least he don't look all comfortable in a fancy woman's bed."

It was my turn to blush. I had never known Beulah to scold me in front of anyone before.

"Do you need me to help you get Mr. Donnelly back to the house?" Tad asked.

Beulah nodded and together they assisted me into my boots.

That was about all the redressing I needed. At some point, my puff tie had been loosened and the top two buttons of my shirt undone; otherwise, I was still in the clothing I had worn the previous day. I suspected it was Belle who decided that I should not be further undressed. I would have to thank her for that later, if I got the chance. It would have been awkward to need assistance getting back into my breeches.

"How are you feeling, Mr. Donnelly?" Tad asked, as he tied my bootlaces.

128

"Oh, like somebody knocked me upside the head," I said. "Has anyone found Miss Belle?"

"No sir," he said, his head dropping. "I offered to help search, but Cousin James said to help you. Not that you'll be doing much today. I guess he just don't want me underfoot."

He was probably right. The Commander didn't seem to be giving him much of a chance to prove himself. But I had decided that Commander Slayton was underestimating the lad's potential.

"I don't expect the police will be looking for Miss Belle today," I said. "They will have their hands full handling the Centennial events."

"He don't want me there either," Tad said, looking entirely dispirited.

"Well, there is something you could do for me today," I said. "It is not detective work, but I am one of the judges for today's events. I'm certainly in no shape to review the parade or do any of this other stuff."

I took the list of events I was supposed to be judging and my parade credential out of my vest pocket and handed them to Tad.

"Since you are my assistant, why don't you take my place? You'll have a great view of the parade from the reviewing platform at Cheapside. It will also have about the best view of the crowd that can be found. While you're up there, you can keep a lookout for Mr. Peltmutter and that burly man we saw in Frankfort. I think he might be responsible for my present condition. At least, my attacker was about his size and build. I would like to know if he shows any signs of being in a fight."

Tad's eyes lit up.

"You want me to represent you? Maybe, investigate the killer?"

"Why not?" I asked as Beulah helped me to my feet.

"Golly. Is that allowed? I mean – I'm not really your assistant. Will they let me on the platform?"

Beads of sweat formed on my brow as I tried standing for the first time since the beating. I closed my eyes and waited for the room to stop spinning.

"We can fix that, if you'd like," I said, when I felt sufficiently steady on my feet, "unless you're attached to working for your cousin."

"No, sir," he replied, with such eagerness that Beulah laughed aloud.

Tad's face flamed with color.

"I-I didn't mean that I…"

I cut him off.

"You'd like the job?"

"Yes, sir."

"Good. We'll consider the parade your first official duty. Once I am better we will discuss money. If that's amenable to you."

He grinned at me. "Yes sir!"

His smile reminded me of Ness. How young and eager he had been when he first started working for Mr. Pinkerton. It struck me that we had begun working for Pinkerton before Tad was born. I shivered at the thought.

"Do you need to sit a spell, Mr. Donnelly?" Tad asked.

"No, just take me home, before I fall over. Contrary to popular opinion," I said, looking meaningfully at Beulah, "I would much rather be sleeping in my own bed."

Beulah responded by deliberately turning her back to me. I could hear her muttering something about fancy women under her breath. There was no point in pursuing a fight.

I sighed and made another attempt to get her to take the day off.

"I mean it," I said. "I intend to curl up and sleep all day, and I don't want any noise around the house to disturb my rest. Could you please find something else to do today, Beulah?"

Beulah turned around and eyed me suspiciously. "You ain't just gettin' rid of me so as you can go out detectin' again, are you?"

That was the most absurd question I had heard in a long time.

"Let me put it another way," I said.

I reached into my pocket and took out a couple of silver dollars, then held them to her and Tad.

"I was hoping that you would go out and have enough fun for both of us at the Centennial Celebration," I said. "Go to the parade, or the brass band concert. Attend the fair or one of the dances. See the circus. Tomorrow when I am feeling better the two of you can tell me all about the things I missed."

Neither of them looked particularly eager to leave. I closed my eyes for a moment trying to decide what I was going to do.

"Listen to me, both of you: there are a hundred events planned for this party, one for every year that Lexington has been here. There must be something you two want to attend. Besides, I don't need either of you fussing over me. There is nothing to be done for a concussion but rest. The swelling will go down in a day or so and I'll be fine."

"Well," Beulah said. "If you're sure you don't need me I would like to see the folks off that are leaving for Kansas in the mornin'. They is havin' an ice-cream social for them at church."

I pressed the coin into Beulah's hand.

"I assure you, Beulah, the only thing I want to detect is the most comfortable spot in my bed today. Now will you two please take me home, then go enjoy the shindig?"

Beulah had prepared a makeshift bed for me in the back of the rented wagon. She climbed into the back of the wagon and stood up next to the straw pallet she had covered with thick quilts.

"Now you just sit down on the edge, Mr. Donnelly," she said. "The doctor don't want you ta do no climbin'"

"I think I can sit up for four blocks," I said.

"The doctor said you was to lie down," she said in a tone that brooked no disagreement. "I done made you this nice pallet. You just sit you'self down and let us take care of you the way the doctor done told us to."

I didn't try to argue. My head was throbbing. My weakness made me feel foolish. I had seen men go into battle before with concussions, but they must have been made of stronger stuff than me. It was all I could manage just fighting back the wave of nausea threatening to overcome me after walking downstairs. I didn't even protest when Tad and Beulah picked me up like a sack of potatoes, carried me to the wagon, and deposited me among a mountain of pillows.

While Tad walked around to the front of the wagon, Beulah leaned close. "Mr. Donnelly," she whispered. "I has ta tell ya, you won't exactly be alone at the house. Miss Brezing's there."

My eyes shot open and I turned my head much too fast. I clenched my jaws tight and forced back the rising bile.

"Don't get all worked up, Mr. Donnelly," she whispered. "If you don't want her there I'll tell her to leave. But it didn't seem right to turn her out last night. Seein' as how you is workin' for her."

"No!" I said, loud enough for Tad to hear.

"You okay back there, Mr. Donnelly?" Tad asked. "I'm trying

not to jostle you."

"I'm fine," I lied.

I lowered my voice. "No, I need to ask Belle some questions. You go say good-bye to your friends. I'll be fine."

Beulah gave me a dubious look, but thankfully let the matter drop.

"Beulah," I said, a moment later.

"Yes sir?"

"I am glad you and Amos decided to stay."

Two rows of perfect white teeth smiled at me.

"I told Amos that we couldn't go off and leave you. Sometimes you ain't got no more sense than God gave a mule, but you got a good heart. Don't make no difference in folks either."

"Difference?"

Her smile seemed to spread up into her eyes.

"Mr. Donnelly," she said, shaking her head. "When you was givin' the day off to us to go to the shindig you handed me and the boy a dollar apiece and said go have a good time. Maybe you think that don't mean nothin' much. But you'd be wrong. Because them kind of things tell me you don't think that skin the color of coffee makes me worth less than that pink-cheeked boy you just hired."

"Beulah."

"You just hush up now," she said. "Ain't nothin' need to be said."

I squeezed her hand.

"Yes there is," I said firmly. "There is something I have felt bad about for a long time. Something I need to do."

I looked up into the puzzlement playing across her face. Her dark eyes stared back at me.

"Mr. Donnelly, you ain't fixin' to go do somethin' foolish while I ain't lookin'?"

"No," I said quietly, "but when this mess with Belle is over, you and I are going to go dig through the records of slave sales. We are going to do our best to find out what happened to your children. If they survived the war, I think they should know that their parents did, too."

"You'd do that?" she said, large tears forming in the corners of her eyes.

"I should have done it long ago. I guess I was just afraid of what we might find."

"Whatever you find, you'll tell me. Even if both my babies is dead, or if you don't find nothin' at all."

"You have my word," I said, squeezing her hand again.

"Lordy," she said, wiping her eyes as the wagon pulled to a halt outside my house. "They can keep the whole state of Kansas."

CHAPTER FIFTEEN

Belle popped her head through the door shortly after Tad and Beulah had gone.

"Feeling better?" she asked.

"Could I trouble you for a glass of water and a headache powder?" I asked.

"Where do you keep your headache powders?"

"There's a water closet through that door," I said, pointing to the door on the far end of the room. "The powders are on the shelf under the looking glass."

She grinned as she came back into the room.

"A razor and shaving soap. Isn't that taking this act of yours a little too far, Miss Nessa?"

"Not really," I said. "There's not much hair on my face, but Sergeant Hamm started teasing me about the peach fuzz on my upper lip about the time I turned thirty. I had to get rid of it before it became obvious that I was never going to develop a crumb duster like he wears."

Belle tilted her head from one side to the other examining my face for a long moment. Then she laughed.

"Nope, she said, still giggling, "Even if you shave every day, you are never going to have a mustache like Sergeant Hamm. Maybe you could grow one of those little thin ones the gamblers like. The kind that makes it look like your upper lip is dirty."

"Just give me the medicine," I said, grumpily.

"Oh, don't be mad," Belle said.

"I'm not mad."

"Yes you are."

I was peeved, but was not going to admit that to her. The lengths I went to in keeping up my disguise were my business. There was no point in talking about shaving the hair from my face, or the heat rash that plagued me each summer as I sweltered under the heavy padded tunic. The fact that I did all of the gardening and chopping wood to harden my muscles enough to make the ruse believable was nobody else's business.

She handed me a glass of water, then opened the headache powder.

"Miss Nessa," she said. "Are you going to be able to figure out who killed Mr. Buckner?"

I fought back the dizziness and sat up.

"I am getting closer to why he was killed," I said, meeting her earnest eyes. "The killer knows that. He wouldn't have jumped me at the cemetery if he wasn't aware that I was closing in on the truth. But this case is more complicated than anything I have ever investigated before."

"Complicated?"

"Yes," I said. "Every time I think I am getting a handle on the investigation, something else happens. I was hoping you could help."

"Me?"

"Belle, there are some very dangerous men tangled up in Mr. Buckner's murder. Maybe, if you told me what you saw at the cemetery, I would have a better idea of what they are up to."

"I didn't see much," she said. "I wouldn't have seen anything at all if I hadn't gone looking for you."

"Why were you looking for me?"

"We was watching from the upstairs windows when the undertaker's carriage rolled by," she said. "I saw Mr. Buckner's son glance up and kind of smile at Rachel. I thought you would want to know."

"That certainly explains his behavior," I said. "When we questioned him, I could tell he was hiding something."

"Do you think his father found out?"

"I don't know," I said, "but I don't think Buckner's son killed him over that. Do you think young Buckner was one of the men who attacked me?"

"No," she said. "They were bigger, and older too. One of them must have been over six foot, with broad shoulders and gray hair. He was doing most of the work of loading Mr. Peltmutter into the wagon. I didn't get a good look at the other one. But I heard them say they would come back for you. I guess there wasn't room in the wagon with Mr. Peltmutter."

"Did you overhear anything else?"

"Isn't that enough?"

"I don't know just how they fit into all this," I said. "I thought Peltmutter was working with them, but he seemed more afraid of them than he was of me."

"Why would someone as important as Mr. Peltmutter be involved with men like those?"

"Because men like Peltmutter don't care whose life they ruin if it brings them what they want. The men who attacked me are the same sort."

"So what do they want?"

"I don't know. I wish I did--if I understood that, I might know why they killed Mr. Buckner. I think he might have been one of them, but I am not even sure of that."

"One of what?"

I weighed my words carefully. The KGC had far-reaching tentacles. It was difficult to know how to broach the topic with Belle.

"Belle, have you ever heard of the Knights of the Golden Circle?"

Her entire demeanor changed instantly. Belle's eyes narrowed, her shoulders tensed as her breathing swallowed.

"You think *they* killed Mr. Buckner?"

"What do you know about them?" I asked.

"Enough to know that if they are behind this, I'm already as good as hanged."

I took the little amber bottle from my pocket and held it up where she could see the small parchment rolled up inside.

"This was in Buckner's desk drawer," I said.

"That don't make good sense. If Mr. Buckner was one of them, why did he get killed? Nobody messes with a Knight and lives."

Her eyes opened wide.

"Do you think someone is trying to kill off some of the former Knights? Did that other gent, the one in Frankfort, kill Mr. Buckner? The Knights maybe killed him. Retribution kinda'. You gonna be able to prove that?"

"I don't think that's what happened," I said. "But could we back up a minute?

I picked up the bottle and held it out to her.

"You didn't bat an eye when I showed you this. Have you seen one of these before?"

Belle made no attempt to touch the bottle. Her head lowered so our eyes no longer met.

"Maybe," she said.

"This is no time to be holding out on me, Belle. In case you have forgotten, the police are looking for you. If they find you here we will both land in jail and maybe hang…together."

"Pa belonged to the Knights," she said softly. "One night he got drunk and said some things that he shouldn't have. He turned plumb white when he found one of those on the counter. I never seen a body so scared."

"Did you see how he opened it?"

"No."

I let out the breath I hadn't realized I was holding, lay back against the headboard, and closed my eyes.

Belle laid a hand on my shoulder.

"I'm sorry Miss Nessa. Pa took it to the icehouse. I never saw it or him again."

My eyes shot open.

"The icehouse? You're sure?"

"Y-yes," she said tentatively.

"Help me downstairs."

"I can't do that!"

"I'll crawl to the icebox if I have to, Belle. It would be much easier if you helped me."

I could almost see the clockwork wheels turning in her mind. Not that my feelings mattered on the subject. Beulah was a formidable woman and not one to trifle with. Belle was weighing the risk of offending my housekeeper by helping me against the risk of offending her by *not* helping.

"Why don't I just bring you whatever you need?"

"Ice! I need ice." I said excitedly, remembering what Doc Haydon had said about lowering the temperature of phosphorus below the flashpoint. "The bottle has to be chilled before it can be opened. That's why your father went to the icehouse."

"Oh!"

138

Belle rushed out of the room.

I hated waiting. I could hear her chipping away at the block of ice for what probably was only a few minutes, but from my bed it seemed an interminable amount of time. Had I been able, I would have been pacing the floor. Instead, I picked up the bottle and looked at it from every angle. By the time Belle finally returned with a bowl of ice, my impatience had reached a level near the screaming point.

Belle hovered over me as I settled the bowl in my lap and plunged the bottle deep into the ice. The education I received from the Sisters of Mercy did not include chemistry. I could only guess at how cold the bottle needed to be before it could be safely opened.

I turned it slowly in the ice, much the way I would have turned a jug of sweet cream I was chilling into iced cream. I reasoned that it was cold enough when the tips of my fingers started turning blue.

"You had best step back," I told Belle. "If this thing bursts into flame there is no sense in both of us getting hurt."

"I trust you, Miss Nessa."

"Well don't," I said, crossly. "I don't know what's going to happen. So move out of the way."

Once she was out of range, I took a deep breath and broke the seal.

Nothing happened.

I gulped air again and pulled out the stopper.

Still nothing happened.

I grinned at Belle as I turned the bottle upside down and let the little scroll inside drop onto the melting ice.

The grin faded when I unrolled the scroll and saw...

"Nothing!"

Bell ran over. "What do you mean nothing?"

Belle and I looked at each other, then back at the parchment. In the places where water had soaked the page there was something starting to appear. I picked up one of the pieces of melting ice and rubbed it over the paper, then waited as the cold water soaked the page. Little by little entire words formed.

I reached for my spectacles, then realized they had been broken in the fight.

"Can you read it?" I asked Belle.

She took the wet parchment from me and read aloud:

"The om-omnipo-tence of right, its own shall save, though hell itself oppose, but an unfaithful son and his foolish knave shall die unnumbered among the rebel foes."

CHAPTER SIXTEEN

Even the excitement of discovering the note proved insufficient to overcome the effects of my head injury. Belle was kind enough to fetch a handful of Ness's old files from my office so I could study them. They were still scattered all around me on the bed, but somewhere between the third and fourth page of an 1861 KGC exposé Ness had saved from the Louisville paper, the headache powder eased my pain enough for me to fall asleep.

I awoke to the clamor of voices and banging doors in the downstairs hall. I wasn't sure what was happening. For a few seconds I was frightened, but Wilfred Hamm's voice was easily recognizable even through the closed bedroom door.

"Careful," I heard Sergeant Hamm say.

This was followed by a loud crash and the unmistakable sound of breaking glass.

"Now look what you've done!" Hamm exclaimed. "You had better hope Mr. Donnelly doesn't ask the department to pay for that lamp."

"Sorry," someone replied. "I was trying not to shake the boy."

"Don't worry about that," Doc Haydon said. "Until the ether wears off, he won't feel a thing. Just take him up to the spare room and put him to bed. I'll be in as soon as I look in on Ness."

I reached for my robe, determined to find out what was going on.

The sleep must have done some good; my double vision had passed. Unfortunately, my head still ached like the devil, and the way Doc Haydon had splinted my arm made getting up a challenge. Once I got to my feet, standing proved to be less difficult than I had expected. I could even move without feeling sick. If I was careful, I might be able to make it downstairs on my own.

I was struggling with the sash on my robe, trying to tie it one-handed when Belle popped her head through the door, her eyes wide.

"Miss Nessa, Sergeant Hamm and Officer Watts are coming up here," she said. "What'll I do?"

I glanced around the room looking for a place to hide. The wardrobe was out of the question. Even someone as tiny as Belle couldn't hope to squeeze in there.

"Just duck in the water closet and stay there until I find out what is going on," I said. "I'll be right back."

I opened the bedroom door just as Doc Haydon reached the landing of the stairs.

"What are you doing out of bed?" he asked. "You were supposed to stay in bed for at least twenty-four hours."

"What are you doing to my house?" I countered. "Even doctors are not supposed to just barge into a man's home without knocking. And what was that noise downstairs?"

"Oh. That," he said. "Nothing."

"I heard something break."

"Watts hit a lamp with the litter. It was difficult to maneuver around enough to carry it up the stairs."

"Litter!"

I tried to look past him to see whom the two policemen were carrying up the stairs, but Haydon pushed me back into the room.

"Give them some room to work," he said. "That turn on the stairs is going to be a tight squeeze. Besides, there's nothing to worry about."

He kicked the door closed with the heel of his boot.

"Just a flesh wound," he said. "The boy will be fine in a day or two."

"Boy? You mean Tad?"

I pushed against him in an effort to get free and go out into the hall.

"Ness, calm down!" he ordered, gripping my shoulders to keep me from leaving.

In all the years we had known each other, he had never spoken to me that way. The two of us just stood there, looking at each other, while Sergeant Hamm and Officer Watts footsteps passed by my room and stopped outside the next door. I heard the latch open, then the squeak of bedsprings as they deposited Tad on the bed in my spare room.

"What happened?" I demanded, glaring at the doctor.

"I didn't actually see it, but Sergeant Hamm said that someone fired a shot at the review stand just as everyone was standing to leave. It may have been fired at the boy, we aren't sure," he said. "It could have just been a stray shot. It isn't every day the city turns a hundred. A lot of people were firing guns in the air to celebrate."

"You said it was a flesh wound?"

He nodded.

"How bad? I heard you mention ether. If he just needed a few stitches, you wouldn't have had to put him out."

"There won't be much of a scar, but the bullet lodged under the skin and traveled along the side of his head. I put him to sleep to remove it," he said. "He'll be fine in a few days."

"I shouldn't have sent him."

"It's not your fault."

"Isn't it?" I asked, looking directly into his eyes. "You have been laughing for days over the way he imitates me. Whoever attacked me yesterday probably mistook him for me today. I was supposed to be on that review stand; the Knights probably thought it was me."

"You still think the KGC is involved in Buckner's death?"

"I'm certain of it."

"Just because of that medallion Malthus had?" he asked. "The man could have picked that up anywhere."

"I got the bottle opened," I said, looking toward the bowl still sitting on my bedside table. "Look at the message, then tell me you don't think they are up to their eyeballs in these murders."

Doc Haydon fished the water-soaked parchment out of the bottom of the bowl and studied it for a long moment.

"So, was Buckner the unfaithful son or the foolish knave?" he asked, in a tone that was at least half teasing.

"It isn't funny," I snapped.

"Get off your high horse, Ness. We are talking about a bunch of grown men passing secret notes and playing at being knights. This is the sort of thing I would expect from a bunch of schoolboys."

"These *schoolboys* are responsible for two deaths."

He dropped the wet note back into the bowl of ice water and stood there looking at it for a long moment before he spoke.

"Three," he said, turning to look at me.

"Three?"

His clear blue eyes studied my face. "I didn't particularly want to tell you, but there has been another murder. That's why we brought Tad here. I sent my assistant to find Beulah and asked her to sit with him. Didn't think you'd be up to playing nursemaid."

"What do you mean, another murder?"

"They found Peltmutter's body laid out on Buckner's grave. From the description we have…this corpse is not one I would want Tad to wake up and see first thing. We decided it would be best to bring the boy here since nobody could locate the Commander."

"You haven't seen the body then?"

"No, as soon as they get Tad into bed, we are going over to pick up the body."

"I'm going with you."

"You are in no shape to go anywhere."

"I'm fine," I lied.

"Ness, be reasonable," he said. "This is the second blow to the head you have suffered in less than a year. Another one, and we'll be picking you up in the death wagon."

I was already opening the wardrobe and taking out a fresh suit.

"I'll be careful," I said, "but I am going to see this body, with or without your assistance."

"Is there anything I can say that will convince you to let us handle this?"

"No," I said. "When they attacked me they made it personal. If I don't take this fight to them, sooner or later they will come here. I don't want anybody else getting hurt."

Haydon shook his head sadly.

"Let me tell the sergeant to go on," he said. "We can meet him there."

Doc Haydon hadn't really put up much of an argument. I figured he had to object to my going; it was kind of a duty for doctors to protest when patients didn't have the good sense to stay in bed and get well. I tried to look as if I were sorry to be so disagreeable as I laid my suit on the foot of my bed where I could more easily manage the buttons one-handed.

Fortunately, once Doc Haydon left the room, Belle came out

of hiding and helped me finish dressing. I felt like a baby for needing help dressing myself, but the broken arm was proving to be more of a problem than I had anticipated. Doc Haydon had set the arm, but it was utterly useless to me. Belle helped me with my shirt, then secured the arm in the sling again. When she had finished she gave me a light kiss on the cheek.

"Thank you," she said softly.

"For what?"

"Everything."

I started to tell her to be careful, but she cut me off.

"Want some help with your tie?"

"Leave it," I said. "Doc Haydon is too smart to believe I tied it with one hand."

She smiled.

"Belle," I said.

She put a hand over my lips.

"Don't worry. I'll stay outta sight. Here all right with you?"

"Here's fine," I said. "Get some sleep if you can. I am liable to be out most of the night."

CHAPTER SEVENTEEN

"Sorry about our transportation," Doc Haydon said, pointing to the unadorned black hearse parked at my curb. "The officer who usually drives the city's death wagon is busy dealing with pickpockets and horse thieves at the fairgrounds today. It was either drive myself in this thing, or try to load a body into my buggy. I don't think Peltmutter would have fit in my little saltbox, and Old Sam sure wouldn't have welcomed pulling that load."

I eyed the tall black wagon dubiously. The driver's box was set high on the front end of the hearse. In my present condition, it would have been easier to mount a horse than to climb up the side of the wagon to get into that seat. There were a couple of bars set into the frame as footholds, but they were narrow and about two feet apart. I grabbed the railing with my right hand and tried hoisting myself up the first step.

Doc Haydon watched me for a moment, then said: "It smells to high heaven in back, but it would be much easier to get into."

That idea, I rejected immediately.

"You won't find me riding to the cemetery in the back of a hearse until I'm stone cold and making my final journey," I said. "Where hearses are concerned, I'll take the front every time."

Haydon chuckled.

"I guess it is a good thing the ether didn't wear off while Young Tad was back there. He might share your opinion of the accommodations," he said as he walked round to the other side and climbed up.

"Can I at least give you a hand?" he asked, reaching down from the box.

"Thanks," I said, taking the proffered hand.

Even with his help I made an awkward job of climbing. I hadn't realized just how hard it would be to do simple tasks with a useless left arm.

Doc Haydon waited until I had settled into the seat, then released the hand brake. The wagon lurched forward, causing me to give an involuntary groan as we rattled down the street toward Lexington's City of the Dead.

I winced with every bump in the crushed limestone road, but said nothing. There was no point in whining when I had insisted in coming along.

It was past six o'clock when we reached the cemetery. The gates were locked promptly at five and the watchman was reluctant to allow anyone in after the appointed closing time. He walked slowly out to the heavy iron gates and looked up at us.

"You here with the police?" the old man asked.

Haydon nodded.

"Doc Haydon, County Medical Examiner. I understand there is a body that needs to be picked up."

"Police said you'd be coming," he said. "Who's your friend?"

"Ness Donnelly; he's doing a private inquiry into the Buckner murder."

He looked me over carefully, then unlocked the chain holding the gates closed and pulled it free of the iron bars. The racket caused by the steel chain broke the stillness shrouding the cemetery. It rattled loudly as it fell to the ground, releasing a small cloud of rust colored dust.

"This is a new one on me," the watchman said, removing his hat in anticipation of the death wagon rolling past him. "First time I ever had to open up so we could remove a corpse from a grave."

"It is a bit peculiar," Doc Haydon called down to him. "Can't say as I have ever been called to the cemetery before. I guess there's a first time for everything."

"Do you know what section the body is in?" I asked Doc Haydon.

The watchman answered for him. "He didn't tell ya? Somebody opened that ta-bakka feller's grave. Plopped the body down on top of his coffin."

My mouth gaped open.

"There's something else I didn't tell you at the house," Haydon said, when we were out of earshot of the watchman. "I've been told the head has been…mutilated. I suppose that's the right word. At least that is the best word I can come up with for what they've done."

"Mutilated?"

"I haven't seen it, of course, but the description I was given is the main reason I didn't put up much of an argument about your coming along. I don't think Sergeant Hamm knows what to make of a murder like this one. He could use some help."

"What sort of mutilation are we talking about?"

"Maybe you ought to see for yourself, Ness. Sergeant Hamm said he wouldn't move anything until I have a look at the evidence."

Haydon halted in the shadow of a large gingko tree near the graveside, one of Henry Clay's donations. The doctor climbed down from the driver's box with the agility of a man half his age.

"Need a hand, Ness?"

"No thanks." I yelled down to him.

I probably needed a ladder, not that I was going to admit that. The effort of descending the hearse made beads of sweat dampen my upper lip, but I did manage to get to the ground without falling. I may have moved about as stiffly as a man more than twice my elder, but I was still moving.

From the looks of Sergeant Hamm, he had to be feeling about as bad as me. Dark circles had formed under his eyes and fatigue marked every angle of his long face. The sergeant was more disheveled than I had ever seen him. The normally creased black pants of his uniform were soggy and mud-soaked. Clumps of mud mixed with what looked like blood clung to his boots. The double-breasted jacket to his uniform had been discarded on a nearby tombstone and his shirtsleeves were rolled up to the elbow.

"I've never seen anything like this, Doc," he said, wiping the sweat from his face with the backside of one grubby hand and leaving a fresh streak of mud across his mustache. "Men do gruesome things, but this…"

Our eyes followed as he waved his arm toward where Officer Watts was climbing out of Nathaniel Buckner's reopened grave. Officer Watts' black uniform appeared to be soiled beyond cleaning. Muddy water poured in a steady stream from the small wooden box he held.

"Got it, Sergeant," he yelled.

"Good work," Sergeant Hamm said. "Just set it there by the headstone; the doctor may want to get a look at it while he is examining the corpse."

Doc Haydon and I looked down into the wet grave. Peltmutter's body had been laid out on top of Buckner's coffin. From the amount of blood splattered over the lid, it appeared that he had been placed in the grave alive and beheaded there.

"I'd never be able to get out of there," I said.

"Considering that that the head has been removed, I don't think there's much point in climbing into that mess anyway," Doc Haydon replied.

The head, or what was left of what I presumed was Mr. Peltmutter's head, was perched on top of Buckner's new headstone. It was hard to tell from what remained that this was the heavy-jawed banker's head. The skull had been stripped bare: hair, skin, muscle…everything was gone save a few small fragments of flesh still stubbornly clinging to the scraped bone. Most remarkable was the hole that had been sawed into the top center of the skull. Through this, a miner's candle had been inserted and still burned behind the fleshless face. The candle cast eerie red gold light through all the openings in the bone.

The grave had sickened me, but it was the sickly sweet smell caused by heating the fresh skull turned my stomach. I quickly stepped behind one of the ancient oak trees where I could recover from my embarrassing weakness out of the line of vision of the others.

Doc Haydon was bending over the skull when I returned.

"Curious, isn't it?" he said. "Someone must have had some knowledge of medicine."

"At least they had some access to the tools," I agreed, looking down at the small wooden box.

I didn't want to look at the head. Focusing on the box didn't help. One glance at the "USA" engraved on its brass plate was enough to tell me why it had been left behind.

"Did you see this?" I asked, pointing to the box. "What do you make of it, Doc? Are there markings of a trephine in the bone?"

"Trephine?" Sergeant Hamm asked.

"It is a surgical instrument. We used them a lot in the war to cut into the skull and remove bullets," Doc Haydon said.

"The murder weapon is probably in here," I said, pointing to the box. "Union Army field surgeon's kit."

"You think this trephine thing was the murder weapon?" Sergeant Hamm asked.

"It could have been," Doc Haydon replied, "but from the amount of blood splashed around the grave, I would say they cut his head off first. There is no way to really know unless we find someone who was involved."

"There's a lot of blood on the stone and the grass here," I said, kneeling to get a better look at the area around Buckner's headstone. I took my broken spectacles out of my pocket and perched them on my nose. The shattered side was useless, but that made little difference, since that eye was still swollen shut. Through the uninjured eye I could see where the sod near both ends of Buckner's gravestone had been trampled. Two people had been involved in mutilating Peltmutter's head. I saw something white in the patch of sod closest to Buckner's stone. When I leaned over to pick it up, my spectacles fell. I reached to retrieve them and felt my stomach heave again at the sight of one of Peltmutter's gray eyes looking up at me from the ground.

"Doc, I think you'd better take a look at this," I said.

Hamm followed him.

"Why would anybody do a thing like this?" Sergeant Hamm asked.

"To send a message," I said.

"A message?" Hamm said, stroking his chin.

"I have suspected for some time that your killer or killers were members of the KGC," I said, "I think there's more than one person involved."

Hamm frowned.

"Donnelly, you see the handiwork of the KGC in half your cases," Hamm grumbled. "It is time to get over this obsession of yours. There hasn't been an active Castle in Fayette County in a dozen years."

"You mean you haven't seen any evidence of them in your cases," I retorted. "I could be wrong, of course, but I have more than enough evidence in this case to believe that the men we are looking for belong to the Knights of the Golden Circle."

"What reasons?" he asked.

"For one thing, they're arrogant. These men aren't really

worried about us as long as the other members of their circle stay quiet." I waved my arm expansively. "This is a reminder. Look at the places where the grass is crushed around the stone. There were at least a half a dozen men involved this ritual. This murder was a show to make sure their fellow Knights don't forget the oath of silence they took."

I looked up into his puzzled eyes and let out an exasperated sigh.

"All members of the Knights of the Golden Circle swore an oath of silence, an oath that contained a promise of what would happen should it be broken," I said.

"Who ever does our cause reveal, shall test the strength of knightly steel, and when the torture proves too dull, we'll scrape the brains from out his skull, and place a lamp within the shell, to light his soul from here to Hell."

"Tell me that doesn't fit this scene." I said. "Peltmutter was one of the Knights. That's the only thing that makes any sense in this whole gruesome mess."

"So you think Mr. Peltmutter talked?" Hamm said.

"Someone thinks he talked or that he was going to talk. They made an example of him in front of the rest of his circle as a reminder to all of the other members to keep their mouths shut." I pointed to the crushed grass. "They were here…and there…and there." They formed a circle around the grave, watching this. With the two over by the stone leading the killing, I'd guess at least six or seven men were here. There isn't a single piece of evidence to indicate that one of them tried to stop this sick desecration of Peltmutter's corpse."

"I would say they have a very effective way of keeping members in line," Doc Haydon said. "I certainly wouldn't be inclined to interfere or answer police questions if this punishment were hanging over me."

"Why would they dig Buckner up and dump the rest of the body in his grave?" Sergeant Hamm asked.

"Who knows? Maybe to let the others know that they were both damned," Doc Haydon said. "It would make sense, considering that they placed that skull on Buckner's tombstone."

Doc Haydon looked at me. "Have you told him about the

bottle, Ness?"

"What bottle?" Sergeant Hamm said.

"I found a bottle with a threatening note inside when we were searching Mr. Buckner's office," I said, not meeting his eyes. "I intended to tell you about it after the funeral, but things moved so fast I hadn't the chance."

Sergeant Hamm looked confused.

"I don't see what one has to do with the other."

"I'm not sure either," I said. "I don't think we can be sure of anything until we figure out why they killed Buckner. But it looks to me like whatever got him killed was something he and Peltmutter were both involved in. Their pals sent them on their way together. The question is, do we have enough to get the Commander to turn his attention to the Knights instead of Belle?"

"I guess we can ask him when we find him," Sergeant Hamm said. "He was supposed to be on the grandstand with Officer Kent, but nobody seems to know where he is."

"How long has he been missing?" I asked.

"You'll have to ask Officer Kent if he came home last night," Sergeant Hamm said. "We asked everyone we could think of after young Kent got shot. He is the boy's guardian. Nobody has seen him since yesterday evening."

"I hope you keep looking, Sergeant," I said. "I wouldn't want to find Tad's cousin like this."

"You think the Commander is one of the Knights?"

"I don't know. Do you?" I asked. "Does anybody outside the KGC know who is or is not a member?"

The muscles in Sergeant Hamm's jaw knotted into a hard ball. He opened his mouth to say something just as the heated bone of Peltmutter's skull cracked from the heat. The noise made all of us jump.

Hamm stared at the skull for a moment, then looked at me.

"Watts!" he shouted. "Put that flame out. Then help the Doc get Mr. Peltmutter into the death wagon. We've seen enough."

I reached over and picked up the carved-out section of Peltmutter's head I had spotted before discovering his eye.

"You might want this, Doc," I said, handing the round section of bone to the medical examiner.

He laid the cutout fragment of bone on the stone beside the rest of skull, then took out his handkerchief and collected the eye from the ground with it.

"You might want to have your men bring lanterns and search the area carefully, Sergeant, see if any more body parts remain. We wouldn't want some unsuspecting visitor to come upon the other eye."

CHAPTER EIGHTEEN

A somber group gathered near Nathaniel Buckner's grave. The sun had long since vanished, making it impossible to continue looking for the missing pieces of Mr. Peltmutter's head. Sergeant Hamm left Officer Watts in charge of guarding the open grave and climbed up beside me on the hearse. He was holding a small pail, which contained the remains we had recovered. There wasn't much: the eye and round section of bone I found in the grass, some pieces of flesh that Officer Watts fished from the muddy water in the grave, and the tongue. To his horror, the sergeant had spotted a stray cat carrying that away from the gravesite. He had chased the poor creature all the way to the backside of the cemetery before he recovered it. We made an exhausting search of the graveyard, but were unable to locate the other eye before darkness forced us to give up. Sergeant Hamm reluctantly picked up the bucket containing those few parts we had recovered.

"Are you sure you want to carry that?" Doc Haydon said. "You could set it in back with the rest of him."

"Might tip over," Sergeant Hamm said. "Wouldn't want to lose anything. There's little enough."

Doc Haydon's lips pressed into a thin line as he turned his attention to the team, guiding the horses back through the main gates and into the heavy traffic on Leestown road. We sat side by side in the box, silently contemplating the murder, as the hearse began its slow journey to Doc Haydon's house. I couldn't help wondering if the others were thinking about the many times each of them had dismissed my concerns about the Knights as an overreaction to my twin's murder. Now that Doc Haydon and Sergeant Hamm had seen up close what the KGC was capable of, neither of them were likely take the organization lightly again.

The hearse had to stop several times to avoid the revelers still crowding downtown streets. Street vendors pushing carts of roasting chestnuts, ham biscuits, and cold cider were all crowded with customers. I could see the muscles in Sergeant Hamm's jaw twitch every time the death wagon stopped to avoid hitting the hoard of people spilling into the street.

"We invited them to come to our anniversary party to spend lots of money," I said. "Can't blame them for taking us up on the invite."

"I didn't invite anybody," Hamm snapped. "Bunch of gawkers. They got no respect for the dead."

"They probably think the death wagon is empty," I said. "Most of them saw us pull out of the cemetery."

As the hearse started moving again, Sergeant Hamm crossed his arms over his bosom and mumbled something that sounded indecent.

I decided to pretend I didn't hear the obscenity.

We wound our way down Main Street and turned onto Upper, then turned the corner and pulled into a long drive lined with budding dogwood trees. Doc Haydon's house was a rambling L-shaped farmhouse that sat back from the corner of Upper Street and Third Avenue. Doc Haydon lived in the Third Avenue side of the house, which was a beautiful two-story white board house with a covered front porch which ran the length of the first floor. Through each tall black-shuttered window I could see the handmade lace curtains reminiscent of the ones every Irish housewife, who could scrape together the money, hung in the windows of her home. I doubted that this part of the house had changed significantly since his wife died.

The Upper Street side of the house was his tiny kingdom. It contained his medical office, some upstairs rooms where patients occasionally stayed, and his surgery. The lawn sloped on that side of the house, allowing a basement which he used as a mortuary and post-mortem room. It was here that we delivered the body of Ambrose Peltmutter for autopsy.

Doc Haydon took the pail from the sergeant, added the skull and candle to its contents, and then handed it to me. He tucked the wooden box under my arm.

"Do you think you can manage the lantern?" he asked, looking me over.

He must have noticed how awkwardly I held the items he had already given me.

"Never mind," he said. "We wouldn't want you dropping anything."

He took the lantern with him and hung it on a hook just inside the cellar door.

"That should give us enough light to see the stairs," he said. "Ready, Sergeant?"

He threw open the double doors of the hearse, grabbed the headless corpse under both arms and began pulling him out of the wagon. Sergeant Hamm latched on to the feet and the two of them carried the body inside. I trailed behind them carrying the rest of Mr. Peltmutter.

Doc Haydon placed the body on a stone table in the center of the cold room. Once he had Mr. Peltmutter situated on the table, Doc Haydon walked over the basin and washed his hands thoroughly.

"Wash up, Ness," he said. "My assistant doesn't keep these hours. I'll need you to take notes while I examine the body."

He found a match and lit the oil lamps mounted to beams near his autopsy table, then took out several pages of stationery and laid them on the small desk.

"We're going to be a while, Sergeant," he said. "Why don't you go home and get some rest?"

"Got to relieve Officer Watts," he said. "Can't leave him wet and muddy all night. Miserable enough duty without being soaked to the skin." He looked down at his own filthy uniform. "I guess I should go home and clean up a mite first."

"Would you like me to take a watch?" I asked. "I wouldn't be worth much in a fight, but I can still shoot."

"I'm used to late hours," Doc Haydon said.

"Thanks, Donnelly, Doctor," Hamm said. "I appreciate the offer. If the Commander don't turn up tomorrow I'll speak to the mayor's office about what I can do, but I don't want to deputize civilians just yet."

"If you change your mind, you know where to find us," I said.

Doc Haydon handed me his stylograph and the paper.

"Don't scuff the nub by letting the ink run out. There's an ink bottle and eyedropper in the desk drawer for refills," he said.

"How do I refill the inkwell?"

"Ness, you need to keep up with the times," Haydon said, taking the strange pen from me and twisting it open. "Just drop the ink in here and screw it back together."

"How long before this new plaything of yours leaks all over your suit?" I asked.

"Just write down what I tell you," he said, annoyed by the reminder that his love of fountain pens quickly diminished when they proved disastrous to his wardrobe.

I settled back into the desk chair and waited for him to begin.

"One coat, Stein Adler, silk lined, black wool with black buttons," he began. "Nothing in the pockets. One banker's vest, red silk, gold pocket watch and chain."

Detail by detail, I listed the articles of clothing and Peltmutter's personal effects as Doc Haydon undressed the corpse.

When he had finished undressing Peltmutter, he covered the body with a sheet and turned his attention to the wooden box.

"Make a note that the police recovered a Union Army field surgeon's kit from the grave of the late Mr. Nathaniel P. Buckner," he said. "Not that which army it belonged to means much. Most every Confederate surgeon managed to get his hands on at least one of these before the end of the war."

I nodded. The South lacked the resources to provide the same quality of instruments to their field hospitals. The wholesale theft of medical supplies was common, but I knew more than one Northern doctor who had traded his field surgeon's kit for a copy of his Confederate counterpart's guidebook to medicinal plants.

Haydon jarred me from my thoughts.

"Note that the afore mentioned surgeon's kit was found partially submerged in muddy water," he said. "Therefore, attempts to ascertain if any of the surgical implements inside were used in the decapitation have been compromised."

Doc Haydon opened the box and examined the contents.

"I think this is our murder weapon," he said, removing the shiny steel chainsaw and holding it by the crosspiece.

He moved closer to the lamp.

"I can't be certain in this light, Ness," he said, but I believe we still have some tissue clinging to the teeth. I'll take it upstairs and examine under my microscope tomorrow. For now, just list it as showing signs of recent use."

He took hold of the other crosspiece and walked over to where the body rested.

"Ness, come move the sheet so I can compare this to the wound."

After comparing the saw to the cut from several angles he laid it aside and went over to the shelf to retrieve a bottle of alcohol and a roll of cotton bandaging. Doc Haydon vigorously scrubbed the neck until all traces of dirt and dried blood were gone, then took out his magnifying glass and looked closely at the exposed bone.

"Yes!" he exclaimed. "Look there, Ness," he said, pointing to the neck. "You can see the rough cuts into the yellow cartilage. A rank amateur. The worst hack surgeon I ever met wouldn't leave that kind of mess."

I took the proffered magnifying glass and examined the area Doc Haydon was pointing out. He was right. Distinct marking of the saw crisscrossed on the exposed spine. The man wielding the surgeon's saw was unfamiliar with the implement. If Peltmutter was awake when this was done, he suffered through at least three botched attempts to sever his head.

"You don't have to sound so gleeful about it, Doc. The man is dead. Probably suffered more in unskilled hands."

"Sorry," Doc Haydon said, "but I was concerned. Medical box and all. Gives a bad name to the profession."

Nothing he could say would make me feel better about this crime. I didn't like Peltmutter, but my mind recoiled from the kind of evil that would allow men to stand watching as he was being butchered.

I sank into the desk chair and closed my eyes for a moment before I picked up the stylograph.

"What should I say about the bone?" I asked.

"Just note that there were cuts to the posterior spine indicative of upward sawing at the base of the neck."

He lifted one arm and dropped it back to the surface of the table.

"Also note the time as seven twenty-two, and the body has not significantly cooled to the touch nor has rigor mortis set in. That indicates a time of death within minutes of the time the body was discovered by the watchman. The man said that he had just come on duty and was making his first walk through the grounds at approximately ten past five this evening when he noticed the light."

"No wonder they left such a mess behind," I said. "They must have fled as the church bells chimed five o'clock."

"Even at that they barely had time to get out before he locked the gate and started his rounds," Doc Haydon said, looking thoughtful. "Wonder how they kept him quiet."

I glanced at the bucket containing the remains of his head. "No way to tell, I suppose. We might want to advise Sergeant Hamm to have his men check around the walls to see if they can find where these scoundrels climbed over, though. Their trail should still be pretty fresh."

CHAPTER NINETEEN

Belle was sleeping in my room when I returned. Rather than waking her, I took my nightshirt and went to the unoccupied room across the hall. Despite the late hour, I slept fitfully. My dreams were filled with images of Ambrose Peltmutter's headless body being lifted from Nathaniel Buckner's grave. In my nightmares Buckner kept reaching out, grasping Peltmutter, pulling him back. Tossing and turning in the strange bed worsened the pain in my side, but I could not find a comfortable position. My discomfort was compounded by an aggravating itch under my bandages. Sometime before dawn I gave up trying to rest.

I lit the oil lamp nearest the bed and crept across the hall to recover the papers Belle had brought upstairs. Belle didn't even turn over when I picked up the files and quietly returned to the guest room.

Ness's handwriting was worse than my own. Without my spectacles, I quickly gave up on deciphering his scribble and concentrated on his sketches. Those were far superior to any drawings of mine. They were not detailed; some must have been sketched very quickly, but Ness had a way of capturing the essence of character with a minimum number of pencil strokes.

About halfway through the second stack of sketch cards my brother had marked "KGC suspects", a familiar face leapt out at me. I picked up the small stack of sketches I had made in Frankfort and fumbled through them until I found the one of the man I suspected of attacking me. Placing my crude drawing side by side with his, there didn't seem to be much of a resemblance. That fact said more about the skill of the artist than it did about the subject of our drawings. I recognized him, though. True, the hair was longer, and he was a good thirty pounds heavier, but the rough line of his jaw and hawkish expression Ness had captured in the young man's face made me certain it was the man I had first seen at the inquest in Frankfort.

My hand trembled as I turned the card over to see if he had added any notes on the reverse side. There was only a notation that he was "Frequently seen in the company of Colonel Groner."

I knew of Colonel Groner, of course; he had been one of the leaders of the Texas KGC when Allan Pinkerton first began investigating their activities. At one time, more than a dozen Pinkerton operatives were dispatched to Texas just to keep track of Groner. Ness had been among those sent to Texas. It was one of the few times in our years with Pinkerton that we had not worked together. Right now, I wished I had firsthand knowledge of their plots. It might give me some insight into what I was up against now. There was a sort of backhanded compliment in the fact that my investigation had attracted the attention of someone so highly placed in the Knights. But having a Knight with no ties to the Bluegrass, and no connection to the local Castle, was a frightening development.

Someone within the castle here had contacted him, brought him here to…to what? Murder their brother knights? Maybe he was here to settle some internal division and establish control of the organization in Kentucky. That would explain why the bodies were left in places that would attract the attention of the newspapers. Miss Hill's bawdyhouse wasn't chosen as a place to dump Nathaniel Buckner's body because of his dispute with Belle. Buckner, known for his moral crusading, had been left in a brothel that catered to men of his social class because it would generate the most newsprint.

Unlike Mr. Buckner, whose death had been quick and clean, Malthus had been brutalized first. Malthus was punished, first by being confined to slave shackles and whipped, then by having salt thrown into his fresh wounds, and then, after death, subjected to a public lynching. The slave shackles, the whipping, the fact that he was lynched, sent a very different message, but I didn't know enough about the man to understand what was being said.

It was incredibly frustrating to realize that Commander Slayton could be in the hands of this fanatic. If Slayton had been taken by the KGC, it was unlikely that I could connect all the pieces in time to save him from whatever fate they might have in mind for him.

The beating had left me so sore I could hardly move at a time when I needed to move quickly. This morning, I envied Allan Pinkerton his army of operatives. I needed help, as much help as I could find. I forced myself to get up and get dressed, then started knocking on the doors of my houseguests.

"Belle," I called through the closed door. "Belle, I need to you to get up and get dressed."

"What time is it?" she said drowsily.

"Almost five. Why?"

"In the morning?" she asked incredulously.

"Yes." I said. "Please hurry."

She groaned, but I heard her feet hit the floor. Belle mumbled something I could not understand through the closed door. I moved on without asking what she said. Miss Hill's girls were just going to work when most folks were turning in for the night. This was probably the earliest Belle had gotten out of bed since Christmas.

I banged on the next door.

"Tad!" I shouted. "Tad, are you awake?"

Tad stumbled to the door and tried to focus his weak eye on me. He was a mess. His suit was rumpled from sleeping in it and had bloodstains that would probably never come out. The black eye patch he usually wore over his good eye had been replaced with layers of white bandaging. In places, blood had soaked through the cotton. From the looks of him, I doubted that he was going to be of much use at all.

"Mr. Donnelly?" he said, his uncovered eye blinking in the light of the gas lamps.

"Yes, Tad."

"Where am I?" he asked, looking around at the unfamiliar hallway.

"My house," I said. "I'll explain later. Right now, I need you to pull yourself together and come downstairs as soon as you can."

I pointed at the door next to my bedroom. "The water closet is there. Don't take too long. Miss Belle is going to want in there as soon as she gets dressed."

"Miss Belle is here," he said brightly.

The change mentioning Belle brought to his countenance might have made me laugh, had I not felt so guilty about asking him to do more after sending him out to get shot the previous day.

"I'm going to go light the stove and get some water on for tea," I said. "Just come downstairs when you get cleaned up. I'm sure Miss Belle will be down soon enough."

I wasn't really sure how much help either he or Belle would be. As far as I knew, Belle was still wanted for murder and likely to get arrested if she was seen by any of the local police. Whatever I asked her to do would have to be something she could accomplish without getting caught. As for Tad, he was still sleeping off the effects of surgery when I returned from the cemetery.

He didn't know that his cousin was missing. That wasn't going to be easy news to break to the boy. I decided it could wait until he had been up for a while.

We were going to be a ragtag group of investigators. If we managed to get through this alive, Sergeant Hamm would have quite a belly laugh over the adventure. Right now, it was the getting through it alive part that concerned me. I was trying to figure out just how to proceed as I headed to the kitchen.

There was already a fire in the cook stove and the teapot warming on the back cap when I entered. I stood there for a moment, scratching my head as I tried to figure out what was going on, then Beulah stepped out of the pantry. The surprise was mutual. She nearly dropped the bag of flour she was holding when she saw me. I, on the other hand, couldn't believe she had overcome her fear of snakes long enough to fetch fire wood from the shed. Beulah might walk through fire for me, but facing the blacksnake that had taken up residence in my woodshed was quite another matter.

"Mr. Donnelly! Why are you outta bed?"

"I think the better question is what are you doing here?" I said. "This is Sunday. You are not supposed to be working this morning."

Beulah rocked back on her heels and placed her free hand on her hip.

"Now, Mr. Donnelly," she said, "Don't you go getting' all riled up with me. Can't I do a body a favor without expecting to be paid for it?"

"But..."

"Now you hush up," she said. "I just stopped by to fix breakfast for some sick folks afore church. I'm sure the Good Lord don't pay no attention to that workin' on his day, any more than he did pluckin' corn to feed his hungry disciples. You an' Miss Brezin' gotta eat, and I don't imagine she is any kind a hand a usin' a cookin' stove."

I knew from experience that Belle was a better than average cook, but somehow I didn't think Beulah would appreciate my saying that just now.

"It was kind of you to think of me on your day off," I said.

"I am just doin' my Christian duty," she said. "And don't you go tellin' me that you is in any kinda shape to be buildin' a fire and fixin' victuals for yourself. You shouldn't oughta be out of bed, let alone liftin' a load a firewood with that busted arm. You're goin' a come down with fever if you don't take better care of yourself."

"Beulah," I said quietly, "did you bring in all that firewood?"

She stopped lecturing and looked at me.

"Yes sir," she said. "Brought it from home. Ain't no snakes in my woodshed."

"Thank you," I said. "But I can't stay in bed."

"Even the Lord hisself took a day off."

"Yesterday, Tad was shot while he standing in for me at the parade. He's going to recover," I added, as her eyes widened, "but the boy could just as easily have died. I think whoever shot him thought Tad was me."

"I could see how they might," she said. "Bless his heart. He's been pretendin' to be you for days. He's right good at it."

"Too good," I said. "From a distance it would be hard to tell the difference."

"You can't blame yourself for the way he is acting,'" she said. "I expect you is goin' to take it to heart anyway, but it ain't your fault."

"She's right, Mr. Donnelly," Tad said from the doorway. "It wasn't your fault. It was mine."

"Tad," I said. "I didn't hear you come down."

His head dropped.

"I never got the chance to tell Cousin James I was leaving the police force," he said. "I suppose there is no point now."

The statement puzzled me.

"Do you know where the commander is?" I asked.

"At home, I reckon," he said, studying the toe of his boot. "He don't usually get up this early. You don't have to tell him you don't want me around anymore. I will."

"Why on earth would you do a thing like that?" I asked. "Is the job too much for you?"

"You mean you still want me to be your assistant?" he said.

Unconsciously, my free hand massaged my temple as I tried to pull my thoughts together. I didn't try to figure out what put the idea that I wanted him to quit into his head. There were too many other questions to occupy my mind.

"Tad. Yesterday, after you were shot. Sergeant Hamm tried to find your cousin. He was unsuccessful," I said. "Doc Haydon tried again later in the afternoon, even drove out to his house to look for him. Finally, he left a message for the commander on the door, saying that you had a gunshot wound and he was keeping you at his house.

"There was an emergency and Doc Haydon brought you here so you wouldn't be alone. Since I haven't heard from Doc or your cousin, and nobody has come by to check on you, I suspect he is still missing. That's why I woke you up. I think he may be in trouble, and I need you to help me find him."

CHAPTER TWENTY

By the time Belle had finished her morning toilette and joined us downstairs, I was on my second cup of tea and Beulah had made an enormous country breakfast. The table was loaded with plates of ham, sausage, salt pork, biscuits, gravy, scrambled eggs, and fried apples. She was about to leave the room when I shocked her and my other guest.

"Please join us, Beulah," I said, "there is plenty of food for four."

For a long moment she stood in the doorway between the kitchen and dining room, trying to decide what to make of being asked to have a seat at the table. Finally, she reached back, untied the strings of her starched apron, laid it aside, and came over to the table.

I stood up stiffly and signaled Tad to do the same.

There was an odd expression on his face as he got to his feet, but to his credit he realized I wanted him to show some respect, and he pulled out Beulah's chair and waited for her to sit down before returning to his own.

Beulah was watching us all carefully as though she thought we might be playing some sort of cruel joke.

I gave her my best attempt at a reassuring look. Considering the condition of my face, my efforts probably did little to put her at ease.

"Tea?" I asked, lifting the pot with my good hand.

"You shouldn't ought to be waitin' on me," she said. "It ain't right."

"You said you were not here as my housekeeper," I reminded

her. "You came to help an injured friend. I don't put one friend above another. This morning I need all the friends I can get. Now eat up everybody, because this is going to be a long day."

"It might not have been so long if you hadn't rousted us out of bed at the crack of dawn," Belle said.

She was baiting me and I decided not to nibble. Instead, I took the two sketch cards out of my pocket and handed them to Belle.

"This man was at the inquest in Frankfort, and at Mr. Buckner's funeral," I said.

Belle's eyebrows shot up.

"This one you showed me at Miss Hill's," she said. "You should have brought the other along. I would have recognized him at the cemetery if I'd seen both of 'em. He was one of the men who beat you up."

"You're sure," I said.

She nodded.

"He's older, but the face isn't so changed. This is the man who was bending over Mr. Peltmutter, when I came looking for you. I hid in the bushes while he and another man…I couldn't see the other one's face, but they carried Mr. Peltmutter to the wagon. The way they were talkin', I think they were trying to figure out how to squeeze you in, but Mr. Peltmutter took up all the room they had. They decided to take him to the house and come back for you. So, I got you outta there quick as I could."

"I'm glad," I said. "Peltmutter is dead. They found his body yesterday afternoon. I would not have wanted to meet a similar fate."

"I'm glad too," Belle said.

"It seems that once again I owe you my life, Miss Belle. Perhaps, this time I can at least get the murder charges dropped."

Belle said nothing, but the fear that had been haunting her these past several days seemed to vanish from her eyes.

"Do you think so?" she asked.

"Just one more question," I said.

"What's that?"

"The other man, the one whose face you couldn't get a look at, what did you see? Maybe a better question is: what was your impression of him?"

Belle looked down at the table for a long moment as she thought about my question.

"He seemed younger than this one," she said, pointing to the sketch I had made. "From the way he moved, I would make him about your age, maybe a little older. Dark hair with a little gray at the neck. Expensive topcoat, black, with a velvet collar. Tailored for him too, though not recently."

She must have noticed my puzzlement.

"Not the latest style," she said.

I took her word for that. I wouldn't know the latest style if I fell over it. Belle, on the other hand, had an eye for fashion and nimble fingers that could duplicate anything she saw in the New York papers.

"Did you see anything else?"

No, that's about all I saw," she said.

Belle held the sketches out to Tad.

"Your turn," she said, smiling at him.

Tad blushed as he took the sketches from her outstretched hand.

I waited for him to compose himself and examine the drawings.

"You think this man killed Mr. Peltmutter and that he plans to kill Cousin James next," he said. His voice dropped. "If he's not dead now."

"Doc Haydon said he would go by the house and check again this morning, but the last news I had from him was that your cousin is missing," I said. "We have three dead bodies, all of whom disappeared in much the same way as your cousin. I hope we can find him before he becomes the next victim."

Tad swallowed hard.

"Have you found the secret, Mr. Donnelly?" he asked meekly. "The one that unravels the puzzle?"

"Part of it."

I looked at Belle.

"Miss Belle was able to help me solve one piece of the puzzle. Together, we were able to discover a threatening note delivered to Mr. Buckner by a fellow member of a secret society. We don't know what he had done to become a target of this group, but whatever it was likely involved Mr. Peltmutter."

I didn't think it was necessary to reveal every gory detail of the ritual killing of Ambrose Peltmutter, but everyone was looking at me expectantly.

"His killer opened Mr. Buckner's grave and placed Mr.

Peltmutter's body on top of Mr. Buckner's coffin," I said. "The sketches you have in your hand, Tad, are of a man very close to the top of the organization. I believe he is working with someone here in Lexington. We have to find this man before he has the opportunity to kill again."

"Can I see them pictures, Mr. Kent?" Beulah asked.

"You can call me Tad, Ma'am," Tad said.

"No sir, Mr. Kent," Beulah said firmly. "I can't do that. The Klan is still mighty active in these parts."

Beulah saw his discomfort and her tone softened.

"Thank you for offerin,' but takin' them kind of liberties with a white man, even one as young as you, would likely get me strung up. We ain't had a lynchin' in weeks, and I am much too fond of this ol' neck of mine to want to have it stretched out on the end of the next rope."

Tad's face turned crimson.

"I'm sorry, Ma'am," he said. "I wouldn't want to cause you trouble."

Beulah smiled at him. "You got no need to be sorry. It's this ol' world that is in a sorry mess. I shouldn't have set down at no table with white folks. An' Mr. Donnelly there shouldn't be puttin' ideas in your head 'bout holdin' my chair and callin' me Ma'am. Maybe one day an ol' colored woman can get treated respectful by a nice white boy. I keep prayin' that'll be the way it is, but that day ain't come yet."

"Mr. Donnelly," she said, meeting my eyes. "I reckon you'd be wantin' me to look at those pictures."

"I need your help too," I said.

"I would have done that without all this fuss."

"I know that," I said, "but sometimes there needs to be a little fuss. You're right about the fact we can't change much. Together, I think we might be able to stop this one man from whatever evil he is planning."

She took the sketches from Tad and studied them carefully. Her face had a peculiar expression when she looked at me, then she looked back at the sketches again, first one then the other.

"Would it be all right with you if I take these to church with me?" she asked, when she finally looked up again. "I ain't sure, but I think I saw him once…I want ta ask somebody who would know."

"I think that's a fine idea, Beulah," I said. "Will you come back as soon as the service is over?"

"Yes, sir," she said, standing to leave.

CHAPTER TWENTY-ONE

Sergeant Hamm was just going off duty when I arrived at the stationhouse.

"Dang it all, Donnelly. I just finished writing out the blasted report," he growled. "Besides, the missus will have my hide if I'm not home in time to take her to church. She's got some fool notion that her cousin should see a real Christian service."

He colored slightly, remembering that Mrs. Hamm's cousin and I shared the same faith.

"No offense, Donnelly," he said. "I didn't mean that the way it came out."

"I thought your wife's machinations were intended to find me a nice Catholic girl as a prospective bride," I said. "Seems a waste of effort, if she plans to convert her."

"Well now, that's a fact," he said, stroking his thick mustache. "She is expecting you for dinner tonight. If I tell her I'll bring you along with me when I come home, it might be enough to get me out of hot water for skippin' Sunday services."

He looked from me to Tad while he mulled over staying to hear us out.

"All right," he said, "Sit down. I'll send Officer Watts to let Millie know I'm tied up with these danged murders."

He returned a few minutes later and sat down behind the battered desk.

"Before you get all het up about it, I'm not looking for Miss Belle."

"Is the murder charge being dropped?" I asked.

"No," Sergeant Hamm said. "I'm willing to concede that Miss

Belle's not the sort to indulge in the sick display at the cemetery, but until I hear from the Commander, I'm obliged to arrest her for the Buckner murder."

"The murders are connected," I said.

"I'm of a mind to agree, Donnelly, but without proof, where does that leave us?"

"I don't know," I said. "Honestly, I thought Peltmutter was the brains behind the murders of Buckner and Malthus. With him dead, I've lost my best suspect."

"Do you have any evidence that he was involved?"

"Not now. At least nothing I could take to court."

Hamm eyed me suspiciously for a long moment while he stroked his thick crumb duster.

"What do you want from me?" he asked.

"Your help."

"Then tell me what you think is going on," he said.

"I think Peltmutter was involved up to his eyeballs," I said. "Once his cohorts realized that he would not hold up to questioning, they got rid of him to save their own necks."

"Maybe he stepped over the line when he killed Buckner and Malthus and the rest of the circle turned on him?" Hamm reasoned.

"Peltmutter struck me as being too cowardly to be the person to pull the trigger. I think he was supposed to be watching over the money. Suppose he and his friends Buckner and Malthus were dipping into the KGC treasury?"

"You can't be serious," he sputtered. "These men were pillars of the community."

"Now they are, but Buckner was a junior partner before the war; the others weren't any better placed. They each rose to prominence after the war. I'll bet that if we get a close look at Peltmutter's business dealings, we'll find proof that he was living above his means."

"If you're wrong, the Commander will have my neck," Sergeant Hamm replied.

"If the Commander is still alive," I said, not daring to look at Tad. "I don't have a good feeling about our not being able to locate him."

"Cousin James might have been investigating this himself," Tad said. "He could be in trouble."

Sergeant Hamm's expression told me how unlikely he thought

it was that Commander Slayton would be found alive. We exchanged glances in a silent agreement that we would not share that opinion with Tad.

"Do you think your cousin doubted Miss Belle's guilt?" I asked.

Tad's face dropped.

"No, sir," he said. "But he wouldn't go off like this."

"It isn't like the Commander to miss the parade today," Sergeant Hamm said.

I had to agree. The Commander rarely missed the opportunity to put on his dress uniform and attend public events. The way he thrived on public speaking made me think he considered this office as a stepping stone to political power.

"I know you're worried," I said, placing a hand on Tad's arm. "If your cousin has been taken by the Knights, the best thing we can do is figure out what they're up to. Let's follow the evidence and hope it leads us to him."

Tad nodded agreement.

I turned my attention back to Sergeant Hamm.

"Think about this, Sergeant," I said. "During the war the Knights stole dozens of Union payrolls here in the Bluegrass. What better way to hide all that money than to set up their own bank and feed the coinage through in small amounts?"

"Donnelly, you are talking about some of the leading businessmen in Lexington."

"Yes, but consider how they each made their fortunes. First Peltmutter gets himself a job at the bank, I'm guessing, but I would bet he arranged the loan to buy Buckner a partnership in the cigar company. If we get a close look at Peltmutter's business dealings, I think we'll find plenty of proof that money from National Bank helped Malthus with his political ambitions. That all fits with the KGC plans to gain power, but I suspect there was more money flowing out than the KGC realized. What if the people in charge of the money used it for purchases the KGC would not approve of?"

"The Commander is touchy about digging into the affairs of our betters," Sergeant Hamm replied.

The idea of any member of the KGC being better than us rankled. I had to bite back the retort that sprang to mind.

"I think the Commander is the least of your worries," I said, not looking at him or Tad.

I didn't know where Tad's cousin was, but if Slayton was trying to investigate the case on his own, the odds were not good for finding him alive. Tad wasn't ready to face the possibility that his kinsman and benefactor might be dead.

Sergeant Hamm looked across the desk and cleared his throat. He had two sons not many years younger than Tad. I suspected he was considering how they would feel if he vanished.

"I'll go find the judge and get a warrant," he said. "You want to meet me at Peltmutter's house, or the bank?"

"The house," I said. "I don't think Peltmutter would have risked keeping the kind of information I'm looking for at the bank."

Peltmutter's two-story brick house held a prominent position on Main Street. The green shutters and sandstone steps were a pale imitation of General Lesley Combs' stately red brick on the corner opposite the Phoenix Hotel. Still, the Peltmutter home was certainly grander than anything I could afford and, with four daughters to provide for, I doubted the banker was living within his means.

It was a short walk from the stationhouse to Peltmutter's front door. I didn't want to arrive before Sergeant Hamm had his warrant, so Tad and I walked around downtown until we saw the Sergeant approaching. The two of us fell in beside him.

"Judge wasn't happy about issuing this," he said. "You better hope we find something."

"Let's also hope we can understand it if we do find something," I said. "These men are powerfully fond of muddling things up with knightly rhetoric and cryptic symbols."

"That's all I need," Hamm said. "Maybe you can get Cousin Mary Kate to sort through their schoolboy games. I've got better things to do with my time."

"Is your wife's cousin fond of knightly adventures?"

"Not that I know of, but she has a powerful fondness for puzzles and ciphers," he said. "She says she uses them in her classroom. If you ask me, this bunch spent too much time with teachers like her."

"They certainly think they are smarter than the rest of us," I replied. "That's a common downfall of criminals."

"Fools," Hamm muttered, as he climbed the front steps.

His fist pounded on the front door.

"Police. Open up," he shouted.

Get the sergeant mad enough, and he forgot all about being intimidated by the well-to-do, I thought, as the same maid presented herself.

"The mistress isn't home," she said in a frightened tone.

She attempted to slam the door but Sergeant Hamm's hand went up quickly, catching the door and pushing it open.

"I have a warrant to search the house," Hamm said, pressing the folded paper into her hand. "You can give it to Mrs. Peltmutter when she gets back."

The sergeant stepped inside, followed closely by Tad and me. Leaving the front door ajar, the three of us trailed through the entrance hall and through the first door we saw. Sergeant Hamm stopped abruptly. The commanding lead he had taken at the front door melted as he looked around the parlor.

I couldn't blame him for being taken aback. One glance around the room made me shudder at the task of searching the Peltmutter house. Although the rooms were large, the Peltmutters had succumbed to the current fashion of filling every surface to overflowing. Layers of organza and lace covered every tabletop. Floral arrangements, figurines, oriental vases, ginger jars, gilt framed photographs, music boxes, and china dolls crowded together. Each chair was adorned with crocheted antimacassars and needlepoint pillows. The variety and array of hiding places available boggled my mind.

"What kind a man keeps all these doodads around?" Sergeant Hamm said.

"I suppose when you are outnumbered five to one by women it is easier to let them have their way," I replied. "Maybe he has an office or library that's a little less decorated."

"Good thought, Donnelly," the sergeant replied. "Let's look for that."

Tad opened a door on the left side of the parlor and discovered a music room dominated by a grand piano, which was nearly buried under the same sort of clutter we found in the parlor. An artist's easel stood on a paint-splattered oilcloth near the east window, its unfinished canvas covered to protect the artist's work. I worked my way through the maze of chairs and lifted the cloth, revealing a half-finished still life. I could almost see the banker's daughters spending their mornings in music lessons and art classes.

Sergeant Hamm cleared his throat.

"You planning to stand gawking at that picture all morning?" he asked.

"I'm coming," I said, dropping the canvas back in place.

Peltmutter's office held a different kind of clutter. Drawers had been pulled from his roll top desk, their contents spilled onto the carpets, books seemed to have been flung hastily from their shelves and lay scattered over the floor. Papers were strewn about, cushions were pulled from the chairs and sliced open, their stuffing scattered over the mess.

"Get the maid," Sergeant Hamm said, looking at Tad. "I want to know who was responsible for this."

"They couldn't be far ahead of us," I said, when Tad had left the room. "Peltmutter was alive this time yesterday."

"Do you suppose they found what they were looking for?" Sergeant Hamm replied.

"I don't know. They wouldn't have torn the room apart if they knew where he kept his records."

"This mess makes it look like you were right about him keeping some kind of log."

"Peltmutter was scared. You saw the way he was sweating at Buckner's funeral. A man that frightened wants protection. He kept records. I'm sure of that. And he is not the sort to leave them where they would be found easily. There is a good chance that whoever burgled his office didn't find what he was after."

"She's gone," Tad said.

"Who's gone?" Sergeant Hamm asked.

"Everybody," he replied, his uncovered eye open wide. "I looked all over and there ain't a soul any place."

Sergeant Hamm's eyebrows drew together. His lower lip disappeared under his thick mustache.

"What do you think, Donnelly?" he said.

I took my derringer out before I replied. "I think we had better do a thorough search of the rest of the house," I said, thankful that it was not my gun hand confined by the heavy splints.

Sergeant Hamm nodded, drew his revolver, and motioned me to go back the way we came.

I headed out the front door and checked the street in both directions. I didn't see the maid. It was impossible to know if she was alone in the house. Since I lacked any knowledge of the rest of the household staff, I had to give up and go back inside.

The sergeant had taken Tad and gone back toward the kitchen. He was just coming back when I entered the house.

"Kitchen door is locked from the inside," he said. "Nobody went that way."

We searched the downstairs room by room. The Peltmutters' passion for heavy draperies and table coverings made progress painfully slow. Tad opened each likely hiding place while the sergeant and I stood ready to shoot. I suppose it was a lucky thing the Peltmutters didn't have any pets. As uncomfortable as I felt in the house, I might have fired at anything that moved.

Nearly an hour into the search, we discovered a small door by the back stairs. Sergeant Hamm kicked it open.

"Police," he yelled. "Anybody down there?"

"I'll go first," he said, giving my derringer a distasteful look. "Next time, bring a real gun."

"Wait," I said, "You're going to need a light."

I found an oil lamp in the kitchen, lit it from the cook stove, and handed it to Tad.

"It will make a pretty target," Sergeant Hamm said.

I swallowed the lump in my throat and tried to sound calm.

"I doubt there is another way out," I said. "Anybody who starts a fire is likely to roast with us."

Hamm might have been smiling as he started down the stairs. Under the brush on his lip it was hard to tell. If he was, the smile had vanished by the time we reached the floor below.

"What's that smell?" Tad whispered.

The shadows cast by the oil lamp made the angry lines in Sergeant Hamm's face fearsome as he glanced up at me.

I was trying not to retch. The smell brought back memories of dry August days when camp fever and infection were at their worst in the hospital wards. I didn't want him to open the stained wooden door in front of us. It took all my willpower not to turn and run.

"Tad, give me the lamp and go get Doc Haydon," I said, with as much control as I could muster. "Tell him to bring his medical kit."

The boy's footsteps had faded on the stairs before Sergeant Hamm reached for the door.

We entered the dark, damp room together, guns ready should anything move. It took a few seconds for my eyes to adjust to the near darkness. Whatever compassion I had for the way Peltmutter died vanished the instant I saw the horror he hid in this underground prison. The room had no windows or hearth to offer a moment's warmth to Peltmutter's captives.

A heavy chain measured out in iron rings ran the length of one stone wall. Along the chain, manacled with arms fastened above their heads, hung the bodies of four of the most wretched colored men I had ever laid eyes on. It was impossible to ignore the stench of disease and human excrement. I stood for a moment looking into eyes fixedly staring out at me from their emaciated faces. The accusation forever locked in their gaze burned its way indelibly into my memory.

"Mother of Christ," I said.

When I glanced at Sergeant Hamm, I could see the thick knot of muscle in his jaw quivering with rage. For a long moment he just stood there, pistol drawn, gripping it so tightly that the knuckles of his right hand turned white.

"Take them down," Sergeant Hamm ordered. "I don't care what Doc Haydon says about leaving the bodies where we find them. Nobody should be left like that."

I held the lamp high, searching the room. There was a table on the far side of the room had an oil lamp and some papers. Above it, a wooden shelf, set with nails held a ring of keys and a locked box. I set the lamp down and grabbed the keys, testing them in the shackles until I found one that opened the damnable locks.

The sergeant holstered his gun and came over. As I unfastened the shackles of each body, he flung it over his shoulder and carried it upstairs, then returned to carry the next man away.

When the last man was removed, I stuffed the keys in my pocket along with the papers, then grabbed the locked box before leaving. The horrors of Peltmutter's private hell followed me up the stairs and into the kitchen where four bodies lay sprawled on the floor.

I looked down at them, committing each face to memory. Wondering what kind of evil controlled Peltmutter's mind. What allowed any man to do this to another?

CHAPTER TWENTY-TWO

I was certain that Mrs. Peltmutter would have my hide if she ever found out I had stripped the covers from her mattress and lined the bed of our rented wagon before Tad and Doc Haydon loaded it with filthy corpses. It gave me a certain satisfaction knowing how much it would offend the Peltmutters. The banker was one of the city's citizens that protested the medical examiner's use of the city death wagon to transport non-white bodies. It seemed that, even in death, some men needed greater privilege.

"Are you coming over to help with the autopsy?" Doc Haydon asked. "Won't be before morning. Considering they've all had their throats cut, it will probably be straightforward. Not that they would have lived in the condition they were in. Poor devils."

"Where's Sergeant Hamm?" I asked. "He should attend, too."

Doc Haydon gave me a strange look and shook his head. "I sent him home to get some sleep while you were in the kitchen. He's not likely to show up in the morning unless I send for him. The sergeant is a good man, but he's got no stomach for that sort of work."

"How'd you get rid of him?"

"Oh, he wasn't about to leave until I promised you would be presentable and at his door by five o'clock." He shrugged. "The presentable part was a stretch, considering the broken arm and battered face, but you have time to get a bath."

I groaned. I could throw away my ruined clothing, and scrub my skin raw without avail. Just knowing that I had been turned away from Peltmutter's door while these men were still alive made me feel dirty in a way no warm bath would clean.

"What are we going to do about those four men?"

"If the Peltmutters were coming home, they would have been here by now. We might as well take them to my autopsy room. If they were from around here, perhaps Beulah will be able to find out who they were. She was here earlier. Said to tell you that feller was at the city Freedman's Bureau. I hope you know what she was talking about."

"Umm," I said, not wanting to explain about the sketches she had taken to church with her. "You might want to ask some of the colored men at the Freemen's Bureau if they can identify these bodies."

"Good idea," he said. "I'll send my assistant over soon as we unload the wagon."

"Did Beulah say anything else?"

He smiled. "She's a gem," he said. "Worried that the Klan will come after me. Offered to fetch a colored doctor to do the autopsy."

"I'm sorry Doc," I said. "I shouldn't have sent for you. I wasn't thinking."

"Ness," he said, putting a hand on my shoulder. "Klan or no Klan, I don't pass off my job as medical examiner just because the victim's skin is a different color. County pays me a thousand dollars a year to investigate unattended deaths. All of them."

He gave me a friendly push toward the street.

"You, on the other hand have done your job. Now, get out of here. Go take a bath. Splash on some bay rum. Then pick up some posies or something for Mrs. Hamm. Womenfolk expect a man to show up at their door with some sort of remembrance for the hostess."

I hesitated, looking back at him. "Did Sergeant Hamm take the locked box we found downstairs?"

"No," he said, "but don't go getting ideas. No digging through evidence tonight. And don't worry about Slayton, either. The Buckner case is getting so much public attention he is probably off trying to investigate the murder on his own. He has to make some sort of show of being involved. Besides, Mrs. Hamm won't give the Sergeant a minute's peace if you stand up her cousin."

"Don't you think this case merits our full attention?" I growled. "There are seven people dead now, maybe eight."

"There's going to be nine if you don't show up at the

Hamms'," he replied. "You might be able to avoid Sergeant Hamm, but I can't. I gave him my word you would be there."

"All right. I'll leave it until after dinner," I promised, going inside to retrieve the box. "Just take Tad with you. He can help unload the wagon. Tell him I'll see him in the morning."

Doc Haydon wasn't the only one needing help. Bathing with a broken arm took a good deal of help from Belle. She cleaned me up, then powdered the bandages to cover the stains and smell. After dressing me in my best suit and tying my tie for me, she dashed off to the kitchen.

Belle came back as I was stuffing the papers from Peltmutter's house into my coat pocket. The mingled scents of apple butter, sorghum, and cinnamon drifted through the lid of the cake box she carried.

"Beulah baked this for us," she said, "but you might want to take it to Mrs. Hamm. It isn't polite to show up empty handed."

"I'd rather not show up at all," I said. "I have work to do."

Belle giggled. "You never know, you might just like this girl. We're not all bad."

I stuck my tongue out at her, which made her laugh harder as she ushered me out the front door, only a few minutes late.

Tomorrow, when I had more time, I would have to have Doc Haydon replace the binding on my arm. Bell had done her best to clean it up but the filth was pervasive. The scent even clung to the papers I carried. Under the present circumstances that thought offered a little comfort. If I were lucky the lingering scent would be strong enough to offend the delicate sensibilities of my dinner companion.

That was a little cruel. It was not Mrs. Hamm's cousin's fault I was in the awkward position of posing as a suitor. Deep down, I knew my own determination to find my brother's killer had cast me into the role I played. Having dinner with the latest cousin Mrs. Hamm thought would be the perfect wife for me was just part of the price I paid for assuming a man's identity.

I felt a twinge of guilt over still having the papers from Peltmutter's secret jail in my pocket. I should have left them in my bedroom with the locked box, but the brief glance I had given them intrigued me. Symbols and numbers lined each page, making me think it was important enough for Peltmutter to try to obscure their meaning. I was hoping to get a moment or two to try deciphering them before nightfall. The evening would certainly be better spent at home figuring out Peltmutter's cryptic notes than meeting another of Mrs. Hamm's endless string of single female cousins. These thoughts were still churning in my brain when, armed with Beulah's cake, I turned the corner onto Fourth Street.

The section of Fourth Street where Sergeant Hamm lived was a typical working class neighborhood, made up of rental properties and small family homes. The Hamms had purchased one of the shotgun houses that dotted side streets all over town. Although their house resembled most of the others when he first purchased it, Sergeant Hamm had worked very hard to improve the property. Like his uniforms, the house was spotlessly clean inside and out.

A flagstone walkway led up to a sturdy front porch with white, spindled railings, and turned columns. Two oak rocking chairs and a small round tea table sat on the side of the porch most shaded from the afternoon sun. The sergeant had saved up a month's pay to buy those. I could still remember how proud he had been to provide his wife with a cool place to visit with other womenfolk in the neighborhood. A little wistful sigh escaped at the domesticity of what those empty chairs represented. They made my new house with all its modern conveniences seem poorer in comparison.

Through the front window, I spotted the sergeant pacing with military precision the length of his small front parlor, pausing on each pass to gaze out the window then turning to walk back toward the dining room. There was a visible relaxing of his shoulders when he spotted me on the walkway. His head turned and I saw the rest of the boys run up toward the window, before their mother came to shoo them away.

Unable to wave, I nodded my head toward the house and Sergeant Hamm disappeared briefly, then reappeared as the front door opened.

"Donnelly. Come in. Come in," he said.

It seemed odd to see him in his Sunday-go-to meeting-suit instead of the black wool uniform with its polished brass buttons. The string tie, which his wife had no doubt made him wear, looked tight enough around his thick neck to cut off his circulation.

"Good evening, Sergeant," I said. "I hope I haven't kept you waiting long."

"Not at all," he lied. "The missus is just setting dinner on the table."

The dining room door opened and aroma of pot roast wafted through the room, reminding me that I hadn't eaten since breakfast.

"Something smells wonderful," I said, as Mrs. Hamm stepped into the room.

"My goodness!" she exclaimed, at the sight of my bandaged face and broken arm.

"I'm sorry," I said. "I must look a fright."

She glanced quickly at her husband, then forced a smile.

"I had heard there was an altercation," she said. "I do hope you are feeling well enough to be out and about, Mr. Donnelly."

"Thank you for your concern," I said. "Doc Haydon assures me that my injuries will heal quickly. But if you would like, we can make this another evening."

"That won't be necessary," an unfamiliar voice said.

I looked across the room to where a rather bookish woman sat knitting. Her dark hair was pulled back severely and knotted at the nape of her neck. Her gown was equally austere, dark gray and unadorned. I would have supposed she was in mourning save for a small gold locket pinned near her bosom. I watched for a second or two as her needles moved deftly, her attention focused on her work.

"Mr. Donnelly," Mildred Hamm said hastily, "I don't believe you have met my cousin. This is Miss Mary Katherine McGuire."

"Miss McGuire," I said, trying to sound more composed than I was feeling.

"Forgive me for being so forward," she said, laying aside her work and standing up. "Cousin Mildred has been cooking all afternoon, and it would be a shame to deny you such a fine meal or the company of my cousins."

The mischief in her gray eyes defied her otherwise somber appearance. I liked the way they crinkled at the corners and reflected the dancing firelight. But it was frightening the way she could see right through my attempt to escape. I shifted uneasily under her glance.

Miss McGuire seemed amused by my discomfort.

"Would you like me to take that?" She reached for the cake box.

"Allow me," Mrs. Hamm interjected, taking the box from her. "Is that apple butter I smell, Mr. Donnelly?"

"Yes, Ma'am," I stammered. "Beulah baked a stack cake this

morning. I thought you might enjoy it."

"Wasn't that thoughtful of him, Mary Kate?" she said. "I'll just put it on the sideboard until after dinner."

I could feel the color creeping up the back of my neck at Mrs. Hamm's blatant attempt to solicit a compliment on my behalf.

"Very thoughtful," Miss McGuire agreed, her voice carefully schooled to hide the laughter in her eyes. "Shall we come to the table, Cousin Mildred?"

"Yes, do," Mrs. Hamm called back over her shoulder.

Out of the corner of my eye, I could see Sergeant Hamm watching us as I offered Miss McGuire my good arm and guided her to the table.

I am sure Mrs. Hamm prepared an excellent meal, but with the possible exception of Miss McGuire none of us seemed to be enjoying dinner. Out of the corner of my eye, I watched Sergeant Hamm unconsciously run a finger around his tight collar as I tried to think of something to say. Silently, I swore that I was never going to let him put me in this position again.

"I understand you are a private investigator," Miss McGuire said, breaking the tension. "It must be very interesting work."

Sergeant Hamm cleared his throat loudly. "It is not the sort of work we should be discussing in polite company," he said pointedly looking at me as though I were going to go into graphic detail of the day's activities.

"Oh come now, cousin," Miss McGuire said lightly. "Mr. Donnelly's work sounds so much more interesting than trying to teach mathematics to bored schoolgirls."

"You teach mathematics?" I said.

"Yes," she said. "It is rather unglamorous work, but not all of us can enjoy the kind of excitement your occupation affords. I content myself with the occasional gifted student."

"My work is mostly tedious and sometimes heartbreaking," I said, remembering the bodies we had carried out of the Peltmutter home only a few short hours ago.

"You don't need to be modest, Mr. Donnelly," she said. "The papers are full of reports about your adventures."

"I assure you, Miss McGuire, the papers are not to be relied upon on for giving a true report of my activities," I replied. "It would violate the privacy of my clients to speak with the press. I doubt that any news story you may have read was garnered from a reliable source."

"Womenfolk shouldn't be reading those trashy rags anyway," Sergeant Hamm grunted. "The way it coarsens polite discourse is shameful."

Miss McGuire smiled sweetly at him, but appeared unaffected by his rebuke.

"So the press is wrong about Mr. Donnelly getting into fisticuffs at the Buckner funeral, and surviving the altercation through the tender ministrations of his dear friend, Miss Belle Brezing?"

Sergeant Hamm choked on his iced-tea.

His wife gave her cousin a look that would have curdled milk.

From the amount of heat coming off my own face, I was sure it had turned a brilliant shade of scarlet.

"I would not call being set upon and beaten senseless by three thugs fisticuffs," I said coldly, my eyes locked with hers. "As for Miss Brezing, she has proven herself a friend on more than one occasion. I owe her my life."

"Wilfred, do something," Mrs. Hamm exclaimed.

"Donnelly…" Sergeant Hamm began starting to stand up.

"Cousin, please," Miss McGuire said, placing a delicate hand over the sergeant's enormous one. "I deliberately provoked Mr. Donnelly. If you must intervene, it is I who am at fault."

"Please accept my apology," she said, turning her attention back to me. "The accounts my cousins have given me of your character was so utterly different from those in circulation about town, that I wanted to see for myself which was true."

"Am I really such a curiosity, Miss McGuire?"

She smiled. "Sir, is it possible that you are not aware of your own reputation?"

"Mary Katherine, please," Mrs. Hamm implored. She gripped the edge of the dinner table so tightly her knuckles turned white.

"Now, cousin," Miss McGuire said. "Mr. Donnelly has spoken plainly, it is only fair that I do the same."

"Please do," I said.

"Mr. Donnelly," she said, "I have been warned by nearly every woman of my acquaintance that that I should on no account expect to hear from you after this evening."

"Is that so," I replied.

"Indeed it is, sir. Some think you are in love with Miss

Brezing. Others think you have no interest in anything but work." Her eyes twinkled with amusement. "There were even a few that, since their charms had failed utterly with you, believed that your proclivities were not for the fairer sex."

Mrs. Hamm's expression was pure horror as she shot to her feet.

"Mary Katherine, that is quite enough!"

I stood out of courtesy to my hostess. Somewhere deep down, I knew I should be angered by the baldness of Miss McGuire's report, but I found her apparent disinterest in pursuing me too intriguing. She had to be nearly as old as I and, considering the acute shortage of marriageable men our generation had created by the late war, prospective husbands must be few and far between.

"Mr. Donnelly, let me apologize profusely for my cousin," Mrs. Hamm said. "I don't know what's gotten into her this evening."

"It is quite all right, Mrs. Hamm," I said, glancing at Miss McGuire. "Perhaps we could save this topic for another time and find one more amenable to our hostess for this evening."

"Yes," Miss McGuire answered. "Millie dear, please sit down. I promise to behave."

"Another time. Really?" Mrs. Hamm said, suddenly relieved.

I swallowed hard, realizing the enormity of what I had said.

"Yes, well," I stammered. "That is, if Miss McGuire is willing to be seen in the company of a man with my reputation."

The gray eyes that had been toying with me all evening were suddenly fixed on her half-finished dinner. Miss McGuire was clearly not expecting to see me again. I took a perverse satisfaction in watching as color crept into her cheeks.

CHAPTER TWENTY-THREE

Once the ladies had excused themselves to tend to dishes, I took out the notes I had recovered from Peltmutter's house and showed them to Sergeant Hamm. He looked at several pages, then handed them back to me.

"It is all a bunch of gibberish," he said. "Makes no sense at all."

"I think his symbols represent people," I said pointing to the tiny pointed leaf shape on the page. "My guess is that this one is for Buckner; the shape of it is similar to a tobacco leaf."

"In that case, who's the oak?" Sergeant Hamm asked, pointing to a different shaped leaf.

"I don't know," I admitted, "but the lines of numbers look like some sort of cipher. If we can crack that, maybe we can figure out what they were up to."

He took an oil lamp off the sideboard and set it near where we were working. Together we decided that the tree stump was probably Malthus; political stump speeches, we reasoned. That left a star, an oak leaf, and a circle, none of which resonated with a single individual. It was possible the circle represented the group as a whole, but I wasn't sure of that definition. The two of us were still trying to decipher the tangle of numbers and symbols when the ladies returned.

Sergeant Hamm gave his wife a guilty look, but she didn't rebuke him for working. I surmised that her mood was much improved from having succeeded at presenting a dinner companion that I was willing to see on a second occasion.

I stood up and started to collect the papers we had scattered over the table, but Miss McGuire stopped me.

"How interesting," she said, examining one of the pages. "I haven't seen a column cipher in years."

"What?" I asked.

"A column cipher," she said, pointing down at the page. "See how each line has exactly seven words."

"You can read this?" Sergeant Hamm asked in astonishment.

"My Morse Code is a bit rusty," she said, "and I am not sure what the pictograms mean. But if you have a code chart, I would be happy to help. You have quite a lot of pages."

"You could help immensely if you would just tell me how you see Morse Code in these numbers," I said, "and why you are sure there are exactly seven words in a row."

"Look at this" she said, setting the paper so I could see the rows of numbers. "It is fairly simple. There are exactly seven threes in each row. Whoever wrote this is using the three to indicate the end of a word. Most of the rest of the line is fours and sixes. Those are the dots and dashes of the code. These entries that have digits other than three, four, or seven are probably amounts of money. They each have a four, a dot, as the third digit from the end."

"It doesn't sound simple to me, Mary Katherine," Sergeant Hamm said, "but it does appear you're right."

"Perhaps you weren't as guilty as I of passing secret messages in school, cousin," she replied. "I wasted a good amount of lamp oil hiding in my room at night deciphering messages from my girlfriends."

"I wouldn't consider it a waste when you have provided us with such a valuable service," I said. "We are in your debt."

"Should I see if the telegraph operator is willing to translate this for us?" Sergeant Hamm asked.

"I believe I have a copy of the code chart at home," I said, as I gathered the last of the pages and put them in my pocket. "We've seen enough death in this case."

"I would be happy to assist," Miss McGuire said.

Mrs. Hamm looked appalled.

"Don't you think there is enough gossip circulating about me?" I said.

"Oh," she said, realizing the impropriety of her offer. "Cousin Millie, could you chaperone? I am sure I could decipher this much faster than Mr. Donnelly."

"Well," Mrs. Hamm said uncertainly.

"Good. It's settled then," Miss McGuire said. "Give us just a moment to fetch our wraps, Mr. Donnelly."

Sergeant Hamm and his wife exchanged one of those married couple looks that seem to communicate volumes without uttering a word.

"Let me change into my uniform, Donnelly," he said, standing up. "I'll walk with you as far as the stationhouse."

The sun hung low on the horizon, casting long thin shadows onto the cobbles and repainting the white and yellow clapboard houses in shades of pink and orange, as the four of us set out for our destinations. Mrs. Hamm and Miss McGuire walked arm and arm ahead of me, chattering amiably about nothing. The sergeant and I trudged along silently behind, he looking as though he sorely missed the days sleep this case had cost him, and I wishing desperately I had some way to warn Miss Belle of the guests I was bringing home with me. I prayed she was not downstairs when we arrived. Considering Miss McGuire's behavior this evening, I had no idea what reaction she would have, but Mrs. Hamm would be mortified.

"When does the Doc think he'll have a report ready?" Hamm asked.

"He won't get started on the autopsy before tomorrow. Probably late at that. Unless the commander turns up. We're headed out to his place to investigate first thing in the morning."

"You'll let me know what you discover," Sergeant Hamm said.

"Of course," I replied.

"Officially the Commander's house is outside the city, but if he is really missing, the location won't stop me from looking into the matter."

"Didn't expect it would," I said

He paused outside the station house.

"You'll see the ladies home safely," he said.

It was more statement than question. I nodded agreement.

"Take care, Sergeant," I said.

His lower lip disappeared under his mustache, making his long face seem even more serious.

"Depend on it," he said. "I don't like the way this case is

shaping up. Too many dead."

"Entirely," I replied.

As I turned to go, I noticed Miss McGuire watching us. Our eyes met for just a second before she lowered hers. It was as though a curtain had been lowered, shutting me out of her thoughts. It was disturbing to realize that I wanted very much to know what she was thinking.

I desperately needed time and quiet to sort through the turmoil that crowded my mind. My brother's ghost haunted me. Each unfolding secret of the Knights drove me to finally put him to rest. I reached into my pocket and touched the folded papers as I wondered if the key to his murder, as well as Buckner, Malthus, Peltmutter and those four nameless colored men, resided in these cryptic notes.

What if I did discover Ness's murderer? What would become of me then? I glanced at Miss McGuire and wondered if the austere dress and severe hairstyle of an aging spinster might have been mine. It could not be now. I was too coarsened by years of living as a man.

Lost in my own thoughts, I hardly noticed turning the corner onto Short Street until we passed the doors of St. Peter and Paul School. I realized I was a sorry escort when Mrs. Hamm stopped.

"Which is your house, Mr. Donnelly?" she asked.

"Oh, sorry," I said. "It is on the next block, third house from the corner."

"It's charming," Mrs. Hamm exclaimed when we neared the house. "I wouldn't have expected a bachelor to think of a summer kitchen or window garden."

"The window garden was Beulah's suggestion," I admitted. "She believes that most every dish benefits from a touch of fresh herbs. She helped me plan most of the kitchen. She chided me for spending so much on the cook stove, but I thought being able to keep a fifteen-gallon supply of hot water was a luxury worth the investment."

I opened the gate and waited as the ladies entered, and then slammed it loud enough to alert Belle before following them up the walk. From the upstairs window there was a flutter of curtains and I hoped that Miss Belle had seen us. At least there was no trace of her presence when I entered the front hall.

"My office is through there," I said, indicating the door to their left as I turned up the gas lights. "Beulah has Sundays off, so you might want to keep your wraps until I rekindle the fire."

I busied myself with the fire and tried to ignore the way Mrs. Hamm was appraising my house. I had no doubt her appraisal was calculated with an eye toward her cousin's future. It was a little more comforting to see that Miss McGuire's interest seemed to be in my bookshelf. I didn't have a large library, but each volume was carefully chosen and well loved.

I lit the oil lamp on my desk to give us more illumination for our work, then walked over to where she was standing.

"I believe the code tables are in this," I said, pulling a slender blue volume with the faded gold government embossing on the stained cover.

"War memento?" she asked.

"You could say that," I said. "It was a gift from a dying friend."

"I'm sorry," she said. "I didn't mean to pry."

"Do you enjoy reading?" I asked, not wishing to delve into memories of the war.

"Oh yes," she said with enthusiasm, and then colored slightly as she caught sight of Mrs. Hamm's expression.

Her eyes turned back to the row of books. "Mark Twain, George Eliot, Jules Verne and Benjamin Franklin," she said. "You have somewhat varied taste in literature, Mr. Donnelly."

"There are some who would argue I have no taste at all, Miss McGuire," I replied. "Mr. Twain is the subject of much controversy, and Mr. Verne is considered to be more suitable for children, though I do hear his English translations compare most unfavorably to volumes in his native French."

"Much," she said. "His translators did not understand mathematics and did a poor job with the science."

"Then it is a pity that I must rely on the translators," I said. "I hope our own work this evening provides better translation of Mr. Peltmutter's writing."

"We had best get to it then," she said, smiling at me as I pulled a chair close enough for us to share the Morse Code Tables. "Cousin Mildred can only occupy herself for so long with her knitting."

"Don't mind me," Mrs. Hamm said, without glancing up from her work. "I seldom get to read anything more interesting than the children's schoolwork. Mr. Hamm has no interest in books. I have found your conversation a refreshing change."

"If you would prefer reading to your needlework, you are

welcome to help yourself to any volume you find interesting."

"If you're sure you don't mind," she said, already rising from her chair.

Miss McGuire and I settled into deciphering the notes, pausing now and again to allow the other to finish examining the code tables. Little by little I became so engrossed in work that I forgot everything else. I had chosen a set of papers holding mostly entries with the tobacco leaf, I was fairly sure that account was in Nathaniel Buckner's name. Now that I understood Peltmutter's system, I was able to discover he had systematically transferred money into several accounts at his bank. Only one large withdrawal had been taken from the account in the early years, but over the past year or so he had been making withdraws in continually larger amounts.

"Pardon me," Mrs. Hamm said, "I hate to interrupt, but it is getting rather late."

"My goodness," Miss McGuire exclaimed, glancing at the darkened windows. "I hadn't realized."

"Well, the boys do have school in the morning," Mrs. Hamm said.

"As do I," her cousin agreed.

"Forgive me for the imposition, ladies," I said. "Apparently the rumors of my thinking only of work have more merit than I realized. I'll see you home immediately."

Miss McGuire handed me a stack of papers more than twice as thick as the one in front of me.

"I think it is fairly clear these are accounts of some type," she said. "This latter part is different. I only got a page done, but it appears to be some sort of journal. I would be happy to finish the decoding if you would like."

"It would be a great help," I said. "With the police commander missing, I am going to be helping young Kent look for him."

"I'll be proctoring exams tomorrow," she said. "I should be able to work on this most of the day."

"Thank you, Miss McGuire," I said. "You've been a great help."

CHAPTER TWENTY-FOUR

I detested Frankfort Pike, not that the road had any fault. Thanks to the tolls that had to be paid out every five miles, the pike was one of the best-maintained oiled roads in the state. Most of the road between Lexington and Frankfort was broad enough for three wagons to run side by side without any driver being forced from the highway. The scenery was breathtaking. Horses and cattle grazed in the white fenced fields of bluegrass that ran all the way to the horizon. Stone fences, a legacy of the influx of Irish stonemasons, lined much of the road. Unfortunately, the pike also held reminders of another legacy. It gave travelers a close up view of Kentucky's former slave farms, small log cottages, and stone or brick windowless jails, sitting close to the stately farm owners' homes.

Commander Slayton's house was on one of those farms. His slaves had been the bulk of his wealth. Once they were freed, the Slayton family was left without the necessary wealth to maintain their lifestyle. An observant person could quickly spot the signs of economic distress. Slayton still kept the three-story brick house in adequate repair, but recently replaced roof shingles didn't exactly match to the original color. Outbuildings, particularly the no longer useful slave cabins, were running to seed. Here and there, his stone fence was in need of mending. Slowly, prairie grass and wild berry vines were reclaiming fields, save those closest to the house.

I glanced back at the little buggy I had rented for Tad and Miss Belle as we approached the house. It was hard to tell how he was feeling behind the bandages. Even if they were close enough to speak, I didn't know what to say. I could hardly reassure him that his cousin was safe. Both of us had come close to death at the hands of

KGC members. So I sat beside Doc Haydon, pretending to admire the scenery, while Tad followed along behind, making no effort to hide his admiration of Miss Belle.

Just past the house, Doc Haydon turned off the main road and entered Slayton's farm road. Tad pulled his buggy alongside the doctor's, no doubt to protect Miss Belle from dust now that we were on a simple dirt lane.

"This is your house?" I heard Belle say, and glanced over at the astonished face of the young courtesan. "Why, it's bigger than Miss Hill's."

Tad's neck turned red.

"It's not mine," he said. "I'd never been in such a grand house afore I came to live with Cousin James. Ma's whole house would fit in his ballroom."

"I'd lay odds you like your Ma's place better," she said.

"That's a fact," Tad said.

Belle giggled.

"Not that this ain't a nice place," Tad quickly added, turning a deeper shade of red. "But kind of big and empty. Cousin James don't use more than three or four rooms."

"Well, if he doesn't answer the door, we'll look through those rooms first," she said. "His house looks deserted."

"His horse ain't here. He keeps her in the first stall."

"Maybe he's away on business," she suggested.

"He wouldn't a left on the Centennial. He was supposed to be on the grandstand with the other judges."

I didn't think it was likely that Slayton would voluntarily miss the Centennial parade either. From what I knew of James Slayton, he liked nothing better than being at the center of a social gathering. His ability to charm seemed to be his main attribute for being chosen Commander of Police.

"Does he leave messages for you when he goes away?" I asked.

"I don't know. Cousin James never went away. He hardly ever leaves the house unless he has some official duty to perform."

Belle placed her delicate white-gloved hand through the bend of his arm.

"Perhaps we should go inside," she said softly. "He mighta left a note."

The only note we found was the one Doc Haydon stuck into

the doorframe to let him know Tad had been shot. Doc picked it up and put it in his pocket.

"It doesn't look like the Commander has been home," he said, as Tad opened the door.

The three of us followed him into the entry hall.

"Tad, you know the house best. Where should we start?" I asked.

"I don't know," he said. "What are we looking for?"

"Anything that might tell us why he is missing," Doc Haydon said. "Where does he keep his personal papers? Does he have an office?"

"There is a library through there," Tad said, pointing to the right. "He doesn't keep many interesting books. Mostly farming, horse breeding, geography, that kind of stuff."

"Horse breeding sounds pretty interesting to me," Doc Haydon said.

I tried not to smile, remembering Tad's dime novel with its heroic officer emblazoned on the cover. I imagined that anything less action-filled would seem tedious to him. Tad tried too hard to appear grown up, but at seventeen he was still on the cusp of manhood.

"Someone's been here," I said when Tad opened the door to the library. "There's been a fire recently."

Instinctively, my eyes searched out the fireplace. One glance confirmed that the fire had not been built for warmth. An ample supply of firewood was at hand, but the ash littering the grate was mostly paper.

"See anything missing, Tad?" I asked.

He looked around the room carefully.

"Some of his books," he said. "And there was a picture of him and his pa in his uniform on the desk."

Tad looked confused.

"Why would anybody take that? The frame was silver, but it wasn't very big."

I had a bad feeling that I had been wrong about why Tad's cousin was missing. A family photograph and a few favorite books were the sorts of items a man could easily grab if he were in a hurry packing.

"Perhaps you should check the rest of the house, see if anything else is missing," I suggested.

Tad seemed reluctant to leave the room until Belle put a hand on his arm.

"I'll go with you," she said. "Maybe make a list."

"Doc, do you have your magnifying glass with you?" I asked.

"I think so," he said, fishing around in his coat pocket. "Ah! Here it is."

The doctor came over to where I was sorting through the ashes with the tip of my pencil.

"Finding anything useful?"

"I'm not sure," I said. "I haven't had time to get new spectacles."

"You need to get yourself one of these," he said, as he handed me his magnifying glass. "It wouldn't hurt to spend a little less time reading in bad light either. You ought to have some respect for your eyes."

"You aren't going to join Mrs. Hamm in telling me how to live my life are you, Doc?"

He laughed.

"I hear that Mrs. Hamm has found you a nice Irish Catholic girl this time."

"Miss Mary Katherine McGuire," I said, "I had dinner with her and the Hamms last night."

"Ah!" Doc Haydon said, laughing. "And how did that go?"

"It was interesting," I said. "She teaches mathematics at one of the ladies' academies. I forget which one. It turned out she had some knowledge of ciphers and did a large part of translating those papers we found yesterday, even took some with her to work on today."

Doc Haydon's blue eyes reflected the humor in his voice.

"Sounds like you're going to have trouble finding a reason to avoid this one," he said. "Mrs. Hamm isn't easily deterred."

I grimaced, making the side of my face hurt.

"Don't do that; you'll tear the stitches," the doc ordered.

"Sorry," I mumbled. "I got maneuvered into taking her and Mrs. Hamm to next weeks' concert in Woodland Park."

"I don't think reinjuring yourself is a good way to get out of it," he said between chuckles.

"It's not funny."

"That depends on whether you are the victim of a matchmaker's machinations, or merely an innocent bystander. From where I stand, it's hilarious."

"I don't have time for this," I said.

"Dating or marriage?"

I glared at him.

"You never know, Ness," he said, "it could be the best thing for you."

"Doc!"

"Oh, don't look so shocked. You know I'm right."

I didn't answer. Instead, I picked up the poker and shoved it under the mound of ash a bit harder than necessary, striking something soft in the center ash the fire had not consumed. I fished it out with the hooked edge of the poker.

"Holy Mother of Christ!" Haydon swore as I stood up, still holding my discovery on the hook.

My face blanched as I watched the layers of damp clothing unrolled. The breeches were coated in the same mix of muddy clay and blood Sergeant Hamm and Officer Watts had been covered in while searching Nathaniel Buckner's grave.

Doc Haydon and I just stood there looking at each other, neither of us eager to voice what we were both thinking. Commander Slayton had to have been in that grave. Not with us, not when the body was discovered, which only left the time of the murder.

"I don't want Tad to see this," I said, "not yet."

Doc Haydon searched the room until he found an old newspaper.

We bundled the scorched clothing inside and he took it out to the wagon.

While he was gone, I picked up the paper fragments and read through the text that remained. They appeared to be mostly invoices. Not enough survived the flames to tell if they were paid. I wrapped them in a piece of paper and put them in my pocket just as Tad and Belle came rushing into the room.

"Mr. Donnelly," Tad said excitedly. His words came out in a rush. "Cousin James must have had to go somewhere. His trunk and most of his clothes are gone. I guess he just didn't have time to tell me. He must be all right, though. He packed and all."

"Looks like he wasn't kidnapped anyway," I said. "Why don't we go back to town and start checking with the livery stables and depots? If he took a trunk, he must have either rented a wagon or taken a train."

Belle arched an eyebrow at my expression, but didn't ask.

I didn't like the way this was all coming together. The portion of Peltmutter's papers we had deciphered indicated there were five men, besides himself, for whom he had made regular weekly deposits for at his bank. If Miss McGuire's calculations were correct, the combined sum of those deposits exceeded three quarters of a million dollars. Sergeant Hamm and I surmised that two of those men were Nathaniel Buckner and Isaiah Malthus. It now appeared that the star represented Police Commander James Slayton. For Tad's sake, I wanted to be wrong.

We had gone less than a mile when I spotted Sergeant Hamm hunkered low on his horse and riding at full gallop.

Doc Haydon halted the buggy and waited for the sergeant, who practically leapt from his horse and ran over to where we were sitting.

"Donnelly," he shouted, "The Missus came by with a note from Mary Kate. You better see this."

He thrust the note at me and waited impatiently while I read through it.

Mr. Donnelly,

Please forgive the lack of details in my message. I write this note in haste, as I must get it to Cousin Mildred quickly. It is urgent that someone get word to the Nicodemus wagon train departed this past week with those colored settlers, who must be nearing the Ohio by now. They are in danger of being impressed into slavery. Mr. Peltmutter writes of a large tract of land purchased in the Amazon where a slave state will be reestablished and a plan to capture these poor souls at the river where they and their goods can be easily transported south.

I urge you go at once, or send someone trusted. I would telegraph the western authorities, but we both know law cannot be relied upon to take seriously the protection of colored persons. If they could, Lexington would not have its current problems with the Klan.

Most sincerely yours,

Miss Mary Katherine McGuire

Unable to believe the words on the page, I read through it again, then wordlessly handed it to the doctor.

"My duty is here," Sergeant Hamm said, somewhat

defensively. "I do take the protection of the colored as seriously as anyone else, but can't leave the city unprotected to chase down a wagon train. You've got to catch up with those colored folks, Ness. Let 'em know what they're riding into."

"They've had more than two days' head start," I replied. "We'll be damned lucky to catch up before they're ambushed."

Muscles in Doc Haydon's jaw tightened, and his face turned an angry red. The arteries in his neck protruded and seemed to turn dark purple under the red skin as he read Miss McGuire's note.

"Old Sam might not be able to catch up," he said, looking at his horse, "but he can get us to Midway Station before the Louisville train arrives."

Sergeant Hamm lifted a gun belt from his saddlehorn and took a box of shells from his pocket. "Borrowed these from the stationhouse," he said. "You might need a sight more than two shots."

"Tell Tad to see Miss Belle home," I said, as Doc Haydon's little piano box buggy lurched forward.

Doc drove Old Sam hard all the way to Midway, but when we reached the livery stable he paid extra to have his standard bred given special care until we returned. I couldn't blame him for that. Sam had faithfully driven him to medical emergencies at all hours for more than a dozen years. Today he had brought us on another lifesaving mission, though not the medical kind.

We heard the train whistling at the station stop just as we turned the buggy over to the liveryman. I slung the gun belt over my shoulder and headed for the depot.

"Two tickets to Louisville," I said.

The agent looked at my battered face, then the gun.

"We don't want no trouble on the train," he said.

"I think my friend has seen enough trouble," Doc Haydon said, in a friendly tone. "Don't you?"

The ticket master laughed.

"He does look like he came out on the worst end of it," he said.

He pushed the tickets through the window at us just as the train rolled to a stop. "That'll be four-fifty," he said.

I handed him five dollars and waited for impatiently for my four bits before running to catch the train.

Doc Haydon barely let me sit down before he pulled out Miss

McGuire's note and demanded to know everything.

"It's a long story, Doc," I told him.

"We're a good four hours out of Louisville," he said. "I've got nothing but time."

"I don't know where to start," I replied.

"The beginning is usually a good place," he said dryly.

"You won't like it."

Doc started to turn red again.

"All right," I said. "From the beginning. That would have been about August of sixty-three, when the Knights started stealing payroll shipments from the trains."

"Don't tell me Buckner was killed over that," he snapped. "Nobody in their right mind would leave a man buck naked in a whorehouse over a payroll."

"Considering everything that has gone on, I think it is highly questionable that any of these men are in their right minds," I growled at him. "Besides, you said start at the beginning. That was the robberies."

I must have gotten a little loud. I noticed several of the passengers look at us askance. One lady traveling with a passel of children got up and moved to the opposite end of the car.

"Okay," Doc said in a lower voice, "how do these robberies fit into Buckner's death?"

"To understand their motives, you have to understand what they did with the stolen gold. The Union Army was offering a hefty reward for information on the thefts. While the military was in charge, they couldn't do anything but hide all that money and wait for the army to move out of Lexington. Then there was the depression. Anybody in the state throwing around large sums of money would have raised questions. That's where Peltmutter stepped in. He was only a minor officer at National Bank, but it was the perfect position to allow him to set up accounts. Little by little, Peltmutter, fed the stolen money into special accounts he set up for each of the surviving members of his Circle."

"So Buckner and Peltmutter both belonged to the same Circle," he said.

"Yes," I replied. "They used the stolen money to buy Buckner his partnership in the Lexington Cigar Company. That fit very well with the Knights' plan to control all of the New World crops. Lexington is the largest tobacco market in the world, and Buckner had his fingers into every aspect of the business."

"Then killing him makes no sense," Doc said. "Buckner's business partner has one foot in the grave, and his son is barely of age. I doubt the boy even knows his pa's involvement with the Knights."

"Killing him may not have been in their best business interest, but the Knights are an unforgiving lot. Buckner had his fingers in the till. He started using his account at National Bank as if the money really were his own. The Knights didn't like him using their money to fund his personal spending. My guess is, he was using it to fund his campaign to run all the prostitutes and saloonkeepers out of Fayette County. I believe that's why he was left at Miss Hill's bawdyhouse; to send a message. For a man of Mr. Buckner's austere habits, and venomous view of Miss Belle Brezing, being found naked and in her company was the most personally humiliating death they could give him. It was a warning to the others to not make the same mistake."

"What about Malthus?" Doc asked. "Why was Buckner trying to reach him?"

"Probably the same reason, I'll bet if we look at the account set up for Mr. Malthus we'll find that he was dipping into the money for personal use."

"I don't recall Malthus being involved in the Abstention activities," Doc said.

"I think Mr. Malthus did something far more egregious. Compared to Malthus, Buckner got off easy. A gunshot wound is a sight less painful than being horsewhipped and having salt thrown into the wounds."

"What did he do to deserve that?" Doc asked.

"I have reason to believe he used his position on the National Bank Board of Directors to divert their funds to the support of his colored mistress and their bastard son. It must have been an astonishing revelation when his fellow Knights discovered Malthus was keeping a colored woman in such luxury. But it would have been particularly galling to see the boy passing as white. Malthus even sent him to the military academy to attend classes where some of them had graduated."

Doc Haydon stared at me in open-mouthed disbelief. After a moment, he closed his mouth then opened it as if to speak, but no words came out. Haydon turned his head and sat there staring out the window at the scenery.

I shifted uncomfortably on the wooden seat. My broken arm was itching fiercely and the constant rocking of the railcar issued painful reminders of every blow my body suffered. I wished I knew what my friend was thinking. It bothered me that he didn't even look my direction.

"What do you think will become of the boy?" Doc said, after a long while.

"I don't know," I replied. "In the picture his mother had, he looks to be a few years younger than Tad. Not old enough to strike out on his own yet. Why do you ask?"

Doc shrugged. He took a silver flask out of his breast pocket and offered me a drink.

I took a swallow of his bourbon and passed the flask back.

He drank it dry, wiped his mouth with his handkerchief, and retreated back to his thoughts. The demons his mind unleashed were not the sort he wanted to share with me.

CHAPTER TWENTY-FIVE

I awoke disoriented and unsure of what was happening. Doc Haydon was still sitting by the window looking out at the lengthening shadows.

"Where are we?" I asked.

"Still about an hour from the station," he said. "Have a good nap?"

"Can't say these seats are made for sleeping," I said, knocking on the hard wooden benches.

He gave me a wry smile.

"When did you start thinking Commander Slayton was behind the murders?" he asked.

The question came from nowhere. I had to think about how to answer. There were actions that should have made me suspicious, such as the way he had planted Tad in my investigation. The boy had told me his cousin was helping him with his reports. Pumping him for information was more like it. He had used the lad to follow my every move. At the Buckners' funeral, he had deliberately pulled Tad and Sergeant Hamm away to prevent me from questioning Peltmutter. Slayton had been behind the beating I received. He probably stayed away from the Centennial because the bullet hole I left in him would have raised questions he couldn't answer. I felt like a fool for not suspecting him sooner.

"This morning," I admitted. "I should have realized sooner."

Haydon shrugged.

"What are you going to tell the boy?" he asked.

"I guess I'll deal with that when the time comes," I said.

"Tad looks up to his cousin," Doc said. "It won't be easy to break the news."

"I know," I said miserably. "He hardly knew his own father. His cousin James is his hero."

"Speaking of Cousin James," Doc said, "what do you plan to do when we catch up to him?"

"Do you think I could get away with stringing him up on the spot?" I asked.

"Right now I would be happy to help," the doctor said dryly. "But seriously, Ness, what do you have in mind?"

"I was thinking we should head toward the river. If they aren't at the ferry crossing yet, they should be soon."

"What then?" he asked. "There's two of us, and who knows how many of the Knights are involved?"

"Let's hope we catch up with the settlers before they reach the crossing. If I can convince them that they would be safer crossing somewhere upstream, it would help. It would be easier to look for Slayton if we didn't have to worry about innocent people getting caught in the crossfire."

"And if we don't reach them before they get on the ferry landing?" Doc asked.

"I don't know," I said. "Those people left Lexington because they wanted to determine their own destiny. They didn't even want to live where white people were in charge. I expect they'll fight to the death to remain free."

We arrived at Louisville's Union Station just as the sun was setting. I stood up stiffly and fastened the gun belt in place. As Doc Haydon and I made our way through the throng of passengers waiting to board, I found myself constantly reminded of the seriousness of our business by the unfamiliar weight of the revolver. At least it was the left arm that was broken; handling the heavy weapon would be difficult enough with only one hand.

The livery stable was on the river side of the depot. Since I lacked Doc Haydon's eye for horseflesh, I paid the liveryman while he picked out mounts for us. I'm sure the entire transaction took less than ten minutes, but it seemed an eternity before we were riding west in search of the wagon train.

On Fourth Street, we realized the enormity of the job we had taken on. There were more than two hundred settlers instead of the seventy or so people I expected to find. Wagons and carts of every shape and size lined the road all the way down to the banks of the Ohio River. Some looked so old and poorly constructed that I couldn't imagine them surviving the trip west. Crude, hand painted signs gave badly spelled words of encouragement to the hundreds of colored settlers waiting for the ferries to dock and carry them away.

Here and there I picked up snatches of conversation, dreams of Kansas, and wild expectations of the lives awaiting them there. My first thoughts were of the disappointment these innocents were bound to have when they faced the endless miles of untamed prairie that would be their new home. Then I remembered the men who would steal that dream, and the reasons so many wished to live far from any white man.

The ferry was large, but not big enough to accommodate all of the settlers waiting. I wondered how many would squeeze onto tonight's crossing. Unless the doc and I were successful, those left on the shore cursing their luck would be far luckier than the ones who boarded the steamer.

I pushed on, angry and determined to find Slayton.

This would be the last ferry crossing of the day. Slayton would have to make his move now. I turned my collar up and pulled my hat down low over my brow, to conceal my face and hide the mop of red hair that could so easily allow Slayton to recognize me.

Doc Haydon followed my lead, and together we boarded the ferry and made our way up the ramp to the level reserved for white people.

A handful of other passengers milled about the deck or hung near the railings waving good-bye to loved ones watching them go. Doc and I found a place further along the railing where we could see the stream of settlers pouring into the lower deck. I kept a close eye on the road leading to the river, looking for signs of trouble, but spotted nothing suspicious.

The crewmen loading passengers were getting ready to rope off the gangplank over the protest of those being left waiting. I was starting to worry. With the ferry nearly loaded and preparing to cast off, I was beginning to wonder if Miss McGuire had sent us on a wild goose chase. One of the crewmen lifted his arms and pushed one of the less subservient colored men back as he tried to gain entry to the boat. The man backed down rather than risk an altercation with a white man in front of witnesses, but I noticed a short barrel shotgun holstered under the crewman's coat.

"They're running the boat," I whispered.

"What?" Doc asked.

I tried to keep my voice low.

"Look at the crewman pulling up the gangplank," I said. "Can you see the shotgun?"

His face was grim when he looked back at me.

"No river boatman would carry that kind of weapon. It would be a nuisance when he was trying to do his job."

I nodded.

"How many men do you think they have?" Doc asked.

"Not counting the boiler room, maybe four or five." I replied.

Doc Haydon ran his hand over the rough red gray stubble on his chin.

"We could probably block the boiler room door, but I don't cotton to going up against shotguns," he said.

"Maybe if we make the first move, we could take one or two out before they know what we're up to," I said. "At the moment, they aren't close enough together to help each other."

The whistle sounded as the two of us drifted back toward the steps. The other white passengers didn't seem to notice as we headed down to the lower deck and the guts of the steamer. I leaned against the bulkhead, my hand near the butt of my pistol, standing watch while Doc Haydon latched the steel door leading into the belly of the vessel. Over the mechanical racket of the engine, I doubted if the crew in the boiler room paid any attention to the sound of the latch sliding closed.

"Shouldn't be any trouble from that quarter," Doc said, coming up beside me. "What now?"

"I don't want to start a panic," I said.

"With all those children and animals, it could get ugly," Doc said, taking a lethal-looking knife from his pocket. Let's see if we can take out one or two quietly."

We didn't try being inconspicuous as we moved through the crowded lower deck, looking for the Knights pretending to be members of the ferry crew. Blending in was impossible for the two of us among a sea of colored faces. But, most of the people were either at the rail or tending to their animals. They ignored us with the studied practice of those accustomed to staying out of white folks' way.

The two Knights securing the gangplank and closing the heavy steel doors were far from their compatriots. With so many wagons crowded together they couldn't even see each other. Nervous animals and frightened children added to the general confusion, making it all too easy for us to approach men busy with preparations for getting underway without being seen until it was too late.

Perhaps there is a learned callousness in a surgeon that hardens them to the necessity of cutting human flesh. Or maybe the years of carving secrets out of the bodies of the dead killed off any revulsion the doctor may have had to sinking a knife into another man. I only know that Doc Haydon handled his knife with a cold, surgical efficiency that made me appreciate the fact I was not an enemy of his.

The first man crumpled without a sound.

"Get his gun," Doc said quietly. "I'll take care of his friend."

This was a side of Doc Haydon I hadn't seen before and wasn't sure I liked, but I did as he told me. After I took his shotgun, I did a quick search of the body for other weapons, and then shoved him behind the spools of rope near the hull.

There wasn't a lot of light at this hour, but if anyone saw what we were doing, they made no effort to stop us. Still, I didn't want to leave the body where it could be easily spotted. By the time I managed to hide the murdered man one-handed, Doc was back. The shotgun in his hand and the revolver tucked into his belt told me all I wanted to know about what had happened to the other Knight.

"What do you suppose they did with the real crew?" Doc asked.

"I'm hoping they are somewhere on board," I said.

"Not interested in trying to dock a steamboat?" he asked.

"No," I said, "but I don't think we are headed for the dock."

He gazed over the railing at the gathering darkness for a few seconds considering our direction.

"Could just be turning," he said.

"Picking up speed," I replied, giving him a doubtful look.

Doc shrugged and headed toward the steps with me close on his heels. Behind us were two dead men and a deck full of passengers unaware that they were caught up in the madness of a group of men determined to enslave them. I didn't know what lay ahead, but there was no turning back now. We had made our choice before we boarded the westbound train at Midway. Either we would see these people safely on their way west, or die in the attempt.

Unlike the settlers below, most of the people on the upper deck crossed the river regularly and knew the riverboat should have begun the turn toward the west bank. We were met with suspicion and anger when we stepped onto the deck. The doctor didn't hesitate. He leveled the shotgun at the cluster of men glaring at us.

"This boat has been taken over by a pack of criminals," he said in a menacing tone. "We aim to take it back. Any objections?"

In mass the cluster of passengers took an involuntary step back.

"Good," I said. "You might want to stay out of the way. There's likely to be some gunplay."

One man stepped forward.

"I reckon you could use some help," he said.

"Count me in," said another.

I glanced at the doctor.

Doc Haydon nodded agreement just as two others stepped away from the group.

I balanced the barrel of the shotgun across my broken arm and led the way up the dark stairway to the pilothouse. Unlike the deck below us, only two oil lamps burned near the pilothouse door on the top deck. A sign heavily decorated in carved French scroll hung between the two smokestacks, and the polished brass back plates of the lamps reflected patches of light into the ornate sign, casting long distorted shadows across the plank deck.

I recognized Slayton from his stance. He was standing to the right of the pilot, just inside the cabin. Shooting was too good for him. I wanted him to suffer as he had made me suffer. It took all my willpower to fight back the urge to rush headlong into the pilothouse and wrap the gun around the side of his head.

Common sense won out over the rush of emotion. Somewhere up here there was probably at least one other man. I turned my head slowly as I searched for him. Behind me I could sense the restlessness of the men. I had to move soon.

Staying to the shadows as much as I could, I crept out onto the deck.

The first shot sent my hat rolling across the deck. I don't know how many followed. Oblivious to my old injuries, I hit the deck and rolled. Pain shot up the side of my injured face as the stitches ripped loose. My head hurt so much from rolling across the deck, that I was briefly distracted from the complaints of my broken arm. Once behind the corner of the pilothouse, I tried to sit up and assess the situation. For a long moment I just sat there with my back against the bulkhead trying not to be sick. Bullets seemed to be flying from every direction with little effect.

"Make those shots count," I heard Doc shout from behind a cargo store to my left.

The men trying to help us weren't listening. A double-barreled shotgun blast followed his order. Buckshot hammered the sides of the cargo store like raindrops on a tin roof but did little damage.

The shooter, however, had exposed his location while making his shot and paid for the mistake with his life. It is doubtful that any of the men returning fire would ever know which bullet hit the fallen man first.

I breathed a sigh of relief when the smoke cleared enough to see that Doc Haydon was unhurt.

Clutching the shotgun, I searched for a likely target, but both sides seemed to have taken Doc Haydon's order to heart after the first killing. It was just as well. In the darkness, I couldn't be sure which of the men were with us.

Despite the coolness of the evening a trickle of sweat rolled down my face. I wanted to wipe it away, but dared not move for fear of giving away my position. In the momentary lull I could almost feel the eyes searching for movement. Waiting. Listening to the slow splash of the turning wheel as it propelled us over black water.

Somewhere on the shore, a mother called her children into the house.

Closer, the click of a door latch. My eyes were suddenly alert. The door handle turned slowly. The door cracked open, throwing a shaft of light onto the dark deck.

My finger lay ready, beside the twin triggers of the shotgun, impatient for Slayton to appear.

I wanted to bring him down.

"Mr. Donnelly," Beulah's voice came in a frightened gasp. "Please don't shoot Mr. Donnelly. It's me, Beulah. The commander says to tell you he has me and the crew here and he's gonna kill us all if you don't give yourself up."

"You've got five minutes to decide," Slayton shouted somewhere behind her, as the door slammed shut.

My brain ran through every expletive I had ever heard. All of them together didn't seem obscene enough for the situation.

Beulah was like a mother to me, but giving myself up wouldn't help. He would take greater pleasure in killing her in front of me. Besides I knew Beulah would prefer being lowered into a pit of rattlesnakes than be returned to slavery and there wasn't a woman alive more afraid of snakes than her.

Afraid of snakes…I told myself it was a crazy idea, but even as my brain argued it wouldn't work, my eyes were on the yards of cotton bandages holding my broken arm in place. I unlaced my boots and pulled off the thick wool socks under them. I had the better part of five minutes to fashion a pair of black socks into a snake that would scare the bejesus out of my housekeeper.

I saw Doc Haydon watching me from his hiding place and motioned him to come closer, then went back to pulling strips of bandaging from my arm.

"Donnelly, what the hell are you up to?" he said quietly. "That bone hasn't had time to heal."

"Get ready to rush the door," I replied.

"Are you crazy?" he asked. "Slayton will kill Beulah."

"Would you rather be dead or his slave?" I replied.

The door opened again, but before Beulah could say a word I flung the makeshift snake at her.

"Snake!" she screamed, grabbing her skirts and dancing around wildly. "Snake. Kill it. Kill it…"

Commander Slayton tried to grab her and pull her back inside, but the police commander was no match for Beulah. Her hysterical screaming and flailing around distracted him. He didn't realize he had left the shelter of the pilothouse until it was too late.

"Get back inside, you fool," his confederate shouted, coming out of his hiding place. "I'll take care of her."

Instinct took over and I emptied both barrels of the shotgun into the man's midsection before it registered that the voice belonged to the burly man I had first seen at the inquest in Frankfort.

Doc Haydon cut off Slayton's escape route, not that it mattered to Commander Slayton. The gunshots fired so close to Beulah had driven her into further hysterics. She turned on Slayton, pummelling him with both fists, screaming at him, calling him every sort of villain, as she meted out abuse.

Slayton tried to fight back, but years of soft living made him a poor match for Beulah's fast, powerful hands. Beulah lashed out at him with all the pent up anger slavery burned into her soul. Oblivious to his ineffectual blows, she struck him about the neck and face over and over again. Under the relentless battering, Slayton was forced back.

"That's enough Beulah," I shouted, "he's finished."

She either couldn't or wouldn't hear me.

Beulah had Slayton trapped against the railing, beating him like a rag doll when I realized what was happening and rushed forward.

Doc Haydon reached her first, grabbing her around the waist with both arms, just as the railing failed.

Slayton screamed as he disappeared from sight.

I saw Beulah's feet slip over the edge as I grabbed for any part of her I could reach. Just as I thought her weight was going to pull all three of us overboard, a strong rope looped around us, drawing us together, and gradually pulling us back toward safety.

Beulah, Doc Haydon, and I landed in a jumble of arms and legs on the hard wooden deck. My heart pounded in my ears. I could hardly breathe with Beulah's weight crushing down on me, but we were alive.

Commander Slayton hadn't fared as well. Someone said he had been run through by the spiked blades of the great paddlewheel driving the boat. I noticed a few men looking over the edge of the railing, but had no desire to join them. My thoughts were of Ness and the shallow unmarked grave I had left him in because of Slayton and his ilk. With so many of the Bluegrass Circle dead, it was unlikely that I would ever find out who had pulled the trigger. It didn't seem to matter as much to me now. I had found the stolen payrolls he was searching for and shattered the Knights' grand plan. Ness would have been content to close the case with that.

CHAPTER TWENTY-SIX

Doc Haydon worked without talking, cutting strips of bandages, dunking them in wet plaster and applying them to my greased arm, which Beulah held firmly in place.

I tried to look contrite, but Doc wasn't buying it and neither was Beulah.

I wasn't surprised that Doc was mad at me. This was the third time he had set my broken arm.

Beulah was another matter. Instead of being grateful that I had rescued her from Slayton, she was pouting over the snake. Never mind that I could have been killed. It didn't matter that it wasn't a real snake, or that I had said I was sorry at least a dozen times. Beulah wasn't of a mind to accept an apology. I wasn't sure I could stand being trapped between the two of them for the four hours it would take for my cast to dry.

Luckily I didn't have to be alone with them that long. Long before Doc finished applying plaster, Sergeant Hamm poked his head through the office door and asked if we could answer a few questions.

Doc nodded, and slathered another layer of bandaging onto my arm.

"Might as well," he said. "Donnelly won't be moving out of that chair for hours."

I rolled my eyes, which brought another glare from Beulah.

"Commander's body's due to arrive on the afternoon train," Sergeant Hamm said, as the door swung open. "The telegram from Louisville is a mite short on details."

Beulah's grip tightened as Tad crept into the room behind the sergeant.

The boy's ill-fitting black suit smelled of mothballs and hung like decay from his scarecrow frame. His hat was pulled low, obscuring his eyes, but nothing could hide the naked grief in his demeanor.

Beulah and I glanced at each other in silent understanding that neither would shatter the boy's illusions about his cousin's character. Haydon confirmed the pact with a nearly imperceptible nod of his head.

"What do you want to know?" Doc Haydon asked.

"Start with how the Commander got hisself killed," Sergeant Hamm said.

"There was a fight on board the ferry," Doc said dryly. "During the ruckus a railing broke and the Commander fell into the wheel."

Tad's features twisted into an expression of pure misery.

"It was quick," Doc said, more for the boy's benefit than Sergeant Hamm's. "The Commander probably didn't suffer at all."

"Just what was he doing there?" Hamm asked.

"Didn't get the chance to ask," I replied. "By the time we got there the KGC had taken over the ferry. We had our hands full taking it back."

"Are you two telling me that the Commander just happened to be on the same ferry the KGC took?"

"Maybe he figured out their plot on his own," Haydon said. "He's had a keen interest in this case."

"He did look over all my reports," Tad interjected. "Maybe that's why he left in such a hurry. He must have been trying to stop them all by himself."

"Huh," Hamm said.

I knew he didn't believe James Slayton was the sort of man to stand up to the Knights alone, but prayed he would let the matter drop.

"Miz Beulah, how do you fit in to this?" Sergeant Hamm asked.

"Me," she exclaimed. "I ain't got no part in this at all. I was mindin' my own beeswax and them scoundrels throwed a sack over my head and dragged me into a wagon. Next thing I know, I was trussed up like a roaster and carried onto the train."

"Did you see who abducted you?"

I drew in a sharp breath at the question. I had never known Beulah to tell an outright lie and wasn't sure she could.

"A body can't see nothin' from inside a tater sack. That ain't no way to treat a poor ol' colored woman. What do you reckon they would want with me, anyhow?"

"That's a good question. Donnelly? Any bright ideas?"

"It is no secret that I am fond of Beulah," I replied. "Her kidnappers knew I was getting close. They thought I would back down if they hid behind her. Cowardly, but that's hardly surprising."

"So they went to all that trouble just to get you to back down?"

"These men like hurting people," I said. "Beulah is about the closest thing to family I have left."

"Speaking of family," Doc said, "did you find the families of those four men downstairs?"

"Between Mr. Peltmutter's journal and the city's Freedman's Bureau records, we were able to identify them," Hamm said. "We haven't been able to locate any kin. Seems all four of them were traveling around the state raising funds and organizing coloreds to move west. Nobody I've located knows where they live."

"How much money were they supposed to have raised?" Doc Haydon asked.

"According to Cousin Mary Katherine, they had raised over six thousand dollars for seeds and supplies," he said sadly. "I guess that's the last those folks will see of their money."

"I wouldn't say that," I replied. "I haven't had the chance to count it, but there was box full of money with that journal. The question is, why did Peltmutter want it?"

"That's a lot of money," Tad said.

"Yes," I replied, "but not nearly as much as they had stashed in his account. The reward money for recovering what he and his confederates stole is more than he took from those men."

"It was enough to put back what he had taken," Hamm said. "He knew that Buckner and Malthus were done for. All he cared about was saving his own skin. I guess he didn't have time to put it back before his brother Knights caught up to him."

"They didn't kill him for the money," I said. "I doubt that they even knew about that underground jail of his. Peltmutter was a coward. He had already given them Buckner to save his own skin. The KGC killed him to shut him up. They made an example of him to keep anyone else from talking."

"Do you think you can prove that in court?" Hamm asked.

"What's the point?" Doc asked. "There's nobody left alive to prosecute."

"Can we at least drop the charges against Miss Belle?" Tad asked.

Beulah turned toward me so Tad couldn't see her grin.

"Donnelly, when you get home, you can tell Miss Belle that the charges have been dropped," Sergeant Hamm said, looking directly at me. "But next time you hide a fugitive from the law under your roof, don't expect me to look the other way."

CIRCLE OF DISHONOR
AUTHOR'S NOTES

One of the questions I am often asked about writing historical mystery is: "What's real?" The question isn't an easy one to answer. Novels are works of fiction. Nessa Donnelly and her world exist in my imagination, and hopefully that world becomes real in the minds of readers. It is a place I would like to see people visit again and again. The borders of that world are the covers of my books.

Lexington, Kentucky and the other places mentioned in my book are actual places. Telling a good historical story means that fact and fiction have to be carefully shaped to fit the plot. Throughout the book, I have tried to remain true to the documented history of Kentucky and to the historical figures presented in this work.

Countless hours of research have gone into the writing of *Circle of Dishonor*. I am grateful to the University of Kentucky and Transylvania University for opening their Special Collections to me. I also owe a debt of gratitude to the Lexington Public Library for the wealth of historical newspapers in their Kentucky Room. The Kentucky Digital Library and the Lexington History Museum's online collections were invaluable to my work. All of these sources contributed to my writing.

In answer to "What's real?" The Pinkertons were active in Kentucky during the Civil War, and they did have female agents. The Sisters of Mercy and the Sisters of Charity are doing the work attributed to them in my book. Buildings and events named in the book are based on true accounts in the historical records. Where possible, I have consulted the actual words of historical people in an effort to capture some facets of their personalities.

There are holes in the historical record and disputes among

scholars. Where that has happened, I used the prerogative of a fiction writer to take liberties with the truth. In other words, when I could not find any information on a subject, I made stuff up to fit with the characters in my story.

Below are more detailed notes on what was pulled from the pages of history:

KNIGHTS OF THE GOLDEN CIRCLE

The Knights of the Golden Circle were a secret society of Southern sympathizers who united to promote the interest of Southern slaveholders. The KGC drew a circle on a map of the Americas encompassing the Southern United States, the islands of the Caribbean, Mexico, Central America, and portions of South America (particularly a large portion of Brazil). The idea behind the group was to control the world through controlling the production and sale of the major New World crops, i.e. rice, sugar, cotton, tobacco, coffee, and indigo.

George Bickley, the Virginia-born founder of the KGC, organized the first castle in Cincinnati, Ohio in 1854. During the Civil War it is estimated that in Kentucky alone there were about 400,000 members. (To place that number in perspective, the entire free male population of the state was roughly 500,000.) The KGC ran on secrets. Secret handshakes, symbols, codes, ciphers, and rituals are all part of the mystique surrounding the Knights. The ritual used in *Circle of Dishonor* is based on fact. It called for a gruesome death for those who revealed KGC secrets.

One of the primary objectives of the KGC organization was the annexation of Mexico and the division of the country into fifteen new slave states. It was an ambitious goal, and one that made them particularly popular in Texas. During the years leading up to the Civil War, at least thirty-two castles of the KGC formed in Texas.

The KGC fell out of favor when their attempts to annex Mexico failed, but members still remained active throughout the Civil War. Lincoln often referred to the KGC as the fifth column, which is perhaps where the term originated. It is believed that the KGC was involved in stealing hundreds of Union Army payrolls and often using the gold to fund the purchase of large tracts of land in Central and South America. But many treasure hunters still believe there are stashes of gold secreted away by the KGC in the United States and Canada.

ASSASSINATION OF JUDGE JOHN ELLIOTT
(5/6/1820 – 3/26/1879)

Kentuckians were somewhat accustomed to the almost daily reports of violence, but the assassination of a sitting circuit court of appeals judge in broad daylight at the state capital was unusual even by Kentucky standards.

The judge had ruled against Colonel Thomas Buford's sister in a court case costing her possession of the last remaining farm property in the once vast Buford family estate. Buford's sister, Mary, committed suicide following the ruling. The colonel made up his mind to kill both Judge Elliott and Judge Pryor.

Buford later changed his mind about killing Judge Pryor, who had small children. He was less forgiving toward Elliott, whom he believed responsible for his sister's death.

At about 1:00 PM on March 26, 1879, Judge John Elliott and colleague Judge Hines were meeting for lunch when the pair was approached by Buford. Buford was carrying a twelve gauge shotgun and shot Judge Elliott to death in front of hundreds of witnesses.

BELLE BREZING
(6/11/1860 – 8/11/1940)

Belle Brezing continues to raise questions long after her death. She was born Mary Belle Cox in June of 1860 (her gravestone sets the year as 1859). A year later her mother married a saloon keeper named George Brezing and Belle was given his last name (the name was never legally changed to Brezing). It is widely reported that she began her life as a prostitute on December 24, 1879 (this date is taken from her obituary, but is contradicted in her personal papers).

In September of 1875 Belle married a cigar manufacturing worker named James Kenney. Just nine days after the wedding, John Andrew Cook was found dead at the couple's back gate. Belle's mother's Derringer was at his side, and a photograph of Belle and love letters from her were in his pocket. Whether his death was suicide or murder is still debated as is the true parentage of her daughter. Her husband James couldn't face the scandal and left Lexington shortly after the shooting. The couple never divorced, but there was no further contact between them. Belle only used her married name when traveling.

One of the questions about Belle is whether the character of Belle Watling in *Gone with the Wind* was based on Lexington's most famous madam. Margaret Mitchell denies it, but the controversy continues.

JENNY HILL'S SPORTING HOUSE

Jenny Hill, the madam in *Circle of Dishonor*, was famous in her time, but she and her house of ill repute are barely a footnote in Lexington's history. Miss Hill is remembered not only because she gave Kentucky's most famous lady of the evening her start, but also because she chose to locate her bordello in a house that was once the residence of our sixteenth president's wife.

The house was built in 1803 as an inn and tavern called "The Sign of the Green Tree". The inn closed in 1806 and the building was purchased by Robert Todd, Mary Todd Lincoln's father. He moved his large family into the house in 1832.

The Mary Todd Lincoln House still stands on Main Street in Lexington. It is listed on the National Register of Historic Places and opens to tours Monday through Saturday.

The Kentucky Mansions Preservation Foundation was largely responsible for the restoration of the property. They opened the home of the former first lady to tours in 1977. The house and enclosed garden are restored to represent how it may have looked when the Todds were in residence. There was an inventory made of the contents of the Todd home before the estate auction. Most tour guides prefer not to talk about the home's less reputable occupants.

Though we have no definitive records on Jenny Hill's years in the house, it is known that her most famous girl, Belle Brezing, lived there until July of 1881. The fact that Jenny Hill took Belle in has given her the dubious and somewhat undeserved distinction of being the madam who introduced a teenaged Belle Brezing to the life of a professional prostitute. Before her marriage to saloonkeeper George Cox, Belle's mother was a part time prostitute. Belle's background prepared her for little else than a life of prostitution.

Perhaps what Jenny Hill prepared Belle for was being good at her profession. Belle left Miss Hill's to open her own sporting house in July of 1881. She quickly became Lexington's most famous (infamous) brothel keeper.

LEXINGTON POLICE FORCE

Lexington police of the 1800's were a mix of constables, night watchmen, local militia, and city guard. By the 1870's Lexington had grown too large to effectively be policed by piecemeal police forces. The lack of organization was made abundantly clear when Kentucky's 1871 election season erupted into riots and brought US marshals into town to arrest local officials. When the dust cleared Lexington's county clerk, chief of police, deputy chief of police, captain of the night watch, and two police officers were facing charges in US district court.

Lexington disbanded the night guard and reorganized into a new Lexington Police Force. For the first time officers were uniformed and expected to wear badges so the public could clearly identify them as policemen. This did not end the corruption. Graft was a way of life in Lexington politics. Book was made openly in the Phoenix Hotel's billiard room and the proprietor handed over $500 per week to insure that police officers turned a blind eye to the gambling.

Citizens never strenuously objected to sporting houses, illegal saloons, or the gambling venues making regular protection payments to the city. Time after time they had voted down increases in city taxes. Moreover, Lexington's city government officials were bound by ordinance to make up any deficit in spending from their own pockets. Someone had to pay the salaries of the new police force. It made sense to city government that the whorehouses, gambling establishments, and saloonkeepers paid the bills for the "real" police work of arresting thieves and murderers. Kickbacks were a kind of "sin tax" that lawmakers and lawmen tried not to think too much about.

PHOENIX HOTEL

In 1797 Postlethwait's Tavern opened on the site which would become the Phoenix Hotel. The original building was expanded from two to three stories and went through several name changes before it became the Phoenix. When the hotel was rebuilt after being burned to the ground in 1820, the owners named it for the mythical bird that burns every five hundred years and resurrected from its own ashes. In May of 1879 the Phoenix lived up to (or down to) its name when it was again consumed by fire. The hotel was rebuilt in 1914, this time as a 90-room brick building eight stories tall that advertised a "fire proof" dining room. The Phoenix Hotel operated as a premier Lexington hotel until 1974.

The prominence of the Phoenix Hotel in Lexington's history dates back to stagecoach days when such notables as Aaron Burr, James Monroe, and Andrew Jackson were among its guests. Meeting rooms at the Phoenix were a favorite of local residents. Henry Clay hosted his poker games at the Phoenix. The Lexington Club was formed in the hotel dining room. General John Hunt Morgan's men planned his reinternment and organized the Morgan's Men Association there.

The hotel and the Lexington Club had a strong influence on Kentucky's horse racing industry. Several stakes races were named for the Phoenix. The most prominent of the races, the Phoenix Stakes, is still run at Keeneland.

Though the old hotel was demolished by Wallace Wilkinson in 1981 to make room for his failed World Coal Center project, the memory still lives on in Lexington. Today the main branch of the Lexington Public Library, the Park Plaza apartment building, and Phoenix Park occupy the site of the old Phoenix Hotel. The camel statue which once stood outside the hotel as a symbol of hospitality still graces Phoenix Park, though the park is now in danger of vanishing for the somewhat dubious dream building of yet another downtown developer. We don't yet know what will happen to the old camel or Phoenix Park.

NICODEMUS COLONY

The Nicodemus Colony was founded by former enslaved African Americans who left Kentucky and organized colonies at the end of the of post-Civil War Reconstruction period. These men and women wanted a place entirely free of white people's rule. They eagerly accepted the opportunity to experience freedom and take up a new life on the free land offered by Kansas.

The Klan was very active in Lexington, as were other secret societies, and the police offered little protection to black families. When the Freedman's Bureau closed in 1872, Lexington tried to run an independent organization to assist African American victims of violence. Few records of this organization exist today. I was unable to determine what it was called or how successful it was. Lexington citizens did assist the black community in setting up their own towns on the outskirts of the city, but this was met with resistance by poor white citizens who resented blacks owning land they could not afford. It was not surprising that many African American families longed for the kind of independence Kansas offered.

Nicodemus, Kansas represents the quest for freedom and the involvement of African Americans in the western expansion. Wagon loads of men, woman, and children, abandoned Kentucky for these settlements on the Great Plains. In 1879, more than one of these wagon trains organized in Lexington and headed toward Kansas with dreams of a life free of white domination. I drew on this information in the writing of *Circle of Dishonor*. Although there was no known plot organized against these settlers, they did face threats of violence on an individual basis. Many died before reaching their destination.

Life on the plains was difficult, and many of the settlers were unprepared for the hardship. Some gave up and returned to their former homes. Others stayed and made successful independent towns in their new home. Over time, some of the towns became integrated, and some failed to thrive. Today, the Nicodemus Colony is the oldest and only remaining one of the Black Townships formed west of the Mississippi River.

KENTUCKY'S REGULATORS
(POST CIVIL WAR)

It is important not to confuse the Regulators of the 1800's with the Regulators of the 1700's. In the post-Civil War era, the Regulators were a vigilante group that resembled their Revolutionary War counterparts in name only. The men who joined the Regulators were reacting to the lawlessness of their time and the criminal activity of roving bands of military deserters and other outlaws.

Over time, the Regulators have been lumped in with the Klan and other vigilante groups. This is also a mistake, even though many members of one vigilante group belonged to others. Unlike the Klan, Regulators were not particularly believers in white supremacy. They were organized to bring order to the mountainous regions where law officers were few and far between. In Kentucky, they were particularly active in the coal fields of the eastern and western parts of the state.

On the night of October 20, 1879, about 200 armed men took two prisoners (John W. Kendall and William "Bill Muck" McMillan) from the Martinsburg jail and hanged them from a tree in the court house square. The hangings started a virtual vigilante takeover of local government. Hundreds of men joined the Regulators and thousands of families lived in fear of their version of law enforcement. During their vigilante governing of Eastern Kentucky, these masked men acted as the legal and moral police of the region. They took it upon themselves to discipline not only lawbreakers but drunkards, abusers, derelicts, loose women, adulterers, etc. Regulators would swoop in on horseback, threatening, beating, and often driving offenders from the community.

Circle of Dishonor is set in the spring of 1879, several months before the powder keg of frustration in Eastern Kentucky erupted into the Regulator Uprising of 1879. The violence spread from Elliott, to Boyd, Carter, Lewis, and Rowan Counties before Governor Blackburn was able to persuade the vigilantes to put down their arms.

LEXINGTON CENTENNIAL CELEBRATION APRIL 1879

In 1879, Lexington was a city of about 25,000. During the Centennial Week, visitors increased the population to more than 50,000. Centennial Week included a wide range of events, formal balls, lectures, concerts in the public parks, a circus, ice cream socials, picnics and, of course, horse races.

Hotels could not accommodate the visitors flooding into Lexington and tent cities were built on both the white and colored fairgrounds. A bed in one of the tents on the Lexington fairgrounds cost visitors 75 cents per night. A shared bed in one of the local hotels went for three times that amount, if one could be found.

The city council voted to honor Daniel Boone in the festivities. Along with the American flags, and red white and blue bunting decorating the parade route, a large banner with Daniel Boone's name and picture was hung across Main Street. Store windows were painted with images of him and filled with merchandise related, however remotely, to Daniel Boone. Downtown, street vendors lined the sidewalks selling coonskin caps and wooden rifles. Buckskin was the favored dress at the festivities. One frustrated socialite complained that never before had so many frontiersmen been seen in Kentucky as there were at the Centennial.

FAYETTE COUNTY MEDICAL EXAMINER

In reading through county records from 1879, I ran across a notation that the county had set aside the sum of $1000 for payment to a county medical examiner. The record stated only that the doctor hired would be a resident of Lexington and would be responsible for examinations of all unexplained deaths occurring in Fayette County and investigate suspected cases of murder. The commissioners specified that the county medical examiner would be afforded the same dignity, respect, and immunity from suit given any judge in the Commonwealth.

I have been unable to locate further information on the office of medical examiner and have no knowledge of who held the position.

The medical examiner in Circle of Dishonor is fictional, with the exception of the name. For many years I worked with Dr. Richard Haydon at the University of Kentucky and, with his consent, named the character of Dr. Haydon after him.

CREATING NESSA DONNELLY
SARAH EMMA EDMONDS
AKA: FRANKLIN FLINT THOMPSON

Sarah Emma Edmonds is one of the women I used as a source for creating Nessa Donnelly. There were more than four hundred women who posed as men to join the military during the American Civil War. Hundreds more worked as nurses, one served as a doctor, and at least a dozen worked as Pinkerton agents. My detective, Nessa Donnelly, is loosely based on a blending of those brave women.

Some of the women who took on male identities went back to life as a woman; others chose to spend the rest of their lives risking arrest for "impersonating a man." Space considerations prevent me from commenting on more than one of these brave, resourceful women.

Sarah Edmonds entered the country through Canada to escape an arranged marriage to a man she loathed. After working for a while as a door to door Bible salesman, she joined the Flint Union Grays, which later became the 2nd Michigan. Sarah spent a good portion of the war posing as a man named Franklin Flint Thompson.

In the course of her military career she moved from posing as a male nurse, to fighting as a soldier, and finally as a army spy for General McClellan. In the latter role she not only posed as both men and women, but as black and white. In the guise of a black laundress, she discovered important military documents left inside an officer's jacket that were of great interest to General McClellan.

Sarah was forced to give up her disguise when she developed malaria while on a mission in the south.

ABOUT THE AUTHOR

Gwen Mayo is passionate about blending the colorful history of her native Kentucky with her love for mystery fiction. She currently lives and writes in Safety Harbor, Florida, but grew up in a large Irish family in the hills of Eastern Kentucky. Her stories have appeared in anthologies, at online short fiction sites, and in micro-fiction collections.

Circle of Dishonor, her first novel, is set during the turbulent political upheaval of post-Civil War Kentucky at a time when murder was more common in Kentucky than it was anywhere else in the United States. The sequel, Concealed in Ash, will be released later this year.

Learn more about Gwen at: gwenmayo.com